"Have you made any progress with the names on my wife-candidate list?"

So they were back to that. Hank certainly didn't seem to be harboring any lingering feelings for her. "A little. But trying to be both discreet and thorough takes a bit of time," Janell responded.

"Then perhaps we shouldn't worry so much about discretion and just focus on thoroughness. Keeping secrets is a lost cause in this town anyway."

"If that's your wish, then of course I'll do what I can to speed up the process." She knew he was right—the sooner he had a wife, the better, for both of them.

"I need to move on with establishing a 'normal' household for Alex and Chloe as soon as possible. They are already getting too used to having you around—it'll be difficult for them when you move on and another woman takes your place."

The words stabbed at her with a keenness that surprised her. She'd known that's what would happen, that another would replace her. She had in fact encouraged it. So why did it hurt so much?

Winnie Griggs is the multipublished, award-winning author of historical (and occasionally contemporary) romances that focus on Small Towns, Big Hearts, Amazing Grace. She is also a list maker and a lover of dragonflies and holds an advanced degree in the art of procrastination. Winnie loves to hear from readers—you can connect with her on Facebook at facebook.com/winniegriggs.author or email her at winnie@winniegriggs.com.

Books by Winnie Griggs

Love Inspired Historical

Texas Grooms

Handpicked Husband
The Bride Next Door
A Family for Christmas
Lone Star Heiress
Her Holiday Family
Second Chance Hero
The Holiday Courtship

Visit the Author Profile page
at Harlequin.com for more titles.

WINNIE GRIGGS

The Holiday Courtship

HARLEQUIN® LOVE INSPIRED® HISTORICAL

Recycling programs
for this product may
not exist in your area.

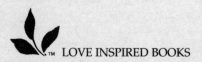

™ LOVE INSPIRED BOOKS

ISBN-13: 978-0-373-28339-2

The Holiday Courtship

Copyright © 2015 by Winnie Griggs

www.Harlequin.com

Printed in U.S.A.

The Lord Himself goes before you and will be with you; He will never leave you nor forsake you. Do not be afraid; do not be discouraged.
—*Deuteronomy* 31:08

Dedicated to my wonderful editor Melissa Endlich
whose insightful suggestions were invaluable
in helping me get the story on the paper
to match the story in my head.

Chapter One

Turnabout, Texas
November 1897

Hank Chandler hefted the two carpetbags he carried as he tried to usher his niece and nephew down the aisle of the train toward the exit. He needed a shave. And a good night's sleep. And a cup of coffee that didn't taste like tar.

But most of all he needed for Enid, his sister, not to be dead.

Chloe paused a moment, as if confused. "Alex, keep a tight hold on your sister's hand, please." It seemed wrong to put an eight-year-old in charge of his ten-year-old sister, but for now that was how it had to be. His niece didn't want anything to do with him at the moment.

Here he was, returning home to Turnabout, with two scared orphans. With a *cat* in tow. Why couldn't they have a sensible pet, like a dog?

Even with Aunt Rowena's help, how would he be able to care for all of them?

Especially Chloe.

He glanced down at his niece. With her straight brown

hair, slightly pointed chin and expressive green eyes, she looked so much like Enid at that age that it hurt. He knew the girl's angry, defiant demeanor was just a front she'd put on to deal with all she'd lost. But how was he ever going to get through to her if they couldn't even communicate properly?

He still had difficulty coming to terms with the fact that his life had changed so drastically in such a short span of time. A month ago—it seemed a lifetime ago now—he'd been a bachelor with a very orderly, uncomplicated life. A life he'd been quite content with. Then he'd received that telegram that had sent him hightailing off to Colorado.

And his life had been irrevocably changed.

But he couldn't waste time feeling sorry for himself. What had happened was over and done with, and there was nothing to do but move on. Besides, his niece and nephew were facing much bigger, more traumatic changes to their own lives. He had to do what he could to help them feel at home here.

The weight of that responsibility pressed down on him again. The one thing he could do for them in the short term was provide a sense of order and routine to their lives. To make them feel safe again.

They reached the exit and Hank maneuvered around to step out on the platform first. He set down the bags and turned up his collar. Turnabout's weather had turned blustery and colder than it had been when he left. Of course, that had been late October and it was now late November.

Hank helped Alex down first, swinging his slightly built nephew out of the train and onto the platform easily. Then he turned to Chloe. The girl stared at him defiantly as she hugged her cat tighter, as if daring him to try to swing her down the way he had Alex.

His heart went out to her but he didn't know how to make things better for her. With a smothered sigh, Hank offered her his hand. She took it and stiffly stepped down. As soon as her feet touched the platform, she released his hand and took Alex's.

Would Chloe ever learn to accept him? Like it or not, both kids were in his care now. And they were not happy about it. Not that he blamed them. He'd torn them away from everything they found familiar—their town, their home, their friends—to bring them here, to a town they'd never set foot in before, to live among strangers. And at a time when they most needed the comfort of the familiar. But he hadn't had much choice.

Thank goodness Aunt Rowena had agreed to help him out, at least for the next couple of weeks, until he could make a more permanent arrangement.

He'd think about just what that *more permanent arrangement* meant later.

Aunt Rowena should already be at his house, getting the rooms ready and preparing a nice hot meal to welcome them home. That ought to make this first day in Turnabout easier for all of them.

Hank raked a hand through his hair as he looked around. He'd asked his aunt to have a wagon waiting for them, but there was no sign of any such vehicle. Normally he'd just walk, regardless of the weather—after all, it was just a little over a mile away. But this homecoming was anything *but* normal.

He hoped that Aunt Rowena hadn't encountered problems. Regardless, there was no point in keeping the kids out in this weather while they waited.

Hank touched Chloe's shoulder. When she looked

up, he very slowly and deliberately explained. "Let's go inside the depot." He used hand gestures to make his intentions clear.

"Yes, sir," Alex responded. He gave his sister's hand a little tug and started moving in that direction. Hank picked up the bags and followed.

With two kids, especially two tired, travel-weary kids, the sooner he got everyone home, the better. He hoped Aunt Rowena had had time to get the children's rooms ready.

But the lack of waiting transport had him wondering what else might have gone wrong today.

When they reached the door, he stepped forward and pulled it open quickly, ushering the children inside and out of the wind. From the corner of his eye he noticed someone sitting on one of the benches that lined the far wall of the depot. The woman seemed to be reading a book, and a closer look revealed it was Janell Whitman, one of the town's two schoolteachers.

Her presence reminded him, that was one more thing to add to his list of tasks—getting the kids enrolled in school.

The woman looked up just then and he tipped his hat in greeting. He wondered for a moment if she was going on a trip. Then he turned back to the counter and dismissed her from his thoughts.

The stationmaster gave him a smile of greeting. "Hi, Hank. Welcome back."

Hank nodded as he ushered the kids up to the counter. "Thanks, Lionel." He gave the man a mock grimace. "You sure could have ordered up some better weather to welcome us home."

"This damp chill just rolled in yesterday. It was downright pleasant two days ago for the Thanksgiving festival, though. Too bad you missed it."

They'd been on the train Thanksgiving Day. Not that he regretted missing the festival. Neither he nor the children had been in the mood for any sort of celebration.

Lionel smiled at the children. "I see you brought some friends back with you."

"This is my niece and nephew, Chloe and Alex."

"Welcome to Turnabout." Then Lionel's expression sobered. "I'm right sorry about your ma and pa."

Alex shifted closer to Chloe's side, but neither kid said anything.

Then Lionel held out a slip of paper. "By the way, a telegram came for you this morning."

Hank reached for the telegram, unable to repress a sense of dread. The only telegrams he'd ever received had contained bad news. The last one had brought him word of his sister's and brother-in-law's deaths.

He slowly unfolded the paper and read the missive.

Tom Parson taken ill. No other driver available to transport me to Turnabout. Will likely be Monday before I arrive.
Rowena Collins

Today was Saturday, so that meant he was on his own for at least two days. And there would be no warm, clean house or hot meal to greet them. This wasn't the homecoming he'd expected at all.

Hank resisted the urge to crumple the telegram and toss it away. Instead he focused on figuring out how to deal with this new setback.

One thing at a time. The immediate concern was that there was no wagon on its way to transport them.

He glanced back Lionel's way. "I need to fetch a wagon to get the kids and their belongings back to my place. There are a couple of trunks in the baggage compartment that belong to us. If you could just leave them on the platform when they're unloaded, I'll take care of them when I return." The livery was only two blocks away but hiring a horse and wagon was an expense he could ill afford right now. Could he ask Lionel to keep an eye on the kids while he took care of business at home?

"Excuse me, Mr. Chandler?"

Startled, Hank turned to find the schoolteacher standing behind him. "Ma'am?"

"I'm sorry, but I couldn't help overhearing what you said just now. These two children appear to be exhausted and the wind is picking up outside. I would be glad to keep them company while you see about the wagon."

"You're not here to catch the train?"

She shook her head with a smile, as if the thought was absurd. "No, I'm just waiting to see if any mail arrived for me."

Hank sent up a silent prayer of thanks for this good news in an otherwise miserable day. He couldn't have asked for a better caretaker for the kids. The schoolteacher would naturally be accustomed to dealing with uncooperative children. Of course, she probably hadn't had to deal with anyone with Chloe's particular problem before.

"I appreciate the offer, ma'am, and I'd certainly like to take you up on it." He made sure he was turned so Chloe didn't have a clear view of his face. "But there's something you need to know before you take them on."

"Oh?" Her green-flecked brown eyes studied him patiently.

"I'm sure you heard about their parents." News of that sort normally spread fast in Turnabout.

Her expression softened. "I did. My condolences on the loss of your sister and brother-in-law."

He nodded. "Well, the accident that killed the kids' parents also damaged Chloe's eardrums. She's become totally deaf."

Her reaction surprised him. There was a sudden flash of something in her expression that seemed more than sympathy or mere surprise.

Whatever it was, it seemed to be very personal.

Everything inside Janell stilled.

Deaf. Not again.

The terrible memories of that nightmarish time came tumbling back.

But this wasn't about her. This little girl needed help— help she was uniquely qualified to give. How fortuitous that she'd wandered in this morning to check on the mail. But then, God's timing was always perfect.

A moment later, Janell realized Mr. Chandler was studying her, concern digging furrows in his brow. "Ma'am, are you okay?"

She straightened and met his gaze, determination stiffening her spine. "As it happens, I actually have some experience dealing with the deaf."

Surprise and relief flashed in his dark gray eyes before he resumed his businesslike expression. "Miss Whitman, if that's true, then you are truly a godsend to us right now."

He glanced at the children. "And I'll take you up on your generous offer to watch them while I'm gone."

"It'll be my pleasure."

He stared at the children for a moment, appearing to

be at a loss for words. For just a moment she sensed a vulnerability in him that tugged at her.

Poor man. This was a difficult situation for anyone to be put in, much less a man who'd seemed happy with his bachelor status. He looked as if he hadn't slept in ages—and she didn't think it was just travel weariness. There was at least one day's growth of beard on his chin, enhancing rather than detracting from its square ruggedness. And his dark brown hair was in need of a trim.

Not surprising—it just meant he cared. And she could empathize. When this had happened to her sister, her entire family had been impacted. How much worse must it be for someone who had to deal with the situation on his own? It did him credit that he'd stepped up to do what he could for the children. There was a lot to admire in a man who would do that.

Of more concern right now, however, were the children themselves. It was obvious they needed a mother's touch. Like his uncle, the little boy's straw-colored hair was also just a tad too long, and he kept tucking it back behind his ears as if it bothered him. And Chloe's rebellious attitude, a natural reaction to what she'd been through, would only be healed through an abundance of patience and love.

Mr. Chandler straightened, rubbing his jaw. He tapped Chloe's arm and waited until she met his gaze, then explained the situation to them. "Alex, Chloe, this is Miss Whitman. She's one of the schoolteachers here in Turnabout. I'm going to go home to fetch a wagon, but I'll be back as soon as I can. Miss Whitman will be staying with you until then."

She approved of the way he spoke slowly and enunciated each word. It showed he understood Chloe's limitations and cared enough to try to get through to her. Not that the girl seemed able to read his lips just yet. But in time, she might be able to learn.

Janell gave him a reassuring smile. "Don't worry—we'll be just fine." Then she turned to the children. "Won't we?"

Alex gave a tentative nod. Chloe merely ignored them.

But Janell refused to be put off by their lack of enthusiasm. She turned to Mr. Chandler, her smile still firmly in place. "There, we three are already friends. So you can go take care of this wagon business. I have nothing pressing to tend to today." Then she looked around. "But perhaps we can find someplace more comfortable and interesting to wait."

The sawmill owner gave her a questioning glance.

"I was thinking perhaps the children would be willing to take a short walk," she explained. "Say, just as far as the Blue Bottle?"

His expression cleared as understanding dawned. "Now, that's a very good idea." He turned to the children. "Miss Whitman is offering to take you to the town's sweet shop. What do you think—wait here or brave the wind for a couple of blocks to reach the Blue Bottle?"

Alex perked up. "You mean a candy store?"

Janell nodded. "And a very good one. You can find all sorts of tasty treats—chocolate drops, sugared pecans, pumpkin brittle, caramels and much more."

"I like candy just fine." Alex took his sister's hand. "And Chloe does, too."

Chloe looked up then, her eyes darting back and forth as if trying to make sense of their conversation.

Yes, this girl definitely needed her help. Janell straightened. "Well then, if you don't mind taking a short walk—" she glanced toward Mr. Chandler "—and if your uncle doesn't mind, why don't we go see what the Blue Bottle sweet shop and tea parlor has to offer this morning?"

"I don't mind at all," Mr. Chandler assured her. Then he turned to the stationmaster. "Lionel, if you don't mind, I'll leave our bags here and get them when I come back for the trunks."

While Mr. Chandler took care of business, Janell noticed Alex trying to help his sister understand what was going on, but Chloe merely looked confused and frustrated. The girl hefted the cat higher, resting her chin against his furry back.

Janell touched Chloe's arm. When the girl met her gaze, she pointed to the cat. "What's his name?" she asked.

Alex answered for her. "His name is Smudge."

Janell thanked him. She knew he was trying to help his sister, but somehow she had to make the boy understand that he wasn't truly helping her by always answering for her. Her own sister, Lizzie, had been that way as well, rarely speaking. And at first they'd compensated for her, answering for her so that she hadn't had to figure out what had been said. But they'd eventually learned that was the wrong approach.

Chloe would need to learn to reengage with the people around her or she would turn into a sad, lonely hermit.

"Ready?"

Mr. Chandler's question brought Janell back to the present. With a nod, she followed the children outside while Mr. Chandler politely held the door open.

As they stepped off the platform and onto the sidewalk, a gust of wind swooshed down on them. Janell quickly took off her shawl. "Here, you two, you can share this." She draped it over both their shoulders, then smiled at the picture they made.

Mr. Chandler frowned. "Now *you'll* be cold." He shrugged out of his jacket and held it out. "Here, take this."

She smiled but shook her head. "Thank you, but that's not necessary. It's a short walk to the Blue Bottle."

His brow drew down and she got the impression he was irritated. "Surely you don't expect me to escort you through town wearing my jacket while you give your wrap to my niece and nephew. What kind of oaf do you think I am?"

She held her hand out to accept his jacket. As she shrugged into it, she realized it felt surprisingly nice. Some of his warmth lingered, and though it was larger and heavier than she was used to, those very masculine qualities somehow made her feel more feminine than she had in quite a while.

Pushing that fanciful—and dangerous—thought away, she turned her attention back to the children. "I'm so glad you've moved to Turnabout," she said cheerily. "It will be nice having two new students in my class."

There was no response except a half nod from Alex.

"They're not very talkative." Mr. Chandler's tone held a hint of apology.

"I imagine they're weary from so much travel. But I can do enough talking for all of us."

"I'm sure you can."

She ignored the hint of sarcasm in his tone—after all, it was a schoolteacher's job to reach even the most recalcitrant or guarded of children and engage them in the learning process.

"It's a good thing we ran into you," Mr. Chandler said. "And I don't mean just because you came to my rescue."

"Oh?"

"I need to speak to you about getting the kids enrolled in school as soon as possible."

Did he really think these two would be ready to return to school right away? "Of course. But there will be time enough for that after the children have settled in."

He frowned, but she didn't give him a chance to say anything. Instead she turned to the children. "So, is there a favorite treat you're hoping to find at the sweet shop?"

Alex nodded decisively. "I like lemon drops and licorice whips."

"I'm afraid you won't find those at the Blue Bottle, but I believe the mercantile has an excellent selection. No, the kind of treats you'll find at the sweet shop are more along the line of bonbons—chocolates, caramels, taffies and brittles. I'm certain we can find something you like."

During the three-block walk, she kept up a running dialogue, describing the various buildings and points of interest in the town, aware that Chloe wasn't benefiting from the commentary. But she also knew that Chloe *would* benefit, even if only in a small way, from any easing of tension in her brother.

And all the while she was *very* aware of Mr. Chandler strolling beside her and of the warmth of his jacket on her shoulders.

She'd forgotten how special this kind of consideration could make a woman feel.

Chapter Two

When they reached the Blue Bottle, Hank quickly stepped forward to open the door.

Miss Whitman hadn't been exaggerating when she'd said she could do enough talking for all of them.

But he noticed Alex seemed more relaxed now, which meant Chloe's tension should ease as well. He'd noticed she was taking many of her cues from her brother when she couldn't tell what was going on around her.

His attention shifted back to the schoolteacher. His coat should have looked ridiculously large on her, but for some reason it didn't.

In fact, she looked quite nice—in an impish kind of way.

Hank pulled himself up at that thought. The strait-laced schoolteacher, impish? What a strange notion—he must be more tired than he'd thought.

He stepped inside with them for a moment, just to make certain they would be okay here while he was gone.

Miss Whitman started to shrug out of his jacket and he moved forward to help her. When she smiled up at him, he found himself wondering why he'd never really noticed her before. Not that he'd been looking for a wife before current circumstances had made it a necessity.

Then she turned to Chloe with an apologetic purse of her lips, giving him the nudge he needed to step back.

"I just realized it's probably not a good idea to bring a cat into a sweet shop." She glanced back his way. "Perhaps you should take Smudge with you."

He swallowed a retort. She was undoubtedly right, but that didn't mean he had to like it. "Chloe won't let him out of her sight."

"I'm sure Smudge provides her with a measure of comfort. But she must learn that she'll be okay without him for short periods of time."

The schoolteacher planted herself squarely in front of his niece and stood silently until Chloe met her gaze.

Miss Whitman touched Smudge lightly on the head, then held out her arms, her meaning obvious.

Chloe replied by hugging Smudge tighter against her chest and lifting her chin defiantly.

But Miss Whitman didn't drop her hands or her gaze, and Chloe finally handed over her pet. The girl's shoulders slumped, and she looked as if she'd just lost her best friend, but Miss Whitman patted her arm and gave her an approving smile.

Chloe turned away.

He thought he heard Miss Whitman sigh as she turned and held the cat out to him. "Here you go. Make sure he doesn't get away from you since he's not familiar with the town yet."

Great—now he was responsible for the well-being of not just the children, but this creature as well.

His hesitation was duly noted. Her eyes turned hard without her smile ever leaving her face as she continued to wait for him to take the animal from her.

Hank reluctantly held out his hands and accepted the gray feline, who looked snootily down his nose at him and sneezed. Great—even the kids' pet didn't like him.

After telling Miss Whitman to let Eve know he'd settle the bill when he returned, he headed out the door.

Feeling ridiculous carrying a cat through town, Hank set a brisk pace. But his thoughts remained on the kids.

He had to get through the next few days without his aunt's help, and that meant he probably wouldn't be able to spend much time at the sawmill. He trusted Simon Tucker to do a good job in his absence, but the business was his, not Simon's. And he'd already been away too long.

If only he'd been more successful convincing Willa Booth to return with him. Willa, a good friend of his sister, had cared for the children during the time it had taken him to get from Turnabout to Elgin Springs.

As soon as he'd realized his best recourse was to find a woman to marry, someone to serve as a mother to the children, he'd thought of Miss Booth. The children already knew and liked her. She was not only single, but also seemed to have a fondness for children. The fact that she was a few years older than him hadn't particularly bothered him—in fact, it had the advantage of assuring him she was going into this with her eyes wide-open and not holding out any romantic aspirations.

He'd discussed the situation with her in a business-like manner, explaining that he could offer a comfortable home that she could run as she pleased and a life where she would be respected and her needs cared for. And at first she'd agreed to his proposal. Having a wife to accompany them back to Turnabout would have made everything so much easier.

But at the last minute she'd backed out, and he'd had to leave her behind.

Hank spent most of the train ride back to Turnabout trying to compile a list of acceptable candidates. One by one, he'd considered every unmarried lady in Turnabout he could remember. And he'd mentally rejected most of them for one reason or another. They'd been too old or too young, too slow or too silly, too talkative or too timid. By the time the train had arrived in Turnabout, his list had grown pitiably short. He'd figured—hoped— there were other marriageable ladies out there, though.

Take the schoolteacher, for instance. He hadn't really considered Miss Whitman, mainly because she wasn't someone he'd had much contact with.

But he was definitely considering her now.

In fact, over the past few minutes she'd jumped to the very top of his list.

Once Mr. Chandler left, Janell turned back to the children and found them wide-eyed. The place was tailor-made to be a child's delight. The warmth inside was a welcome counterpoint to the windy outdoors, and the smells were mouthwateringly tantalizing.

Not only did Eve Dawson make delectable sweets, but her husband, Chance, carved wooden toys and fanciful decorations that he displayed around the shop. His woodworking area was visible across the room, separated only by a low rail.

He was there now and looked up when they entered and welcomed them with a smile. Then he bent over his work again.

Eve, her rounded stomach betraying the fact that she was expecting a child, stepped out of the kitchen, wiping her hands on her apron. "Hello, Janell. Who are these two fine-looking young'uns you have with you?"

"This is Chloe and Alex, Mr. Chandler's niece and nephew. They just arrived in town and I thought I'd treat them to some of your candies."

She saw understanding and sympathy flash in Eve's expression. Everyone in town knew why Mr. Chandler had headed for Colorado a few weeks ago.

"Well, as first-time customers, you're allowed to sample anything in the shop for free. Just let me know what you want."

Alex and Chloe were already eyeing the treats on display with hungry eagerness. Much better than the scared and woeful expressions they'd worn earlier.

Janell turned back to Eve. "While they're trying to decide, would you mind whipping us up some hot cocoa?"

Eve smiled. "Not at all. Three hot cocoas, coming right up."

Her husband, who'd sauntered over from his workbench, gave them another smile, then dropped a quick kiss on Eve's cheek. "Why don't you let me handle the cocoa while you take care of your customers?" Without waiting for an answer, he headed for the kitchen.

Eve turned back to her young customers. "Made up your minds yet?"

Alex's eyes were wide with appreciation for the treats spread before him. "It just all looks so good."

"And what about you, Chloe?"

When the little girl didn't answer, Eve's smile turned uncertain.

Janell caught her gaze and touched her ear with a shake of her head.

With an understanding nod, Eve turned back to the

children. "I tell you what—why don't I make up a platter with a little bit of everything and bring it to your table?"

Alex's eyes lit up and he nodded enthusiastically.

"That would be lovely, thank you." Janell lightly touched Chloe's arm to get her attention before sweeping a hand toward the tables. "Let's have a seat, shall we?" She led them to one of the round tables that were set out for customers.

As they took their seats, Janell turned to Alex. "How old are you?"

"Eight."

Then she turned to his sister. Touching the girl's arm to get her attention once more, she carefully enunciated her question. "And how old are you?"

Alex immediately jumped in to answer for her. "She's—"

Janell immediately stopped the boy with a raised hand. "Thank you, Alex, but I asked Chloe."

"But—"

"She can still talk, can't she?"

He shifted uncomfortably, shooting a furtive look his sister's way before answering. "Yes, ma'am."

Janell turned back to Chloe with a firm smile. "So, Chloe, how old are you?"

Chloe shook her head, a clear indication that she hadn't understood. Janell knew from experience that even if the girl had read her lips properly, she wouldn't have the confidence to answer. So she took a pencil and a scrap of paper from her handbag and wrote down the question.

Chloe looked at the note, then pursed her lips, as if she would refuse to answer. But Janell determinedly held her gaze and eventually the girl mumbled a reply. "Ten."

Satisfied that she'd got the girl to respond verbally, Janell included Alex in her next question. "Then both of you will be in my class when you're ready to join us at the school."

Eve approached just then with a tray containing a generous mix of treats. "Here you go." She set the tray between the children, then straightened and placed a hand lightly over her stomach. "I hope you enjoy."

Both children leaned forward to examine the goodies. "Yes, ma'am," Alex responded enthusiastically. "And thank you."

Janell waited for Chloe to add her thanks, but the girl remained silent. She knew Chloe was having trouble interacting with folks around her, but it was time she began learning to do so again.

She leaned over and touched Chloe's arm. The ten-year-old glanced up, a guarded expression on her face.

"Isn't there something you'd like to say?" Janell spoke very deliberately, and when she was done she waved a hand Eve's way.

Chloe blushed and pursed her lips stubbornly. Then she turned to their hostess. "Thank you."

Eve smiled at the girl as if nothing out of the ordinary had occurred. "You're quite welcome. Now, I'll leave you to enjoy your treats while I check on how the cocoa are coming."

As Eve walked away, Janell gave the children an encouraging nod. "Help yourselves."

Without further prompting, they each grabbed something from the tray. Janell reached for a piece of pumpkin-seed brittle, her personal favorite.

As she nibbled on it, she wondered how Mr. Chandler planned to deal with his new circumstances. Had he already realized how much his life was going to change, that this was not a temporary situation that he could resolve and then go back to the life he'd had before? As far as she knew, he didn't have any family here in Turnabout. Was there someone he could turn to, or even hire if need be, to help him care for the children?

Before any of them had time to reach for more, the cocoa arrived and Janell let the children drink without further attempts at conversation. The pair gradually relaxed. Alex, whose feet didn't quite touch the floor, swung his legs absently. Chloe fidgeted with her cup.

Perhaps once they'd finished their cocoa she could try again to get them to open up to her. But she found her thoughts drifting to their uncle, wondering when he would return and feeling a small flicker of anticipation at seeing him again.

Mr. Dawson came over and handed Alex and Chloe each their own very small wooden top. Alex's had a green stripe around the middle and Chloe's had a red stripe.

He taught them how to spin the tiny toys and then, with a smile, left them to try it on their own.

Their first few attempts drew smiles and even a giggle or two as they tried to get them to spin correctly. Then they challenged each other to see whose could spin the longest.

While they were still playing, the door opened and Mr. Chandler finally walked in. Janell immediately felt her spirits jump, responding to what, she wasn't quite sure. But the children's reaction seemed the exact opposite.

Was it because his presence reminded them of their loss? Or was there some other reason?

Mr. Chandler had the look of someone ready to do his duty by his niece and nephew, come what may. Perhaps that was what they sensed—that they were a duty, not a welcome presence.

Janell saw hints of weariness etched into the lines of his face and a touch of worry and helplessness in his eyes, and her heart was touched once more. Not only had he suddenly been left with a pair of grieving orphans, but he'd also lost his sister as well. The desire she'd felt earlier to help ease his burdens grew stronger.

"Where's Smudge?" Chloe's question pulled Janell back from those inappropriate thoughts.

The child's tone had been a mix of accusation and apprehension, as if she suspected her uncle of having done something unpleasant to her pet. But the fact that she'd spoken at all was a good sign. It meant Chloe *would* make the effort to speak up given sufficient motivation.

Mr. Chandler, however, didn't seem to share her optimism. Instead he looked resigned. "Don't worry, Chloe—your pet is fine," he said. "He's waiting for us back at the house."

Wanting to reassure the girl, Janell quickly wrote down Mr. Chandler's response so Chloe could read it. Some of the girl's anxiety eased, but not her suspicion. She glared at her uncle and then focused back on her cup of cocoa, idly pushing the toy top around with one finger.

For a moment, as Mr. Chandler studied his niece's bent head, there was a defeated slump to his shoulders, as if he didn't think he'd ever get through to her. Janell had the most unexpected urge to give his arm a comforting touch, barely stopping herself in time. What had got into her?

Fortunately, he didn't seem to notice anything peculiar in her behavior. Instead, he seemed to draw on something inside himself. He straightened, once more the picture of confidence, and turned to her with a nod.

"Thank you for watching Alex and Chloe. It was a big help."

"You're quite welcome. They were no trouble at all."

"I'll settle the bill with Mrs. Dawson and then we'll be on our way," he said, already turning back to the children. "Please don't let us keep you any longer—I can take it from here."

He sounded almost as if he meant that. But she wasn't ready to go just yet—she needed to have a word with Mr. Chandler before he took the lost-looking youngsters home with him, if for no other reason than to give him a better idea of what he'd be facing in the coming days.

She stood and glanced toward the counter. "Eve, would you mind if I took Mr. Chandler to the kitchen to show him your new oven?"

Eve picked up her cue immediately. "Not at all." She nodded. "Take your time. I'll keep an eye on the children for you."

Other than a quick raise of an eyebrow, Mr. Chandler hid his surprise at her odd request quite well. Without a word, he swept an arm forward, indicating she should precede him.

Once the kitchen door swung closed he crossed his arms. "I assume you didn't really intend to show me the oven. So why are we here?"

Janell smiled as she motioned to a chair at the worktable. "I'd like to speak to you about something."

He scrubbed a hand wearily across his jaw and glanced at the door as if he could see through it to the children. He was silent so long she thought he would refuse. But after a moment he nodded. He didn't so much sit as drop into the seat.

"If I understood what you said earlier, Chloe hasn't always been deaf."

He shook his head. "The explosion that killed their parents also stole her hearing."

Janell's hand flew to her throat. *"Explosion!"* She hadn't heard that part of the story.

He leaned forward with his hands clasped on the table. "My apologies for blurting that out—I wasn't thinking. Back in Elgin Springs everyone knows what happened."

"No need for apologies. I can't imagine what those children have been through."

His smile was grim. "Fortunately, Chloe was in a separate room when it happened." He looked down at his hands. "So she didn't actually witness…" His jaw tightened and he raked a hand through his hair.

She impulsively placed her hand on his. "That much, at least, is a blessing."

His hand stiffened under hers and she drew back, feeling her cheeks warm. Had she been too forward?

Blessing? Hank's anger and grief threatened to erupt again. No, there wasn't much about what had happened in this matter that he would consider a blessing. Not for him, and not for the kids.

A heartbeat later he realized Miss Whitman had read something of his feelings. But he could also tell by the flush rising in her cheeks that she'd misinterpreted the reason.

Because he hadn't objected to her touch at all. Quite the opposite, in fact.

Now wasn't the time to be thinking of that, though.

Even if she looked quite pretty with that warm color in her face.

Yes, Miss Whitman had definitely solidified her place on his list of candidates for wife.

Chapter Three

"And what of Alex?"

The schoolteacher's question pulled his focus back to the matter at hand. He was relieved to see she had already regained her composure. "Fortunately, Alex wasn't at home when the explosion happened, so he didn't receive any injuries."

"No *physical* injuries, at least," she amended. "I'm sure emotionally he's hurting a great deal."

He nodded. It was something he needed to keep reminding himself of since he tended to focus more on what Chloe had lost.

"As I mentioned earlier," she continued, "I have experience with Chloe's condition. My sister went deaf at the age of seventeen."

He sat up straighter. Perhaps she *could* help. "How did it happen in her case?"

"Measles."

He saw the sadness in her luminous eyes and felt the urge to comfort her. Instead, he kept the conversation on the issue at hand. "How did your sister handle it?"

"Not very well at first." Her lips twisted wryly. "In fact, much the same way Chloe is handling it right now."

"But she *did* get better." *Please let there be hope.*

"She never regained her hearing. But she did eventually come to terms with what had happened. It took a lot of time, though, and a lot of work, both on her part and by all of us who love her."

"So she's fine now?"

Miss Whitman's expression closed off for a moment. Then she seemed to shake off her melancholy. "Absolutely. For the last five years she's been happily married. She now has two children and leads a very active life."

Could he dare hope Chloe would turn out the same way? Right now that seemed an improbable dream. "But there's a difference between an eighteen-year-old and a ten-year-old."

"True." She leaned forward, propping her forearms on the table. "But that doesn't mean the same approach won't work with Chloe."

"You honestly think you can help her adjust?"

"I'm willing to try." She gave him a direct look. "But it means work for you and Alex as well as Chloe."

He'd figured as much. "Hard work doesn't scare me."

"Good. But first things first. You need to get them home and settled in." She paused a moment, as if something had just occurred to her. "I assume you do have room in your home for them?"

"I do." She certainly wasn't afraid to speak her mind. Must be the schoolteacher in her.

"Is there a separate room for each of them or do you plan to have them share?"

"There are two spare rooms." At one time he'd thought to raise a family in that house. But that plan had been discarded years ago.

Hank mentally grimaced. It seemed he'd be raising a family there after all.

"Are the rooms ready for guests?" she asked, pressing on.

This time, her question got his back up. Sure, both rooms could use a more thorough cleaning. And the smaller one had become more storage room than bedroom over the years. But in his defense, he'd left in a hurry. And he'd thought Aunt Rowena would be here getting things ready.

Still, that really wasn't any of her business. "Close enough for now," he said. "And when I went home I stoked the stove and started a fire in the fireplace, so it should be nice and warm by the time I get the kids there."

She nodded approval. "That was a thoughtful thing to do." Then she turned solemn. "As for the rest, I understand this is a difficult time for you. And I'm certain Alex and Chloe will appreciate having a room of their own and a comfortable bed, regardless of the condition."

"I'm glad you approve." Hank didn't bother to hide his irritation. It didn't matter that the conclusion she'd jumped to was correct; she shouldn't have made any assumptions about him in the first place.

Then he tamped down his ire. None of this was her fault and she was trying to help. "Actually, my aunt Rowena was supposed to come over from Clampton today and stay with us a couple of weeks. The plan was for her to arrive ahead of us and get the house ready for the kids, but she's been delayed."

"I can see why that would make you cross, and more than a little apprehensive. But a grown man such as yourself should be able to take care of the basic housekeeping required."

He wasn't sure how to respond, so he didn't. Time to get this conversation back under control. "What exactly did you do to help your sister adjust? And can you do the same for Chloe?"

Miss Whitman glanced toward the next room again. "Alex and Chloe are tired and very likely apprehensive about their future here. As I said earlier, the best thing for them at the moment is to get them to your place so they can get comfortable with their new home."

Why couldn't she just give a straight answer to his questions? "Does that mean you *can't* help Chloe?"

She gave him a don't-be-silly look. "Not at all. I'm only saying now is not the time to talk about it."

"And just when *do* you suggest we talk?" He was beginning to wonder if she really *could* help his niece after all.

"Since your aunt didn't arrive as planned, are you in a position to provide them with a meal tonight?"

The way she hopped from subject to subject made him dizzy. "I'll take them to Daisy's," he answered, making said plan on the spot.

But she gave a disapproving shake of her head. "Taking them to a restaurant is probably not the best idea. Much better to feed them at home, where they won't feel on display."

And just how did she expect him to do that, especially when she'd already guessed his cupboard was bare? "That's all well and good, but—"

She raised a hand to stop him. Naturally she'd have a suggestion. "There's a simple solution. I can come by your place later this afternoon and cook a simple meal for you."

Her generous and unexpected offer, made with such no-nonsense confidence, set him back a moment. Putting aside the fact that her I-have-all-the-answers attitude set his teeth on edge, it was mighty tempting to accept her offer. After all, a home-cooked meal—and such interesting company—for the kids' first day at his home was more than he could have hoped for just a few short minutes ago. But how far into her debt did he want to go? "I couldn't impose on you—"

She interrupted his admittedly halfhearted protest. "Nonsense. I *want* to do this. And after the meal, the two of us can talk in more detail about how we might best help Chloe."

Her use of *we* made it sound as if she planned to have some long-term involvement in Chloe's life. For some reason that perked him up. "All right. If you're sure it's not imposing on your kindness too much, then I'd certainly welcome your help."

"That's settled, then." She stood and gave him a reassuring smile. "Don't worry, Mr. Chandler—this is something the three of you *will* be able to work through."

Hank stood as well. She certainly had an air of confidence about her—he hoped it was justified. Though he wondered how long *eventually* would take. "Can I give you a ride to the boardinghouse?"

"Thank you, but there's no need. You just get those two children home and insist they lie down for a nap." She looked at him. "And I suggest you do the same."

Sleep *did* sound good, but there was too much to be done for him to waste time on a bit of shut-eye this afternoon.

"By the way," she continued, "the children may decide they want to be together, at least at first. I wouldn't make much to-do over it if they do. It's natural for them to want to cling to something familiar in a situation like this, and right now the only familiar thing left in their world is each other. And Smudge."

"If you're going to shop for the makings of our meal, just have the shopkeepers put the cost on my account."

She nodded. "Very well. I'll see you at your place in about an hour." And with that, she headed for the door.

Hank slowly followed her back into the sweet shop, watching her walk ahead of him. There was nothing tentative about this woman. She moved the same way she talked, with confidence and authority. The knowledge that she planned to help him, that he was no longer facing this alone, gave him renewed energy.

Miss Whitman, for all her I-know-best attitude, had provided him with the first flicker of hope for Chloe since he'd left Turnabout four weeks ago, and for that he was grateful. If the schoolteacher could truly do what she said she could, he'd certainly not begrudge her any amount of superior attitude.

She paused beside the children for a moment, saying something to them, touching Alex lightly on the shoulder, Chloe on the arm. And he could see the children respond to her, if not warmly, at least respectfully.

How did she do it, get them to relax around her like that? For a few moments, when he'd first walked into the Blue Bottle, he'd seen his niece and nephew as they were meant to be—sitting at the table, sipping cocoa and smiling.

Then they'd spied him and gloom settled over them once more.

He tried not to take it personally. It seemed, though, that he was a reminder to them of everything they'd lost.

Would that ever change?

Perhaps with the schoolteacher's help, he could learn the secret to earning their trust.

But first he needed to earn *her* trust.

* * *

Janell stayed behind at the sweet shop after Mr. Chandler and his charges had departed. Over the past year and a half, she and Eve had become very good friends. It was the first time she'd let herself get close, really close, to anyone since she'd moved to Turnabout nearly seven years ago.

"Those poor children," Eve said, putting her hand protectively over her abdomen. "Mr. Chandler is going to have his hands full caring for them, I'm afraid." Then she smiled. "But I can see already that he's going to have some very competent help."

Janell and Eve had shared a great deal about their pasts with each other as their friendship grew, so her friend knew all about what had happened to her sister, Lizzie. "I certainly intend to do what I can to help them. I wasn't able to stay and help Lizzie as much as I would have liked. I feel like perhaps God is giving me a second chance with Chloe."

Eve also knew about her shameful secret, the one that had driven Janell from her family and home in Illinois and brought her to Turnabout. Eve was the only one here who knew.

Because if anyone else found out, it would likely mean the end of Janell's stay in Turnabout, something she couldn't bear.

Eve patted her hand. "What happened was no fault of your own. But we both have scars from our past to deal with, so I'll say no more. Just let me know how I can help."

"Would you mind letting Verity know I won't make it to choir practice this evening and probably won't sing with the choir at church tomorrow?" The choir director and several of the members had made a habit of stopping here for a cup of tea before choir practice on Saturday evenings.

"Of course. I'm sure she'll understand, given the circumstances."

Talk of the choir reminded Janell of something else.

She gave Eve a sympathetic smile. "Is Leo still smarting over what happened at the Thanksgiving festival?"

Leo, Eve's adopted son, was part of the children's choir and had been selected for a small solo part at the festival. However, when he'd stepped forward to sing, his voice had cracked. The boy had turned candy-apple red and rushed off the stage in embarrassment.

Eve nodded. "I'm afraid so. Telling him it's a natural part of growing up for a boy hasn't helped." A touch of worry invaded her expression. "He's already told Verity he won't be taking part in the Christmas program."

Verity had formed a children's choir last spring and had worked wonders with the group ever since.

"As it happens," Janell said, "I've been thinking about working with some of the children to put on a short nativity play in conjunction with the children's choir Christmas Eve program. Do you think Leo might be interested in taking part?"

Eve smiled. "As long as it doesn't require him to sing, he just might."

"Then I'll speak to him about it at school on Monday."

Janell took her leave and headed for the boardinghouse, her thoughts once again focused on Mr. Chandler and his charges. Her pace was brisk, her mind racing. Already she was making mental lists of all the things she could do—in both the short and long term—to help the three of them. The first thing she'd do would be to write a letter to Dr. Carson, the doctor who'd been such a help with Lizzie. Since he worked at St. Matthew's School for the Deaf, he would have access to some of the most current information and materials to help someone like Chloe.

She would also write to Lizzie and get her thoughts on what would help the girl the most from an emotional perspective.

One thing she could do immediately, though, would be to dig through her trunk and find the book she had on sign language. It would be a good place for Mr. Chandler and the children to start.

Twenty minutes later, Janell had the letters written, had retrieved the book and was headed back out of the boardinghouse. She had a number of errands to run before heading to Mr. Chandler's home. Post the letters, stop by the butcher shop and the mercantile and also stop in at the schoolhouse to pick up a few things.

Janell offered up a little prayer of thanksgiving. God was giving her the opportunity to help this little girl, to share what she'd learned with Lizzie with someone else in need. And she was determined to see it all the way through—not turn tail and run as she had before.

Mr. Chandler had appeared to be a little reluctant to accept her help. Thank goodness he'd finally come around—once she explained things properly he'd see that there was merit to what she could offer.

The sawmill owner was someone she hadn't really had the opportunity to interact with during her time here in Turnabout. As a teacher her main interactions were with the schoolchildren and their parents. Being a member of the church choir gave her another social outlet. And being a teacher, she was very circumspect in her dealings with single men.

Of course, that didn't mean she hadn't noticed him before. After all, he was the kind of man one couldn't help but notice. Tall and lean, with a firm jaw and gray eyes, he didn't say much, but there was an air of quiet command about him. She got the sense that he was a man of good character and was well liked in the community.

And now that she'd had a chance to interact with him on a personal basis, she found that he was also a very intriguing man. In fact, she was surprised none of the single ladies or matchmaking mamas here in town had set their sights on him. Being married would certainly make his current situation easier—for both him and the children.

Not that she had any aspirations on that score herself. Her world revolved around the schoolchildren and the choir—that was enough for her.

It had to be.

Because she was living a lie, had been ever since she'd moved to Turnabout. Marriage was not an option for her any longer, something she'd come to terms with a long time ago. It was why she discouraged any attempts by the local gentlemen to come calling. Why she told herself she could live a fulfilling life teaching other people's children, even if she'd never have one of her own.

And most days she could make herself believe that. Being with Mr. Chandler today, however, had stirred up some emotions best left dormant.

Janell brought her wandering mind back to the matter at hand. Yes, the sawmill owner had the makings of a fine family man, and all things considered, the children could definitely have done worse in finding a guardian than Mr. Hank Chandler.

Chapter Four

❧

Hank awoke abruptly, feeling disoriented. It took him a moment to remember he was back in his own home and not still in Colorado.

He hadn't intended to sleep, just rest for a minute. But getting the children settled in had taken longer than planned. He'd shown them their rooms, but unfortunately, the rooms were not quite as ready as he'd hoped.

Alex and Chloe had set their things down and looked around like a pair of lost waifs. He brought in their trunks, which held all the tangible possessions left from their prior lives. The one with their parents' things, at least those items he'd felt they would want someday, he'd carted up to the attic.

When he'd insisted they take naps, they'd complied with almost apathetic nods. A few minutes later, when Alex crept into Chloe's room, Hank had heeded Miss Whitman's suggestion and pretended not to notice. He had to admit, having someone like the schoolteacher in his corner was a blessing.

Hank swung his feet to the floor. Later, after the kids were up, he would set up the new bed he'd ordered for Chloe's room. He'd need it once his aunt arrived anyway, since she'd be sharing his niece's room during her stay. And that fact would probably earn him yet more resentment from Chloe, but there was no help for it.

For now, if Alex chose to make use of his aunt's bed before she arrived, he supposed he could turn a blind eye.

Hank tried to clear the last of the fog from his brain as he stood. He'd come into the parlor intending to check on the fireplace. That done, though, he'd stretched out on the sofa, telling himself it would just be for a few minutes, just long enough to find a bit of peace from the headache that had plagued him since…well, since he'd got that telegram four weeks ago.

How long had he slept? What if the children had awakened before him? He headed down the hall and opened Chloe's door just wide enough to look inside.

To his relief they were still sound asleep. He closed the door, then straightened. Miss Whitman would probably be here soon—he should get a few things in order before she arrived.

But as Hank neared the kitchen, he heard soft humming. A heartbeat later, he picked up the scent of something cooking. What in the world?

He paused on the threshold. Sure enough, Miss Whitman stood at the stove with her back to him. Not only had she made herself at home in his kitchen, but there were also signs she'd been busy cleaning up. And he spotted a large ball of dough rising on the counter. Just how long had she been here?

Normally he was a light sleeper. How had she managed to do all of this without waking him? But there was something satisfying about how at-home she looked here, how right it seemed to have her humming over a meal in his kitchen. It tugged at a long-buried yearning for a

different kind of life... Then he shook his head, irritated
with himself. He wasn't looking for a wife; he was looking for a mother for the children. Besides, just what did
she think she was doing, letting herself in here without
permission?

Miss Whitman finally turned and spotted him. "Well,
hello there. Did you have a nice nap?"

He stiffened at that. "Glad to see you made yourself
at home," he said, pointedly ignoring her question.

She smiled, waving her cook spoon haphazardly. "I
hope you don't mind that I let myself in, but no one answered my knock."

"You must not have knocked very loud."

By her raised brow he could tell his dry tone hadn't
been wasted on her this time.

"Perhaps not. But I figured the children would be
sleeping and I didn't want to disturb them. They needed
to get some rest after your journey. As did you."

"I apologize for not being available to show you
around," he said stiffly. "But you appear to have found
everything you needed on your own."

Either missing the sarcasm or choosing to ignore it,
she nodded. "No apologies needed," she said brightly.
"As you can see, I'm quite capable of finding my way
around a kitchen all on my own."

There was definitely no denying that. He looked
around. Apparently she'd found all the dishes, pots and
utensils she needed.

"I checked on the children when I got here," she said,
turning back to the stove. "The little lambs were sleeping sound as could be."

What had she thought of finding him snoozing on
the sofa?

Pushing that decidedly uncomfortable thought away,

he looked for something else to focus on. "What's that you're cooking?"

"Rabbit stew. I also plan to bake some bread and prepare a peach cobbler for dessert." She glanced over her shoulder at him. "I hope you don't mind, but I took the liberty of picking up a few things for your larder since you'll be cooking for three now."

Cooking for three—something else he hadn't thought through yet. Kids probably required more than the plain fare he normally cooked for himself. But that was his problem, not hers. "Thank you."

She gave him a curious look. "I hope it's not too forward of me, but I'd like to ask a question about your time in Colorado."

He hadn't noticed that being forward was something she worried overmuch about. "Ask away."

"You were gone for several weeks. Were the children in your care during that time?"

"Not entirely. Miss Booth, a friend of my sister's, took them in right after the accident. Chloe needed doctoring and I had to tend to the funerals and to the settling of their parents' business affairs. Besides, I was staying in a hotel. It just seemed best that they stay where they could be more comfortable and have someone familiar to take care of them. I checked in on them every day, though."

"I see."

There was something about the way she said that that raised his suspicions. "And just what is it that you see?"

"That you really don't have much experience caring for them on your own yet. Not that it's your fault. It's just something we'll need to take into consideration."

Then she smiled. "But enough of that. Did the menu sound to your liking?"

"Yes, of course. Let me thank you again for taking the time to—"

She waved his thanks aside. "Oh, you're quite welcome. I'm happy to do it."

Hank rubbed the back of his neck, wondering how she would react if he asked her for another favor, especially since he hadn't been exactly gracious so far.

Before he could figure out the best way to ask, she turned around. "There's no point in you standing around, watching me cook. I figure you're eager to go down to the mill and check on how your business fared while you were away. Since Alex and Chloe are sleeping, now would be a good time. The stew won't be ready to eat for a while yet and the children will probably sleep at least another hour."

How did she always manage to anticipate him like that? "If you're sure you don't mind, I *would* like to drive out to the mill. I'll try not to be gone too long."

"There's no need for you to rush on my account. The children and I will be fine while you are gone."

He bowed. "Once more I'm in your debt."

She grinned. "I'm not nearly as altruistic as you seem to believe. But I really think I can help the three of you, and it would give me immense satisfaction to do so."

He wasn't sure what to say to that, so he merely nodded and headed out to the small carriage house, where he kept his buckboard.

And as he went, he found himself wondering why the schoolteacher, who had such an obvious fondness for children, wasn't married. Sure, she was a bit bossy, but he knew there were men who'd be willing to overlook that, especially given her other attributes.

Unless there was something wrong with her that he hadn't seen yet. He supposed he should keep a close eye on her, just to see if he could figure out what that might be.

* * *

"Where's Uncle Hank?"

Janell looked up to see Alex standing in the doorway, watching her with solemn eyes.

"He went down to the sawmill." She tried to infuse her voice with reassurance. "He'll be back in time for supper."

The boy cocked his head to one side, as if trying to puzzle something out. "Do you live here, too?"

Was she imagining the hopeful tone in his voice? "No, sweetheart, I just came over to help your uncle make your first day here as comfortable as possible."

Alex nodded but didn't say anything. And didn't seem inclined to come any closer. What was he afraid of?

She waved a hand toward the counter, where a couple of loaves of bread were cooling. "I just pulled those out of the oven. I love the aroma of fresh-baked bread, don't you? Why don't you have a seat at the table and I'll cut you off a piece so we can see if it tastes as good as it smells?"

He finally moved forward, but didn't say anything.

"Where's Chloe?" she asked, trying to draw him out.

"She's still in bed." He slid onto his chair, watching as she sliced the bread.

"Is she still asleep?"

He shook his head. "No, ma'am. She's reading."

The way he eyed the bread, one would think he hadn't eaten for days. She placed a thick slice on a saucer and set it in front of him. "Perhaps I should ask her if she wants a little something to eat, too."

Alex popped up out of his chair. "I'll go."

She waved him back down. "Enjoy your bread. I'll go."

Alex slowly sat again, his expression troubled.

The little boy was touchingly protective of his sister. Admirable, but she had to help him focus on just being an eight-year-old.

Janell grabbed the large slate and some chalk she'd fetched from the schoolhouse earlier and headed for Chloe's bedchamber. She paused in front of the door, her hand raised to knock. Such an action was meaningless in this situation. She'd need to find a way to perform that function visually in order to allow the girl her privacy. For Lizzie they'd rigged a system with rope and cloth flags.

Janell opened the door and paused on the threshold, waiting for Chloe to notice her. The girl, who was reclining on the bed with her book, looked up, and Janell saw the flicker of surprise, quickly replaced with a not-quite-genuine frown of indifference. The cat, who was curled at the child's feet, watched Janell with an unblinking stare. Janell stepped into the room and walked right up to the bed. She placed a hand lightly on the book, forcing Chloe to look up again.

"Would you like to join us in the kitchen?" She carefully enunciated each word.

The girl shook her head.

Was she declining the offer? Or had she merely not understood? Janell quickly wrote the same question on the slate and turned it so Chloe could read it.

Chloe again shook her head.

Janell erased the slate and this time wrote *I have fresh bread*. She paused and then added *Your uncle is at his sawmill right now*.

Chloe seemed to think about that a moment, then nodded and set her book down. When she climbed off the bed, the cat uncurled, then gracefully jumped to the floor and followed.

Once in the kitchen, Chloe pulled up a chair next to Alex while Janell sliced off another piece of bread. Once she'd served the girl her snack, she put a bowl of water on the floor near the stove for Smudge.

How was Mr. Chandler going to manage the care of these children? They'd obviously need lots of attention for the foreseeable future, attention he'd never be able to provide on his own. At the very least he needed a housekeeper. A wife would be even better.

Did he realize this? If not, he was in for a rude awakening.

Of course, he might take offense at her bringing up such a topic—she'd noticed he didn't always take kindly to her advice. But to do him credit, he *did* listen, and that was a good quality for a husband to have.

Besides, when it came to the welfare of the children, she was willing to risk his irritation. And if she were to be entirely honest with herself, she rather liked getting the occasional rise out of him.

For just a moment she found herself wondering what it might be like to be married to such a man, a man so different from—

She abruptly pulled her thoughts away from that precipice. Time to grab back on to that control she'd worked so hard to maintain over her emotions since leaving Illinois.

She'd never had this happen before, not in all the time she'd been in Texas. What was it about Mr. Chandler that had allowed him to slip past her control so easily?

Hank headed out of the mill, pausing to give Gus a scratch behind the ears. The sawmill's resident dog was tame with people he knew, but the mostly-boxer was an excellent guard dog. Hank never had a problem with strangers or troublemakers hanging around the mill.

With a last rub of the dog's fur, Hank straightened and headed for his wagon. From what he'd seen of the operation and the books just now, Simon Tucker had done a fine job of keeping the mill running while he was gone. And that set his mind at ease.

He climbed in the wagon and turned Hector, the horse, toward home. Simon had assured him that he could continue to pull double duty as long as Hank needed him to, but Hank didn't want to take advantage of him. Simon had a family of his own to look after, one that included ten children and a wife. So he'd assured Simon he'd be back at the helm by Monday. Surely Aunt Rowena would be here by then.

But of course, that wasn't the final solution. Aunt Rowena had her own home and friends in Clampton. She'd agreed to help him until he could make other, more permanent arrangements. He couldn't see her staying for more than a few weeks—a month at most.

His original plan had been to find a housekeeper, one who would take on the care of the children as part of her duties. But when he'd learned about the sizable debt Enid and her husband had left behind, a debt he felt honor bound to make right, he realized he would no longer have the funds to do that.

The entire situation left him with the rather unappealing option of getting married. Just the idea of going through the motions of finding the right kind of woman and then convincing her to marry him was somehow distasteful.

He rubbed his chin in thought. But if he could convince the schoolteacher to take on that role, it would certainly save him a lot of trouble and time.

Not just that—she was uniquely equipped to deal with Chloe, and the kids already knew her. He admitted he wouldn't mind having her around on a regular basis himself. Yep, marrying Miss Whitman would certainly solve a lot of his problems.

Would the starchy schoolteacher be willing to consider an offer from him?

Well, it certainly couldn't hurt to ask.

As he let the horse have its head, Hank wondered why he hadn't taken much notice of Miss Whitman before. He'd always had the somewhat vague impression that she was a typical schoolmarm—rather spinsterish and pragmatic.

Well, he'd seen now that there was much more to her—a certain spark that lit her up from the inside. Even her bossy tendencies weren't altogether unappealing when it came down to it. And she certainly knew how to deal with children. He'd pick an opportune moment and come right out and ask her. Tonight, if at all possible.

Chapter Five

When Hank arrived back at the house, he tended to his horse and wagon first. When at last he was done, he headed to the pump by the water trough to wash up. He'd been gone longer than he'd planned—how was Miss Whitman faring with the kids?

Probably much better than he would have been.

When he stepped inside, he found her and the two young'uns at the table in the kitchen. Miss Whitman appeared to be teaching them how to do some complicated cat's cradle designs with loops of string laced through their fingers. And the kids—both of them—were actually smiling.

They looked like, well, like a family. And for just a moment he had a keen desire to fit into that picture. The tug of that longing startled him in its intensity.

Then the kids saw him, and the immediate change in their demeanor made it clear that he *didn't* fit, that he was still someone who had yet to earn their trust, much less their affection.

He'd excused that reaction before because of what they'd been through. But this time it was harder to dismiss because he'd seen their relaxed attitude around

Miss Whitman, a woman they'd just met hours ago and who had no blood ties to them at all.

So that meant it *was* personal, at least in part.

When Miss Whitman looked up, she, at least, gave him a welcoming smile. "Mr. Chandler. I trust you found all was well at your sawmill?"

He moved forward with a nod, entering the kitchen fully. "Simon's a good second-in-command." He glanced at the kids. "It looks like you all are enjoying yourselves." He spotted the chalk and slate on the table. Did Miss Whitman plan to leave that here with them? It would sure make communicating with Chloe easier.

But they could discuss that later. "That stew smells good."

Miss Whitman straightened. "I imagine you're hungry." She turned to the kids. "And I'm sure you are, too. Why don't we get the table ready? Your uncle can show you where the dishes and cutlery are stored." She picked up the slate and wrote on it as she talked, and now she turned it around so Chloe could read it.

Hank realized the kids were waiting for him to do as Miss Whitman had asked, so he moved toward the cabinets. He retrieved the dishes and utensils and handed them to the children, who then transported them to the table.

As they arranged things properly, Hank approached Miss Whitman at the stove. "Is there anything I can help with?"

She glanced over her shoulder at him, then nodded toward the counter beside her. "You can slice that loaf of bread and put it on the table, if you don't mind."

"Of course." As Hank grabbed a knife he noticed there was already a portion missing from one loaf. "Looks like someone's been doing some sampling," he said as he began slicing. Then he inhaled the smell of the fresh-baked bread with appreciation. "My grandma used to say that you could always tell how good a cook a woman was by the bread she baked. I think you'd pass even her test with this loaf."

She raised a brow at that. "But you haven't tasted it yet."

"The aroma and how nicely it slices are enough to tell the tale."

He turned to transport the bread to the table and paused a moment. His kitchen table was of a modest size, square with four chairs situated around it. But this evening, the children had rearranged things so that there were two chairs on one side. Should he say something or let it go?

He glanced Miss Whitman's way, wondering if he should let her handle this. But she had her back to them and hadn't yet noticed. There was no way for him to bring it to her attention without the children, or at least Alex, noticing.

He decided to let it go and carried the bread platter to the table as if nothing was amiss.

Later, as they prepared to take their seats, Miss Whitman gave them an apologetic smile from her position at the stove. "I couldn't find a large serving bowl. So for tonight I think we'll just put the pot on the table to serve from."

Hank quickly took the pot from her. He didn't think he actually *owned* a large serving bowl. He rarely cooked more than he could eat in one sitting, so he had no needs in that area. He supposed that was yet another thing he'd have to take care of now that his household had expanded.

Miss Whitman placed a folded cloth on the table and he carefully set the pot on it.

She took her seat and he moved to the other side to take his. He'd barely settled when she gave him a meaningful look.

"Mr. Chandler, would you say the blessing for us, please?"

"Of course." What else could he say? Before he bowed his head, he saw Alex touch his sister's arm and then fold his hands to indicate they were going to pray. That sort of direction was no doubt why Chloe felt the need to keep her brother close.

Then Hank closed his eyes and reached deep for the words. It had been quite some time since he'd prayed aloud. "Lord, we thank You for granting us safe travel home to Turnabout. And thank You for this meal we are about to partake of. Thank You, too, for bringing someone as generous as Miss Whitman into our midst. We ask that You grant Aunt Rowena's friend renewed health so that she may get to Turnabout in the coming days. And in all things keep us mindful of Your grace. Amen."

As he looked up, Miss Whitman softly echoed his *amen* and gave him a warm smile of approval.

That smile touched a spot inside him he'd thought long dead.

Then she sat up straighter. "Rather than passing this heavy pot of stew around, if you'll pass me your bowls, I'll serve each of you."

"Here, let me help." Hank stood and reached for Alex's and Chloe's bowls. He held them up to the pot while Miss Whitman ladled the thick, rich-looking stew into each. Then he set the full bowls in front of the kids and reached for his own.

Alex and Chloe were mostly silent during the meal, but Miss Whitman seemed to take no notice. She kept the conversation going without apparent effort. She asked him some questions about his sawmill and about his home.

He did his part to keep the conversation going, mostly by asking her questions about her life before she'd moved to Turnabout. But she always answered superficially or changed the subject. Was she trying to act the woman of mystery? Or was she truly hiding something?

When the meal was done, Miss Whitman stood to fetch the cobbler while Hank carried the stew pot to the counter.

He saw what was coming a split second before it happened. Miss Whitman had approached the table with the cobbler and was frowning down at the dish, saying something about hoping she hadn't let it bake too long.

At the same time Chloe, who had slipped a bit of bread to Smudge, straightened back up just as Miss Whitman was in the process of setting the dish on the table. Somehow her movement jostled Miss Whitman's arm so that the dish slipped from her grip and landed on the floor with a plop, sending bits of filling and crust splattering in a wide radius.

Chloe slapped a hand over her mouth, a stricken expression on her face. Alex let out a loud *oh*, but for a moment there was no other sound, no other movement in the room. Then Smudge approached one of the splatters and began delicately lapping it up.

Miss Whitman reached a hand out toward Chloe, but before she could reassure or comfort the girl, Chloe erupted from her chair and, with tears flowing, went running to her room.

Hank felt he should follow her, but what was the point? Even if he knew what words to say, she wouldn't be able to hear them.

He looked to Miss Whitman and she returned his gaze with a self-reproaching grimace.

"That was my fault," she said. "I'd forgotten—one of the first rules of interacting with the deaf is to never approach from their blind side if you can avoid it." She looked down at the mess on the floor, then faced in the direction Chloe had run off.

"Go," he said, guiltily relieved she wanted to be the one to comfort his niece. "Alex and I will clean this up."

She gave him a grateful smile. "There's a bit left in the dish. If you set it aside before Smudge gets to it, you and Alex should still be able to have some dessert."

"I don't—"

She made a small movement with her chin that stopped him. Then she glanced toward Alex, who was wearing a helpless, suspiciously watery-eyed look.

Of course—she wanted him to keep the boy distracted.

He rescued the remaining cobbler, placing the pan on the table. "I suppose it would be a shame to let a perfectly good pan of cobbler go to waste," he said thoughtfully. "What do you say, Alex? Let's get this cleaned up for Miss Whitman. Then we can reward ourselves with dessert."

Alex obediently slid from his chair. As Hank placed a hand on the boy's shoulder, he glanced Miss Whitman's way. She gave him a barely perceptible nod of approval, then lifted the slate and chalk and started out of the room. Then she paused, turned back and, with a quick, graceful movement, reached down and scooped up the cat with one arm. "I'll get Smudge out of your way," she said by way of explanation. "And Chloe will probably be glad of his company right now."

Now, more than ever, Hank was convinced the pretty,

warmhearted schoolteacher would make the perfect mother for the children.

If only he could convince her of that.

Janell pushed Chloe's door open and stepped inside to find the girl crying into her pillow. She sat down on the edge of the bed, setting Smudge beside her.

Chloe immediately sat up. When she saw who it was, she swiped the tears from her face and her expression tensed, taking on a prickly, resentful tightness, even as she cuddled the cat.

Janell placed a hand on the girl's knee, giving her what she hoped was a reassuring smile. Then she picked up the slate and wrote *Not your fault*.

Chloe read it, but rather than easing her distress, it seemed to increase it.

Janell quickly erased the slate and tried again. *I should have paid closer attention.*

Chloe rested her chin on her pet's soft fur. "It wouldn't have happened if I could still hear."

Again Janell erased the slate and started writing. *Mishaps happen to everyone. Didn't you bump and spill things before your accident?*

Chloe's expression shifted as a touch of doubt and thoughtfulness crept in.

Feeling she'd done all she could for now, Janell gave Chloe's leg another pat, then stood. It was going to take time, but she was determined to get through to the girl.

When she returned to the kitchen, Janell was surprised to see the worst of the mess had been cleaned up. She gave both of the menfolk a smile. "You've done a fine job, gentlemen. Why don't you let me finish up while you see how that bit of cobbler we salvaged tastes?"

Alex looked up, his worry plain. "Is Chloe okay?"

"She's embarrassed, but otherwise all right."

Alex seemed to accept her words at face value and his mood lightened as he took his seat again. Janell met Mr. Chandler's gaze over the boy's head and saw the relief in his expression as well.

She spooned some of the remaining cobbler into Alex's dish, then turned to do the same for his uncle.

But Mr. Chandler stopped her. "It wouldn't be very gentlemanly of me to eat while you finish cleaning the mess." And he went back to work wiping down a table leg.

Well, well, the man wasn't afraid of housework, nor did he seem to consider it strictly woman's work. A nice surprise.

By the time the two of them had the mess cleaned up, Alex had finished his cobbler.

"May I be excused?" the boy asked. The question seemed to be directed at her, but Janell waved a hand Mr. Chandler's way, letting Alex know she thought it his uncle's place to answer.

Mr. Chandler nodded. "Yes, of course. But carry your dishes to the counter first."

His attempt to instill some discipline surprised Janell yet again. The more she was around this man, the more persuaded she became that he actually had the makings of a good father.

Once the boy left the kitchen, no doubt headed to check in on Chloe, Janell waved a hand toward the table. "Ready for your cobbler?" There was just enough for one serving left.

"Only if you share it with me."

"Oh, but—"

"I insist."

"Perhaps I'll have just a bite." But before she could

serve it up, he performed the task for her and made sure the remaining cobbler was divided equally.

Yet more proof that despite his sometimes gruff manner, Mr. Chandler was a gentleman at heart.

Why *was* this man still a bachelor? Didn't the single women of Turnabout see what a catch he was?

As they dug into the dessert, Hank wondered how he would have handled all of this afternoon's little upsets without Miss Whitman's assistance.

As if reading his mind, the schoolteacher gave him an apologetic smile. "I hope you won't let this worry you overmuch. Such things happen, even with hearing children, and a girl of Chloe's age is easily embarrassed."

Was this what he had to look forward to? "Surely there's a way to minimize these incidents."

"No need to look so horrified. I assure you you'll get through this. Once the children settle in, and get used to having you as their guardian, things will settle down. But first we need to help Chloe realize her life isn't over."

She stood to clear the table, but he tried to wave her back down.

"Don't worry about the dishes—I can take care of that later. You'll want to head home before dark and I'd like for us to have that talk while we can."

She nodded but didn't pause. "Of course. But I can talk while I work."

Stubborn woman. He grabbed their plates and marched to the sink.

She raised a brow. "Do you prefer to wash or dry?"

"Dry." If he was the one to put the dishes away, it might keep her from rearranging any more of his cupboards.

She nodded and began filling the basin. "First of all,

is there someone you have in mind who'll keep an eye on the children while you're at work?"

"Not yet, but I'm hoping Aunt Rowena will arrive by Monday or Tuesday at the latest. I figure, until she gets here or I can make other arrangements, I'll only go to the sawmill while they're at school."

She turned to face him, her eyes wide with disbelief. "You can't possibly be contemplating sending these children to school on Monday."

From the way she asked the question, it was obvious the correct answer was no. But her tone got his back up. "Why not? Attending school is something they'll be familiar with. I would think the sooner I set routines for them, the sooner they'll adjust to their new life."

"School might be familiar to them, but not *this* school and not under *these* circumstances." She looked him straight in the eyes. "Have you forgotten that Chloe will have no idea how to communicate with either the other students or with her teacher?"

"Of course not. But *you're* her teacher and you said you've dealt with this before. And that slate you brought seemed to work pretty well."

She waved a hand dismissively, not seeming to notice the droplets of water she dispensed in the process. "The slate is just a stopgap measure to use here at home. It's not something that will serve her in more public situations."

He wanted to challenge that declaration, but decided to hold his peace. "What about Alex? Surely it would be good for him to go? It doesn't seem right for him to be constantly looking out for his sister the way he does."

"I agree—you absolutely do need to separate the two, for Alex's good as well as Chloe's. Alex can't make worrying about his sister his whole world the way he's trying to right now."

He sensed there was a *but* coming.

"But he *is* worried about her and he *does* feel a sense of responsibility for her."

He sighed.

"You can't just tell him to let it go and expect it to happen," she continued. "Alex needs some kind of assurance that Chloe will be okay without having him constantly by her side before he can focus on class work and on just being a little boy. If we do our job right, I'm hoping he'll be ready by midweek."

He supposed he should be happy that at least they agreed on the need to separate the children. "Just what does doing our job right entail?" She had yet to describe exactly how she planned to help Chloe.

"It means we prove to Alex that we have Chloe's best interest at heart, that even though she won't necessarily be happy with her situation, we are doing whatever we can to make it better for her."

She continued to say *we*, as if she didn't plan to just give him the necessary tools and leave but actually planned to help him wield them. It gave him hope that perhaps he could convince her to make her involvement with the children more permanent.

But now wasn't the time to bring that up. "We keep talking around the main question. Again, how do we help Chloe?"

"We've already started. You're doing what you can to give both of them the stability of a home. But you need to take the next step." She looked at him diffidently, as if she wasn't sure if she should say whatever was on her mind.

"And just what is that next step?" he asked.

"You must show them that you're not only willing to make a home for them here, but that you are *pleased* to do so, that you don't resent their presence in your life."

He shrugged. "That's no problem because I *don't* resent them." Not exactly, anyway.

"Don't you?"

Who did she think she was to judge him? "No. But what I *do* resent, Miss Whitman, are the circumstances that put us all in this position. I resent that some careless yahoo, who was more worried about his schedule than the safety of innocent folk, drove a load of explosives through town instead of going the long way around to the mine like he was supposed to. I resent that my sister died much too young and I will never, ever see her again. And I resent that she will never get the chance to see her children grow up or hold her grandbabies in her arms." He took a deep breath. "And I especially resent that those kids are stuck with me rather than the parents they should have had."

There was a soft sympathy in her gaze now and it made him shift uncomfortably.

He'd said way too much.

Chapter Six

Janell was surprised by Mr. Chandler's bitter outburst. He'd always seemed so unruffled by his circumstances. It was an eye-opener to realize he did indeed have deeper, more passionate feelings. "I'm so sorry for all you've gone through," she said, touching his arm briefly. "That's a terrible loss for anyone to bear. And I have no doubt that you truly care for your niece and nephew."

She meant what she'd said, but he needed to understand the impact on the children. "The problem is, that's not what Chloe and Alex are seeing."

His jaw tightened. "I shouldn't have said all that. And I don't see how it'll serve any good purpose for me to let the kids know how I feel. I need to be strong for them."

His earnestness was touching. "You misunderstand. Of course you don't want to display anger or bitterness."

She saw him stiffen at that. Perhaps she should have been more tactful. "On the other hand," she continued quickly, "I think it *would* be good for them to see how deeply you mourn the loss of your sister and brother-in-law. And even more importantly, you should let them see that you love them and are prepared to take on the role of parent."

"I can't take the place of their parents." There was a suspicious gruffness in his voice, but he'd turned to put away a bowl so she couldn't see his face.

"You're correct. No one can replace their parents."

The look he shot her was one of surprise.

"At least not in the sense you mean," she said to clarify. "But you *can* be a parent figure, someone to care about them, raise them, guide them, just as a loving parent would. Surely you know that to children, especially young children, parents are the most important people in their lives. Parents are the foundation that grounds them and gives them the confidence to try new things, knowing there is a safe haven to return to."

He turned to face her and she could tell he wasn't entirely convinced. "I'm sorry if I keep coming back to this, but it's very important that Alex and Chloe feel both welcomed and loved here."

"Miss Whitman, I am not a demonstrative man. If it's hugs and kisses you're referring to—"

She made a dismissive motion with her hand. "There are other ways of showing love. And like it or not, you have no choice. You can't just say the words—you must show it in your actions as well." She tried to lighten her tone. "But I'm sure you'll work that part out in your own way."

His lips pinched in a thin, rebellious line. "I appreciate your suggestions. But this doesn't address how to help Chloe."

His words had a hard edge to them. It was what she'd meant about how he talked to the children. But he obviously wasn't open to discussing that right now.

"For instance," he continued, "is writing on a slate how you communicated with your sister?"

She nodded as she placed another plate in the wash

water. "We did at first, but as I said, it's a clumsy method at best. My father was determined to do all he could to help Lizzie, though, so we called on the best doctors and teachers who worked with the deaf. With their help we eventually found better ways to communicate."

He raised a brow. "Such as?"

"Teaching her to read lips. And the use of sign language."

He paused a moment. "Sign language—I thought that was a tool for the mute."

"The mute learn to sign in order to communicate what they have to say. But it only works if those around them can read the language. For the deaf it's just the opposite. Those around them must learn to sign and the affected person must learn to understand the signs."

He nodded thoughtfully. "That makes sense."

"Which means, of course, that this is going to be a significant amount of work for all three of you. All of you must learn to sign. If you're not committed to putting in the time to do this properly, then it will never work."

He took the clean plate from her. "I understand."

"Of course, it also means Chloe must *want* to learn."

His brow creased. "Why wouldn't she? After all, she's the one with the most to gain. It will allow her to communicate with the people around her again."

She was glad he understood the ramifications. "Yes, but if she's like my sister, she's going to be afraid of what will happen if she fails. And it reinforces the fact that she will always be different from everyone else around her."

"But surely, on some level at least, she already knows this."

"Of course, but that doesn't mean she's ready to admit it. I didn't say these were reasonable feelings, just that it's likely that she'll be resistant and that that resistance will be based in fear. We need to help her get beyond all of that so she actually *wants* to learn."

"How?"

"By forcing her to communicate that way and not give her other options. It sounds harsh, but once she has a few successes under her belt it will get easier—for all of us."

He rubbed his chin. "Even if we succeed, that means she'll only be able to communicate with us. And you, of course."

"True, but only at first. As she makes friends, they'll want to learn to sign as well. Her circle will slowly grow." She gave him a direct look. "But you're right—it will never include everyone, and it won't ever be like it was before."

He grimaced. "Cheery thought."

"It's important that you understand the reality so you can help Chloe face it." She tried for an encouraging smile. "The next step, however, will help her widen her circle."

"And that next step is?"

"Lipreading. Once she masters that skill it will open many more doors for her." From all accounts her sister had become quite adept at it. It was good to know Lizzie was adapting so well.

"And this is something she can learn?"

"Not everyone does, I'm afraid, but Lizzie did." It still pained Janell that she hadn't been there to witness and celebrate her triumphs. "If we can get Chloe to learn to read sign language, and gain some skill in lipreading, it will open the world back up for her. Right now she's feeling like she won't ever fit in again. The sooner we equip her with these skills, the sooner we can make her see that her future isn't as bleak as it seems to her right now."

He gave her a skeptical look. "But, to be realistic, she will always be different."

Janell nodded. "Of course. But our job is to make her see that different doesn't mean unlovable. She has to see she can lead a very fulfilling life even though she will always be deaf." She gave him a searching look. "And that means you need to believe it yourself and then make sure she sees that you do." She raised a brow. "Can you do that?"

He nodded, then changed the subject. "So tell me a little bit about signing."

Janell dried her hands on a clean rag. "There are two different skills involved. First we'll work on the alphabet." She held her hand up and began to form the shapes. "This is *A*, and this is *B*, and this is *C*."

She was surprised by how quickly the movements came back to her. It had been four years since she'd had occasion to use sign language.

Because that was how long it had been since she'd last seen her family.

As Hank watched her contort her fingers into the shapes for each letter, he wondered if he'd ever be able to duplicate her motions, especially with such grace. He'd have to learn twenty-six of these signs?

"What about Alex?" he asked. "I'm sure he knows his letters, but I'm not sure he can form words yet."

"Unless the school where he's from is significantly different from Turnabout's, at age eight he should at least be able to spell simple words, but you're probably right that he'll have limitations. So that means he won't be able to use very much of that skill just yet. The burden for much of that will be on you. But I'm certain Alex will manage enough to communicate with Chloe. And he *can* learn the other component to signing."

"Which is?"

"There are signs that encompass whole words and even phrases. Some are fairly obvious." She crossed her wrists over her chest. "This is *love*." She shifted, pressing her palms together. "This is *praying*." Then she opened her palms, keeping the edge of her hands touching. "This is *book* or *reading*."

"That seems much more practical than the alphabet."

"They both have their place. There are some things that there's no shorthand for, such as proper names." She gave him a warning look. "And not all signs are quite that obvious. For instance, this means *play*." She held both hands out about chest high, extended her thumbs and pinkies, then wiggled the hands themselves. "And this means *work*." She made loose fists with both hands then tapped the right with the left twice.

"How long did it take before you were able to really communicate with your sister?"

"Well, it certainly didn't happen overnight." She placed the last of the dishes in the rinse water and emptied the washbasin. "Once we found someone to teach us what to do and to provide the materials we'd need, it took a few weeks before we really felt as if we were making progress. The hardest thing with Lizzie—and I think this will be true of Chloe, too—was convincing her that it would truly help make her life better."

Reading between the lines of some of the things she'd said, it sounded as if she came from a well-to-do family. It made sense—she seemed to have the manner, speech and education of someone who'd grown up with certain advantages.

So how had she ended up in Turnabout?

"What were these materials you got access to?" And what had they cost? He intended to do whatever he could to help Chloe. But at the moment he didn't have a lot of money to spare.

She waved a hand. "Mostly texts on sign language and a few academic texts outlining what we as a family could expect and how best to deal with Lizzie."

"Do you still have them?"

She nodded. "In fact, I still have the notebook I made on the subject of sign language. The rest stayed in Dentonville. But I've sent letters to my sister and to Dr. Carson requesting whatever they can spare." She dried her hands again, then moved toward the hall. "I brought my notebook with me so you can take a look at it if you like."

Miss Whitman might be a bit too take-charge for his liking, but she was definitely going above and beyond what he'd expected.

He had the last dish dried and put away by the time she returned. "So when do we start?"

"I assume you'll be taking the two of them to church tomorrow?"

She still seemed to have trouble giving a direct answer. As he thought about her question, though, he shifted. Could he really get the kids ready to go if Chloe pulled one of her stubborn, you-can't-make-me maneuvers?

Seeming to read his mind, Miss Whitman pursed her lips. "You need to be firm with Chloe. She's really more scared than anything else." She set the notebook on the table. "The best thing you can do is to keep the world around her as normal as possible and not let her retreat into herself."

Easier said than done. "I'll do my best."

She smiled. "I know you will. If it's all right with you, I'll sit in the same pew with the three of you so there will be someone else they know."

He moved to the table. "I'm sure the kids will appreciate that." And he wouldn't mind having the extra support nearby, either.

She took a seat at the table, seeming to hesitate for a moment. "There are a few things you should watch out for. The townsfolk here, for the most part, are a friendly and caring group. They will naturally welcome the three of you back and commiserate with you and the children on your loss."

She clasped her hands on the table. "Some will already know of Chloe's condition, but some folks may not. Regardless, there will be some awkward moments and faux pas. It may make Alex uncomfortable, and whether she understands what's being said or not, Chloe will find all of it overwhelming. We'll need to shield them from as much of this as we can."

Hank joined her at the table. He felt an unaccountable urge to grasp those clasped hands of hers just to see if they felt as warm and soft as they looked. Then he gave his head a mental shake and raised his gaze to meet hers. "Perhaps it would be best if I kept her home this Sunday."

But Miss Whitman shook her head firmly. "The sooner she's forced to go out among people again, the sooner she'll learn to adjust. We just need to be careful, however we react to what happens tomorrow, that we don't make her feel singled out or that we are in any way ashamed of her."

Her continued, matter-of-fact use of *we* was reassuring. But he had to be careful or he'd find himself coming to depend on her a little too much.

However, it did bode well for the possibility of convincing her to marry him.

He had to choose the right moment.

But that right moment needed to happen soon.

Janell saw an expression she couldn't quite read flit across Mr. Chandler's face. Had she said something he disagreed with?

"How do you suggest we do that?" he asked.

It took her a heartbeat to remember what he was referring to. Oh, yes, her statement about helping Chloe. "Select a pew near the back of the church so if it becomes necessary to make a quick exit, we can slip out with the minimum of disruption. It's best if Chloe doesn't feel too hemmed in."

"That sounds doable."

His attention to what she had to say was endearing. "Once the service is over, we'll want to try to make certain there are only a few people around us at any one time. Leave that part to me. I'll recruit a few of the choir ladies to help me manage how many folks can approach."

He frowned. "I forgot you're in the choir. I can't ask—"

"Don't worry—they can manage tomorrow with one less singer."

She moved on before he could object further. "This strategy is based on lessons my family and I learned the hard way with Lizzie. Her first few times going out in a crowd were difficult, both for her and for us. I'm hoping we can make things easier for Chloe."

She gave him a direct look. "But you should be prepared, because nothing you do will make it completely without incident."

He nodded and rubbed the side of his jaw. "We've been talking about Chloe, but what about Alex?"

His insightful question surprised her. "I'm glad you understand Alex will need some attention as well. We definitely don't want him to feel left out or that we don't recognize what he's gone through. He's suffered a painful loss, too."

She leaned back. "He's lost his parents, his sister has grown dependent on him and he's been moved hundreds of miles from all that's familiar to him, to live with an uncle he barely knows."

"I take it this is not a situation you encountered with your sister."

She ignored the sarcasm in his tone. "No, but I do have some experience working with children who are dealing with loss. One thing that will help is sending Alex back to school before Chloe. That will allow him to make new friends and gradually find his way back to being a little boy again."

"And here at home?"

"I wish I could give you all the answers, but that's something you'll have to figure out as you go. What he'll need is what any child needs—make certain he knows that he really matters to you. Pay enough attention to commend him when he accomplishes something, and comfort him when he's hurting or feels he's failed in some way."

Mr. Chandler shifted, as if uncertain or uncomfortable with what she'd said. Impulsively, Janell put her hand over his where it rested on top of the table. "You *can* do this."

He stared at her hand on his with an odd expression on his face.

Feeling her cheeks warm, Janell drew her hand back as if scorched.

Had she overstepped yet again?

Chapter Seven

Hank was caught off guard by the soft warmth of the schoolteacher's touch. There had been very few tender, feminine influences in his life these past seven years. He'd forgotten just how pleasant it could be.

When she jerked her hand away, he realized his silence had unnerved her. And this time she hadn't misinterpreted his reaction.

Best to get the discussion back on track. "So I'll try to keep an eye on Alex. How soon do you think he'll be ready to return to school?"

There was still a touch of uncertainty in her expression, but the pink in her cheeks was subsiding.

"I'm hoping by Wednesday." Miss Whitman nodded. "Since your aunt has been delayed, I'll make plans for someone else to take over for me in the classroom Monday and Tuesday, just in case her delay is extended."

He seemed to be getting deeper into her debt. "But what about your students?"

"Since you don't have children—" she shot him an apologetic look "—or at least didn't before now, you may not know that just this year the town hired Patience Bruder to help me and Mr. Parker in our classrooms. She spends an hour with me in the mornings and an hour helping Mr. Parker in the afternoon."

Hank wasn't surprised. The town was growing and so was the number of children attending school. Just last year Simon Tucker had moved into town with no fewer than ten children in his care.

"Anyway," she continued, "Patience has been helping out when needed since school opened in September. I can ask her to fill in full-time for a day or two. Besides, I've only missed two days of teaching since I started here, so I think the town council won't complain if I take a few days off."

He rubbed his jaw. "Miss Whitman, I don't want you to take this the wrong way, because, believe me, I'm more grateful than I can say for all of your help so far and all you've offered to do in the days to come. But I have to ask, *why* are you doing this? I mean, what you're offering here is going way above what one would normally expect."

"When this happened to my sister, we didn't have any idea what to do or how to handle things. As a result, Lizzie withdrew from everything and everyone. If there's a chance I can spare Chloe at least some small part of that, I have a duty to try."

So this was all just out of some sense of duty on her part?

"Besides," she continued with a smile, "I can use the time to work with you all on your sign-language skills."

He had to admit, it would certainly simplify his life to have her here the next few days.

"By the way, I saw Mr. Dempsey earlier today and asked him to deliver a half-dozen eggs here in the morning. I baked an extra loaf of bread tonight so there will be some for breakfast tomorrow. And there's a jar of blackberry jam in your pantry, so you should be able to provide a basic breakfast for the three of you."

Seemed she'd done a better job of thinking ahead than he had.

"After the church service, I'd like to come back here and fix a simple lunch, then sit down with the children and explain to them about our plans for you all to learn sign language. We can even start with a few easy lessons."

Apparently she *did* have it all planned out.

Something of his thoughts must have shown in his face, because she sat up straighter and folded her hands primly. "Mr. Chandler, I hope you don't think I'm being too forward with all of this. But I assure you I'm only trying to help."

"I know you are." Then he mentally grimaced. Had he even thanked her yet for all she was doing?

This time he moderated his tone. "I certainly appreciate your taking such an interest in Chloe's welfare."

"There's no need for thanks." She touched the lace at her throat diffidently. "I know this might sound a bit conceited, but I feel perhaps this is one reason God put me here in Turnabout, so there would be someone here with the skills needed to help Chloe when the time came."

There was a curious air of vulnerability about her as she said that, the first such hint he'd seen in the starchy schoolteacher. And it made him feel suddenly protective. This time it was he who touched her hand. "That doesn't sound conceited at all."

The smile she responded with was sweet enough to make him blink. Then it was gone and she gently withdrew her hand. "I do have one more suggestion."

Of course she did. "I'm listening."

"Just as you don't want to push her too hard, you don't

want to mollycoddle her, either. It's a fine line to walk, I know, but if we act as if we think she is totally helpless, she'll begin to believe that as well."

So he was supposed to both give her time to adjust and nudge her to take some responsibilities? Nothing to it.

He met her gaze and saw the soft concern in her eyes. He decided there was no time like the present. "No matter how this turns out," he told her, "I want you to know that I appreciate your efforts to help us."

Her face pinkened prettily. "Thank you, Mr. Chandler. It's always nice to know one's efforts are being appreciated."

Hank decided that he really did like her smile.

Then he drew himself up short. That was not the direction he intended this to take. It was going to be strictly business.

That was the only way he could face such an arrangement.

Hank cleared his throat. "As you can no doubt imagine, I've had to face some rather stark realities since Enid and Joe died."

Her expression softened further. "I know. And from what I've observed, you are handling the situation quite well."

"Thank you. But there's still another challenge to be faced. Aunt Rowena coming here to help out is only a short-term solution. I need to look for another, more permanent arrangement."

She nodded. "I agree."

"I need to find a wife." He stood and paced to the counter, leaning back against it. Saying the words aloud made it feel more real somehow.

She didn't seem surprised. "I see." Her dry tone made him feel defensive.

"You disapprove?"

"It is not my place to approve or disapprove. May I ask if you have already engaged the affections of a young lady here in Turnabout?"

"No, nor do I intend to." He crossed back to the table, though he didn't sit. "I'm looking to get married because the children need a mother, not because I need or want a wife. And before you voice any objections, I intend to be honest about that with whatever woman I propose to."

Again, she didn't seem particularly shocked. Nor did she seem approving, either. How did that bode for his plans?

"It's not my place to object." She pushed a stray lock of hair behind her ear. "Do you have anyone in particular in mind?"

There was something about her tone that gave him pause. But he brushed it aside—this was his opening and he intended to take it. "I've been giving it a great deal of thought, actually, and there are a few names on my list."

He met her gaze, wanting to see her reaction.

"Right now, *your* name is at the top of that list."

This time it was obvious he'd surprised her. Her posture stiffened and her eyes widened. "I beg your pardon."

He tried to read her, wanting to gauge what her main objection might be. Was it merely being caught off guard? Or did she have objections to him personally?

Or was it something else entirely?

His best course was to keep things on a logical level. "I mean no offense. But anyone can see you and the children are already forming an attachment for each other. And there's no denying you're ideally suited to deal with

Chloe. And as far as I can tell, you don't have any other prospects at the moment."

Her eyes narrowed as she glared at him. "Mr. Chandler, while it is true I have a fondness for your children, it is the fondness of a teacher for her students." She lifted her chin, her expression taking a decidedly chilly turn. "As for my prospects, *that* is none of your concern. But I'll have you know I haven't been without offers since I moved here."

He'd obviously struck a nerve. Perhaps she wasn't as free of silly romantic notions as he'd assumed. He rubbed the back of his neck. It surprised him how hard her refusal hit. And not just because this would have been a convenient solution. He'd convinced himself that the two of them would suit nicely and he'd hoped she'd feel the same way.

But it appeared it was not to be and there was no point in fretting over it.

Right now he needed to smooth her ruffled feathers—he'd rather not get on the wrong side of someone he'd be spending so much time with in the coming days.

He held up his hands, palms outward. "All right. As I said, I meant no insult, but I had to ask. If you're not interested, then you're not interested."

Janell kept her hands hidden in her lap, afraid their trembling would betray her emotions.

How dare he ask her to marry him, and in such a cavalier manner? No matter that they barely knew each other. The way he'd asked—it was clear she was no more than a convenient choice. Someone both close-at-hand and suited—like a nearby rag he'd reach for when he spilled his coffee.

His assumptions about her—that she had no prospects—stung most of all. Vain of her, she knew, but there it was. No woman liked to be thought of as a spinster.

And even if he had no way of knowing it, there had been a time in her life when she'd thought she would have it all—a loving husband, a house full of children, a respected place in the community. The fact that that had been torn from her didn't mean she still didn't yearn for it.

His proposal had brought home to her just how very alive that yearning still was inside her.

Too bad her status as a divorcée made that kind of future impossible.

Chapter Eight

Janell tried not to let her thoughts dwell on that awful, painful time in her life. No one here besides Eve knew about her ill-fated marriage and that was how she wanted it. To reveal her secret, especially after all this time, would jeopardize not only her job, but also her very position in the community. Especially if her neighbors and friends knew the circumstances. Because she wasn't just divorced—the divorce had been all her fault.

She'd taken a chance telling Eve six months ago, but was glad now that she had. Her friend had understood all too well what it was to live under the burden of a shameful past and had not been the least judgmental.

"I suppose I'll have to look elsewhere, then."

Mr. Chandler's comment pulled her back to the present. Thank goodness he seemed to have seen nothing amiss in her demeanor the past few seconds.

Still, she was unexpectedly piqued by his easy acceptance of her refusal. Apparently she was nothing more than one of the names on his list.

Janell gave a stiff nod as she sat up straighter. "So it seems," she replied, striving to keep her tone unemotional and businesslike.

"I wonder if you'd mind giving me your opinion on some potential candidates," Mr. Chandler asked.

"You want my opinion on who would make you a good wife?" Apparently he saw nothing incongruous about asking the woman he'd just proposed to to help him pick a wife.

He frowned as if insulted. "Not a wife. A mother for the children. What I need from you is an opinion on how the lady under consideration and the children would get on."

"I see." The man really didn't have an ounce of romance in him.

He nodded, apparently warming to the idea. "With your insights, you can save me from wasting time talking to someone who's obviously not the right fit."

Janell resisted the urge to roll her eyes. "Assuming you find the right woman, may I ask how you intend to approach her?"

His eyebrow shot up at that.

"If you're wondering if I intend to go a'courtin'—" his tone had a sarcastic bite to it "—the answer is a very definite no, at least not in the usual way. Like I said, I will make it clear right up front what my intentions are. I don't want to deceive anyone into thinking this will be more than a marriage of convenience."

"Your intentions are admirable, I suppose, but I would advise you not to just baldly lay out your intentions and propose."

"Well, I—"

She didn't let him finish. "I understand why you wouldn't want to go through a conventional courtship or mislead the lady as to your feelings. But don't you think you and your prospective bride should get to know each other before you propose? I mean, you must take the time to decide if she's the right one to share your home and the right one to share the responsibility for the children."

He drew himself up. "I consider myself a good judge of character. It won't take me long to figure out if she's a good candidate or not."

"I see." She held his gaze, hoping to make her disapproval obvious.

Apparently it worked. "I assume you'd handle it differently."

"I would."

"Care to elaborate?"

Was she really about to give him pointers on how to find a wife? It seemed she was. "I'd recruit a third party to act as a go-between." She leaned forward, trying to emphasize her point. "It should be someone you can count on to have your and the children's best interest in mind, someone whose judgment you trust."

"And what would this go-between do exactly?"

"Go to the candidate on your behalf, of course. He or she would let the lady in question know the situation in general terms without extending any offers or promises and ascertain said lady's interest in such a match."

"So you agree that a businesslike approach is best, just that I should go about it from a distance."

"It could save a great deal of awkwardness and misunderstanding if you did so."

"Assuming I go along with this plan of yours to use a go-between, and they acted on my behalf, then what?"

"Well, if the lady appears interested, he could ask a few discreet questions that would allow him to form an opinion of how good a fit she would be for you and the children. Then he would report back to you, and the two of you could discuss whether to pursue her or move on to another candidate."

"In other words, you think I need a matchmaker."

"You could look at it that way, I suppose. But you *do* want to approach this in a very businesslike manner, don't you?"

He nodded. "I have to admit, it sounds like a good approach."

Happy that he'd seen the wisdom of her advice, she moved to the next logical step. "Is there someone you could trust to take on this job of go-between?"

He rubbed his jaw, deep in thought. Finally he looked up. "How about you?"

"Me?" She raised a hand to her chest, surprised. "Surely you have some close friend—"

"You're already intimately acquainted with our situation. I have complete confidence that you'd be looking out for the children's best interests. And this was your idea in the first place, so I don't have to do a lot of explaining. In other words, you're the perfect candidate."

"Still, I would think you'd want someone you know better—"

"It also occurred to me that this is a role that would benefit from a woman's touch."

He had a point there.

"Besides, I believe you'll be looking out for Chloe's and Alex's best interests."

"As you said earlier, the children and I have formed an attachment. I'd like to make certain that the woman whose care they are eventually placed in can give them the love and attention they'll need."

He sat back with a smug smile. "Exactly."

Why not? "Well then, if you're *sure* you trust my judgment, I would be glad to assist you in finding a wife." As soon as the words left her mouth, Janell wondered what she'd just got herself into. Was she really going to take on the role of matchmaker for this man?

Suddenly, she had had all she could take for one day. She stood. "It's getting late—we can discuss this in more detail tomorrow."

He stood as well. "Of course. I didn't mean to keep you so long."

Had it been a mistake to agree to this? A better question was, *why* had she agreed to this? She wanted to think it was for the sake of the children alone.

But she had a niggling feeling that the fact that it would mean spending more time with their uncle had played a part as well.

Hank jammed his hands in his pockets and moved to the front of the house while Miss Whitman went to tell the children goodbye. Things hadn't worked out as he'd hoped—he should have known better than to think the straitlaced schoolteacher would agree to marry someone like him, but from the depth of the disappointment he was feeling, apparently he had.

Of course, one only had to be in her company a little while to know that Miss Whitman came from a place of refinement and money. Her circumstances may have taken a downturn, but that didn't change who she was.

Still, he'd hoped her obvious affection for the kids, at least, would offset any reservations she might have about marrying him, and that the knowledge that she was quickly approaching the age of spinsterhood might factor into her decision as well.

The strength of his disappointment surprised him, though. Having her say yes would obviously have made this whole ordeal simpler. And it would also have had the added advantage of him being certain he could share a house with her without her driving him crazy. Strange how certain he was after barely a day in her company.

At least she'd agreed to help him find someone suitable. It made him feel not quite so alone in all this.

He stared out the front door and frowned. He didn't like the idea of letting Miss Whitman walk home unescorted. Dusk was settling in and it wouldn't be much longer until it was full dark.

Not that he believed anyone here in Turnabout would bother the schoolteacher. Still, she deserved more consideration than that. Problem was, he couldn't leave the children home alone, and he also didn't think it would be a good idea to take them out for a long walk right now.

But there *was* one way to handle this without disturbing the children. As she joined him at the door, he said, "I wonder if I could impose on you for just a few minutes longer."

"Of course. What can I do for you?"

"I need to step down to Dennis Raine's house for a moment, if you could stay and keep an eye on the children. I promise I won't tarry long." The Raines were his closest neighbors.

She settled down on the chair near the sofa. "I'll wait right here."

Hank's errand took less than ten minutes. When he returned, he had the Raines' oldest daughter with him. The girl nodded at Janell. "Good evening, Miss Whitman."

"Hello, Glenda." She turned to Hank questioningly.

"Glenda is going to keep an eye on things here while I walk you home."

From the look on her face, she didn't seem to be particularly appreciative of his attempted gallantry. "That's very thoughtful of you, Mr. Chandler, but there's no need—"

He cut her off, determined to have his way on this at least. "Of course there is. And since Glenda is already here, you might as well just go along with the plan."

She rolled her eyes, but gave him a nod of agreement.

"Just give me a minute to let the kids know." As he headed down the hall he smiled in satisfaction. Nice to see she could occasionally allow someone else to take charge.

Then his smile faded. Had he been too quick with his proposal? After all, he'd only arrived back in town with the kids this morning. If he'd given her more time before he proposed, might her answer have been different?

He supposed now he'd never know.

Janell lay in bed that evening, contemplating how quickly her world could change. It was difficult to believe that when she'd got up this morning, she hadn't known of Alex and Chloe's existence and had barely ever spoken two words to Mr. Chandler. Right now they all seemed like very important parts of her world.

Her heart went out to Chloe—she saw so much of her sister in the girl. But the thought of helping this hurting child energized Janell as nothing had in quite a while.

And little Alex—his consuming concern for his sister, despite his own loss, or perhaps because of it, touched her deeply. She had to find a way to help him just be a little boy again. And perhaps she could, especially once she got him in her classroom.

Then there was Mr. Chandler.

She rolled over on her side, trying to find a more comfortable position.

Her opinion of the sawmill owner had certainly undergone a dramatic change in the past twelve hours. No, that wasn't quite accurate. She'd simply given him very little thought before today.

But now that she *had* noticed him, she found him to be a man of intriguing contradictions.

He could be gruff, but he wasn't unkind. While he wasn't classically handsome, his square-jawed ruggedness held more appeal for her.

He seemed unsure of himself around the children, but it was obvious he had their best interests at heart.

He'd also proved himself a gentleman on more than one occasion today.

And he had proposed to her. A marriage proposal was definitely the last thing she'd expected.

Not that it was a true proposal. After all, he was looking for a mother for the children, not a wife for himself. And even though the circumstances were much different than with her husband, she could never contemplate entering a loveless marriage again.

Still, what was most surprising of all the things that had happened today was that she'd found herself, if only for a brief moment, considering saying yes.

Janell arrived for church early the next morning, wanting to get there ahead of Mr. Chandler and the children.

She sought out Eve and another friend, Hazel Andrews, and asked for their help in making certain Chloe wasn't overwhelmed by crowds of people.

She wished she had time to speak to Eve alone for a moment. It would be nice to have a chance to talk over yesterday's surprising development with her friend. Perhaps they'd have that discussion later.

When the church bells rang, indicating it was time for the congregation to move inside, Janell still hadn't seen any sign of Mr. Chandler and the children. Should she check on them? Should she have offered to help him get the children ready this morning?

She'd already taken a few steps in that direction when she caught sight of them, hurrying up the sidewalk. Chloe looked sullen and Alex appeared anxious. Mr. Chandler's usual easygoing demeanor seemed a little frayed around the edges this morning, but they were all appropriately attired and headed this way.

"Hello, Alex, Chloe," she greeted them as they drew closer. "You both look very nice in your Sunday clothes."

Alex said a subdued thank-you. Chloe, as expected, said nothing.

Close up, both of the children appeared nervous. Without her cat, Chloe seemed much more vulnerable.

Janell turned to Mr. Chandler, determined to act as if yesterday's proposal had never happened. And that became easier when she saw the uncharacteristically frazzled look on his face. "Shall we go inside?"

They were the last to enter the church. Fortunately, she had asked Eve to keep the back pew clear for them, and her friend had come through. Janell entered the pew first, then Chloe, Alex and finally Mr. Chandler.

They received several smiles and nods, but fortunately, the service started almost immediately and everyone turned to face front.

Janell knew the service was lost on Chloe and that the girl disliked being here. But Chloe had to learn to spend time among people again, and church was a very safe place to start. For one thing, while the service was in progress she didn't have to interact with anyone. For another, the interior of a church should be a somewhat familiar, comforting place for her.

Once the service was over, she and Mr. Chandler ushered the children toward the exit as quickly as possible. Reverend Harper, who stood in the doorway to greet his departing congregation, gave Mr. Chandler's hand a hearty shake. "Welcome back, Hank. My condolences on the loss of your sister."

"Thank you, Reverend." He drew the children forward. "These are Enid's children, Alex and Chloe. They'll be living with me now."

The reverend smiled at them. "Welcome to Turnabout. We're glad to have you join our community."

"Thank you, sir," Alex said, his tone respectful.

Chloe remained silent.

Janell spoke up then, complimenting the preacher on his sermon. As she'd hoped, this gave Mr. Chandler and the children the opportunity to move on. A moment later she joined them at the bottom of the steps and they moved forward as a group.

Before they'd taken more than a couple of steps, however, Mr. Chandler was hailed from several directions by folks who were eager to welcome him back and express their condolences.

While he was forced to pause, Janell kept going forward. She moved herself between the children and took their hands. Eve and Hazel had recruited some help and several women were positioned strategically around the churchyard. They smoothly intercepted anyone who approached Janell and her charges, diverting their attention.

Normally this would be a good opportunity to introduce the children to others their own age, but Janell knew that Chloe wasn't ready for that yet.

Once they were beyond the churchyard, Alex looked up at her. "Are you coming home with us, Miss Whitman?"

Janell glanced over her shoulder and found Mr. Chandler had kept his gaze on her. As their gazes met, he gave a slight nod and disengaged himself from his conversation with Ward Gleason.

She smiled down at Alex. "I am. But first I need to stop at my place. You don't mind coming with me, do you?"

He shook his head. "No, ma'am. I don't mind at all." He glanced toward his sister. "And I'm sure Chloe won't mind, either."

Mr. Chandler caught up with them about a block down Third Street.

"We're going to Miss Whitman's house," Alex informed him, saying it as if it was some grand adventure.

"So I see."

"If you'd like to take the children home, I can join you there in a bit."

He shook his head. "We're in no hurry. And it's a nice day for a walk."

"As you wish."

They strolled at a comfortable pace, exchanging nods with the folks they encountered but not pausing to chat. When they reached the boardinghouse, Janell motioned to the numerous chairs scattered on the broad front porch. "You're welcome to sit out here while you wait. Or you can sit in the parlor. I won't be long."

"The porch is fine." Mr. Chandler motioned for the children to take a seat. "And take whatever time you need. As I said, we're in no hurry."

With a nod she hurried inside. But even with her back to him, she was quite aware that he watched her until the screen door closed behind her.

Hank watched the schoolteacher disappear through the boardinghouse entrance. Truth to tell, he'd tagged along today because he wasn't ready to be alone with the kids in his house again. At least here there were distractions to be had.

The sight of Mrs. Ortolon, dressed in her Sunday best with a ridiculously embellished hat perched on her head, marching up the front walk, however, made him rethink that decision.

Eunice Ortolon owned the boardinghouse, and while she was a good-hearted woman, she was the town's biggest busybody. He immediately wanted to set the children behind him in order to shield them from her probing. He settled, instead, for stepping forward to greet her. "Good day to you, ma'am. It sure is a fine afternoon, isn't it?"

"Why, Mr. Chandler, how nice to see you." The woman studied him with a broad smile and a speculative gleam in her eye. "It *is* a beautiful day. And what brings you to my front porch today?"

Hank chose his next words carefully. He wanted to avoid having her read anything into the situation that wasn't there. "I'm waiting for Miss Whitman. She's going to work with the children to evaluate where they'll fit in her classroom."

"Oh, how nice." Mrs. Ortolon moved to the side and peered behind him. "And are these the little dears?"

Hank swallowed a grimace as he stepped aside. He nodded to the children, but didn't ask them to step forward. "Mrs. Ortolon, allow me to introduce my niece and nephew, Chloe and Alex. Children, this is Mrs. Ortolon."

"Well, aren't you two just the sweetest things? You look so much like your dear departed mother. I knew her as a little girl, you know." Then she sighed dramatically as she placed a hand to her heart. "I'm so sorry about what happened to her and your father, and to you, too, Chloe."

"Your sympathies are appreciated, ma'am, by all of us."

Luckily Miss Whitman stepped out just then, dressed in a simpler frock and carrying a basket. She paused for the merest fraction of a minute when she spotted her landlady standing there, but then pasted a smile on her face. "Mrs. Ortolon, thank you for keeping my visitors company while I was changing." She turned to him and took Chloe's hand with a cheery smile. "Shall we go?"

Silently thanking her, he nodded, then turned to Mrs. Ortolon and touched the brim of his hat. "It was nice visiting with you, ma'am. Please enjoy your afternoon."

With that, he placed a hand at Alex's back and followed Miss Whitman and Chloe off the porch.

Hopefully, the busybody hadn't noted anything to gossip about. He felt strangely protective of the schoolteacher's reputation. He wouldn't want her getting into hot water due to anything he'd done.

With that in mind, he held back, walking beside Alex rather than trying to hold a conversation with Miss Whitman.

When they arrived at his house, she sent them off to change clothes while she prepared a simple lunch consisting of ham, cheese and pickled green beans.

By the time he returned to the kitchen, she was slicing vegetables into a simmering pot of water. "I thought we were just going to have a simple, cold lunch."

She nodded. "I'm putting a vegetable soup together for tonight's supper."

As usual, she was making decisions for them without consulting him. This time she had assumed he hadn't already made plans to take care of supper. Never mind that her assumption was correct. Again.

However, she seemed unaware that she'd got his dander up once more.

"Did you encounter any problems when getting the children ready this morning?" she asked.

He grimaced. "It was a battle with Chloe. But I think she saw how her attitude was affecting Alex, so she finally gave in."

The schoolteacher glanced his way sympathetically. "I promise it will get better with time. But patience *will* be required."

She said that as if she was doubtful he could pull it off. He *could* be patient when a situation called for it. It was just that he had no patience with tantrums or foolishness. But he decided a change of subject was in order. "I looked over that sign-language book you left here last night."

"And what do you think?"

"I think you were right when you said it would be a lot of work. But if this will help Chloe as much as you seem to believe it will, then it'll be time well spent."

She nodded. "Did you say anything to the children about our plans?"

"No. I figured I'd do that when you were around to answer any questions they might have." And unlike him, she'd be able to do it without putting her foot in her mouth. In fact, he was okay with her taking the lead in that particular discussion—he wasn't such a fool as to think he had all the answers, especially when it came to something like this.

Janell raised her chin. "Then we'll speak to them together, right after lunch."

She wondered why he'd put it off. Had he been afraid

to broach the subject with them? Or had he just not known how to bring it up?

Or was he beginning to think of them as a team, the way she was?

Chapter Nine

After lunch, Janell made certain they all pitched in to clean up. Once the kitchen was put back to rights, Mr. Chandler exchanged glances with her, then turned to the children.

"Alex, I'd like you and your sister to join us in the parlor. Miss Whitman and I have something we wish to discuss with you."

She would have to work with him on addressing Chloe directly in the future, but now was not the right time.

The children sat on the sofa, while their uncle and Janell sat in nearby chairs.

Mr. Chandler cleared his throat. "Miss Whitman has something she'd like to discuss with us."

The children turned to watch her warily. Were they expecting bad news?

She smiled reassuringly. "As I've explained to your uncle, I think I may be able to help Chloe find ways to more easily communicate with the rest of the world and they with her."

There were no changes in Chloe's expression, but

Alex sat up straighter. "You mean you can help her hear again?" he asked.

"I'm sorry, Alex. I wish I could do that, but I can't. However, there are other things we can do."

"Like what?"

"Sign language."

His nose wrinkled. "What's that?"

"I'll show you in just a minute." First she had to get Chloe engaged in the discussion. She took the piece of chalk and wrote *I have a plan to help you* on the slate, then turned it so Chloe could read the words.

Chloe read it, a touch of guarded interest lightening her features.

"My own sister is deaf." She wrote the same words on the slate, and as she did, it hit her, in a way it hadn't before, that that was something she and Alex had in common.

Chloe read the words, then looked up at her with much more interest than she'd shown to date.

"Just like Chloe?" The question came from Alex.

"That's right. Only in Lizzie's case, she went deaf because of an illness." Janell wrote an abbreviated form of that on the slate and showed it to Chloe.

"And did you help her?" Again it was Alex who asked the question.

"*We* did. Because it was not just me. My whole family got involved."

"Involved how?"

"We learned sign language."

Chloe waved a hand, obviously feeling left out of the conversation.

Janell smiled inwardly, encouraged by this show of interest. But she pretended not to notice. Chloe had to learn to speak up, as awkward as it might feel to her.

Finally the girl did speak. "What are you saying?"

Janell wrote on the slate again. *I would like to teach all three of you sign language.*

Chloe read the chalked words and her expression shifted into uncertainty. Janell had expected some resistance, so this didn't catch her off guard.

"Is it hard?" Alex asked.

"It's not a simple thing, but then again, it's not really any more difficult than it was for you to learn to read and write."

The boy nodded thoughtfully at that.

"We're all going to be learning together," Mr. Chandler added. "Even me."

Janell pulled out the book that had the illustrations they would need to learn from. "Why don't we try just a few things today, just so you can get a feel for what it will be like?"

Miss Whitman returned her hands to her lap. "There, that's enough for one day. You've all done quite well. I'm going to leave the book here so that you can pull it out and practice whenever you want to."

She stood. "The soup should be ready in about another hour."

Hank stood as well. How did she think it went? There'd been a lot of fumbling on the kids' part, and his, too, if he was being honest, but she'd done her best to turn it into a game of sorts and not make them feel bad when they made a mistake.

"Do you have to go?" Alex asked.

Hank spoke up before she could answer. "We've already taken up quite a lot of Miss Whitman's time." Though he wouldn't mind if she stayed a bit longer himself.

The schoolteacher gave his nephew a regretful smile. "It was time I enjoyed giving. But I do have some things I need to tend to before I retire this evening. And we've made a good start today."

Alex didn't seem reassured by her answer. "Are you coming back tomorrow?"

"I am. Until your aunt arrives, I plan to be here with you while your uncle goes to work at the sawmill."

That finally seemed to satisfy Alex, at least for the moment.

Hank cleared his throat. He and his would-be match-maker had some things to talk about. "Alex, why don't you and Chloe go to your rooms and rest a bit. Miss Whitman and I have a few things to discuss."

When they had made their exit, Janell sat, while Hank remained standing there, with his hands shoved in his pockets, facing the direction the children had exited from, unsure of how to proceed with her. It suddenly felt awkward between them.

"I think our first lesson went well, don't you?" There was a gentle nudging tone to her voice.

He turned to face her and nodded. "They both seem willing to work at it."

"I think they both have the skill and the desire to make this work."

"Thank you again for all you're doing to help them."

"It truly is my pleasure." She sat up straighter. "Now I suppose it is this finding-you-a-wife business that you wish to discuss with me?"

Her direct approach to the subject put him at ease and he took a seat across from her. "It is."

"You mentioned a list. Shall we start with those ladies?"

"The first is Ada Sanders."

Miss Whitman shook her head. "Ada has a heart for children and would be a good choice. But I'm afraid you're too late. She's been walking out with John Horton lately."

He grimaced. "I suppose that happened while I was in Colorado. Well then, there's Hildie Dalton."

"Hildie is very sweet and kindhearted," she said diplomatically, "but maybe just a little too much so. I would worry about whether she could handle the discipline that's involved in raising children."

Refusing to get discouraged, Hank moved on to the next name. "What about Betty June Latham? She was raised on a farm and her father is a no-nonsense kind of man. I reckon she knows how to be both kind and firm."

Miss Whitman frowned. "I don't really know Betty June well enough to say one way or the other."

He perked up. "She's a possibility, then?"

"Of course."

He rubbed the back of his neck. Might as well mention the fourth name as well. "The other candidate I'd thought about is Alice O'Donnell."

She seemed surprised. "Alice is a fine woman with a heart for taking care of others." She paused a moment, but he could tell there was more.

"But?"

Her expression turned diffident. "It's only that her mother has grown more and more frail the past few months, and Alice is Mrs. O'Donnell's only kin. Her time is likely to be too focused on caring for her mother for her to give Chloe and Alex the attention they will need."

He nodded. "See, this is why I knew you'd be the best person for this job." He leaned forward. "So what's the next step?"

* * *

Janell shifted in her seat, still not entirely comfortable with the role he'd foisted upon her. "If you like, I can pay Betty June a visit in the next day or so and then give you my initial impression."

He crossed his arms. "The sooner, the better. In fact, I'd like to have this settled by Christmas."

She studied him a moment. Something seemed a little off, but she couldn't put her finger on just what. "I know the qualities *I'll* want to look for in a mother to the children. But to do my job properly, I'll need to know what qualifications you'd like this woman to have. Other than the obvious, of course."

"And what do you consider the obvious?"

She tapped her chin. "That she is single, loves children but also knows how to administer discipline when needed, that she has strong Christian values and that she be at least an adequate cook and housekeeper."

He nodded, seeming impressed. "That's a solid list. The other items I'd add to it are that she be of an appropriate age and she not be a ninny or chatterbox."

A smile twitched at her lips. "And just what do you consider an appropriate age?"

He spread his hands. "Old enough to understand what she's getting into and young enough to have the energy to keep up with kids and run a household."

She nodded. "Very well. I'll add those items to my list of qualifications."

As Hank thought over that list of qualifications they'd just come up with, he wondered how in the world they would find anyone who fit them all.

Then it occurred to him that Miss Whitman herself fit that list quite nicely. It was a shame she'd turned his offer down. Was there some way he could make her change her mind?

Before he could think further on that, she stood and brushed at her skirt. "I think we've covered everything we can for the moment. If you'll excuse me, it's time I headed home."

He got to his feet as well. "Of course. Let me fetch the kids and we'll walk you home."

"There's no need." She waved toward the window. "It's a lovely fall day, the sun is still up and it's an easy walk."

The woman would debate with a fence post. "You're right about it being a nice day. And we've been cooped up inside for most of it. I think it would do the kids good to get outside and go for a walk."

"As you wish," Miss Whitman said.

As Hank headed for Chloe's room, he felt his frustration over her refusal yesterday rise a notch. She'd certainly said no quickly and emphatically enough.

Did the woman have a problem with marriage in general? Surely someone who seemed as practical and forthright as the schoolteacher wasn't holding out for a love match?

Or was it just marriage to *him* that she found so distasteful?

And whatever the reason, could he possibly change her mind before it was too late?

Chapter Ten

The next morning, Miss Whitman showed up at his door with a basket of groceries in hand. Hank smiled, feeling more than a little smug. This time she'd made the wrong assumption about his ability to handle things on his own.

"Good morning." He nodded toward the back of the stove. "There's a fresh pot of coffee if you're in the mood for a cup. I've got eggs for the kids here in the skillet. I'll fix some for you when these are done."

"It sounds like you've been busy."

Her voice lacked that satisfactory note of surprise or admiration for his work here in the kitchen that he'd been looking for.

She set her basket on the counter and plucked an apron from it. "How did things go last night?"

"Better than the night before."

She nodded as she donned the apron. "Then they're beginning to settle in."

"I think it was more that they had something to focus on." He gave the eggs a final stir then reached for the platter he'd set nearby. "I found them both looking through that sign-language book and even practicing a few of the movements together."

"Very encouraging." She glanced toward the hallway. "Are they up yet?"

"I haven't checked but I think I heard them stirring a few minutes ago."

"Why don't you let me take over here at the stove and you can go check on them?"

He'd much rather cook. But she was standing next to him with a hand held out for the spoon, so with a nod he headed down the hall.

A knock on Alex's door went unanswered. He stuck his head in, and sure enough, the bed looked as if it hadn't been slept in. Raking his hand through his hair, he moved down to Chloe's room. At least this solved the problem of how to handle gaining entrance to his niece's bedchamber. If Alex was in there, he would hear the knocking.

To his relief, the knock was greeted by his nephew's voice. "Come in." What was he going to do about this when Alex moved into his own room?

By the time Hank returned to the kitchen, the very efficient Miss Whitman had some diced potatoes cooking in the skillet. From the aroma it smelled as if she had also added some onions and bacon drippings to the pan.

She looked up when he entered and gave him a smile. "So are they awake?"

He nodded. "They'll be at the table shortly."

"Have you heard anything from your aunt yet?"

"No, but that doesn't mean she won't show up today or tomorrow. The telegram I got from her was rather vague on when she would arrive."

She nodded and returned her focus to her cooking.

He grabbed plates from the cabinet and set the table. They worked without speaking for a few minutes, but he found himself acutely aware of her presence. Did she realize she was humming or was it an unconscious habit?

And her movements as she stirred the potatoes—efficient, confident, graceful. There was something rather soothing about watching her—

"Do the children know her?"

The question, casually tossed over her shoulder, brought him abruptly back to himself. Good thing she hadn't glanced back and caught him watching her.

He cleared his throat. "They didn't even know me very well before this happened."

This time she did look his way. "Tell me a little about her."

"Aunt Rowena?" At her nod, he leaned back against the counter and crossed his arms. "There's not a lot to tell. She's my mother's older sister. She's a widow and has been since I was a babe. Never had any children, so she spent many of her holidays with us when I was a child, but not as much since Mother passed six years ago."

"So she lives alone?"

"Yes." He waved a hand. "But she's not a recluse. Aunt Rowena likes to keep busy and is very sociable. She owns a hat shop in Clampton and directs the choir in her church. I think she also belongs to a quilting circle." He rubbed his chin. "She leads a busy life with a lot of community obligations. That's the reason I can't ask her to stay for more than a few weeks."

"Oh. When you told me she wasn't a permanent solution, I didn't realize her stay would be quite so short."

"She's just coming to help me until the kids are settled in and I've had a chance to find a wife. I'm grateful for her doing that much."

"Of course. I didn't mean to imply it wasn't generous of her."

He saw her mulling that thought over as she pushed

the potatoes around in the skillet. What was going on in that mind of hers?

"I see now why you want this done so quickly."

"Is that a problem?"

"It makes it more difficult, but it's still possible."

The woman was nothing if not determined. "Good. Now, back to Aunt Rowena. Before we can talk about her departure, she has to arrive."

"True. But don't let that worry you. I'm available all day today to watch the children and tomorrow, too, if need be, so spend as much time as you need at the sawmill."

"I appreciate that, but I don't want to take advantage of your generosity any more than necessary."

She waved a hand as if to dismiss his concerns, then changed the subject. "But I do have a request."

"Yes?"

"Could you come home at noon and take lunch with the children? I have some business to take care of. It shouldn't take me more than forty-five minutes or so."

"Of course. I'll make a point to be here a little before noon." What sort of errand? he wondered. But she didn't offer further explanation and he didn't feel it was his place to ask.

She smiled at him over her shoulder. "I'll have a nice hot lunch ready for you when you get here." Before she could say anything more, the kids arrived and she turned to greet them with a smile. "Good morning. I trust you slept well."

There was no denying the children reacted positively to her. They had yet to offer him the same smiles they gave her so freely.

Granted, Chloe was still guarded with everyone, but

he could sense a certain amount of softening from her when she was in the schoolteacher's presence.

Perhaps he should add that to his list of qualifications for a wife—she must be able to coax smiles from his niece and nephew.

Or better yet, he needed to find a way to make the standoffish Miss Whitman change her mind.

Janell watched Mr. Chandler leave. She found herself looking forward to seeing him again when he returned at noon, even if just for a few minutes.

When she realized the direction her thoughts had taken, she pulled herself up short. That was dangerous ground. He'd asked her to marry him and she'd said no—that was the end of it.

No matter how pleasant the alternative might be.

Much better to focus on preparing herself for her noon "errand."

Mrs. Ortolon's arch comments yesterday had reminded her that as a schoolteacher she had to hold herself to the highest standards. So she'd asked Mayor Saunders to set up a meeting with the town council at noon today for her to speak to them about her intentions. She found it was always best to be completely aboveboard when there were matters that could be misconstrued. Then she grimaced. With one very glaring exception—she'd deliberately held back the information about her divorce when the town had hired her. What would happen if they ever found out?

She turned to see the children watching her curiously. She gave her head a mental shake, clearing away all thoughts of Mr. Chandler as she focused on the children.

"All right, I think we'll take care of a few chores before we tackle those sign-language lessons. Now that this is your home, too, you'll need to help your uncle take care of it."

"What kind of chores?" Alex asked.

"We can start by taking care of the dishes. Then we can straighten your rooms. After that, we'll see what else around here could use a little tender loving care."

She did her best to make a game of cleaning the kitchen and succeeded to a certain extent.

Chloe washed, Alex dried and Janell put the dishes away.

Then they tackled the bedchambers.

Stepping into Chloe's room, she waved toward the second bed. "You know, your aunt Rowena will be here soon and this will be her bed."

Alex drew a little closer to Chloe at that. Was he worried about his sister or himself?

"Why don't we try to make the room as welcoming as possible for her?" she said. "Perhaps, when we're done in here, we can take a walk and try to find some wild-flowers to put on the dresser."

That drew a bit more interest than her other suggestions. Like all children, they needed some outdoor play-time. She doubted they'd had much occasion for that since their parents died.

So she cut short the indoor chores and took them on the promised walk. She directed them toward the open countryside to lessen the chances of Chloe being startled by someone or something coming up behind her.

Janell brought a pail with her and they gathered up some pecans and even managed to find some persimmons.

By the time they returned to the house, the children had color in their cheeks and looked less drawn and frail than they had earlier. She made a mental note to let Mr.

Chandler know he should make certain the children had outdoor time every day.

As soon as Mr. Chandler arrived for lunch, Janell slipped off her apron and headed out the door. Not only was she in a hurry to get this over with, but she also figured it would do Hank and the children good to have their meal without her.

"Well, Miss Whitman, you have our attention. What did you wish to speak to us about?"

Janell sat up straighter. "As you have no doubt noticed, I've been helping Mr. Chandler get his niece and nephew settled into their new life here in Turnabout."

"Yes, and that's quite commendable of you."

She brushed away the praise. "It's more than me helping a family who has lost loved ones. Chloe needs some very specialized help. And as it happens, I have experience dealing with the deaf. A member of my own family was similarly afflicted."

"Then that little girl will be lucky to have you for a schoolteacher. Are you here to ask us to provide some special materials for your classroom?"

"No. At least not just yet." She hadn't really given that much thought, but perhaps she should have. "Chloe will need lots of special instruction outside of the classroom. In fact, so will her uncle and brother, if they are going to learn how to communicate with each other. And to that end, I plan to spend a lot of time in their home, working with them."

"I see."

"As Mr. Chandler is a bachelor and I am a schoolteacher, I wanted to make you aware of my plans and to assure you that the utmost propriety will be maintained."

"And how long do you think this arrangement will last?"

"I should think, if everyone works as hard at it as I think they will, that by the end of the year I should be able to reduce my visits to his home to a few hours a week." And if Mr. Chandler's plans proceeded as he'd like, he should also have a wife by then.

"Miss Whitman, it speaks well of you that you brought this to our attention in such a forthright manner. And your conduct has always been above reproach."

She mentally winced at that statement. If he knew her past he might not be quite so quick to offer such praise.

The mayor leaned back in his chair. "I think the presence of children in the house will be sufficient chaperone for this short period of time under these special circumstances."

He glanced around at the other men in the room. "There will always be those who enjoy a bit of gossip. But I believe I speak for the entire council when I say, in this matter, you have our support." He gave her a steady, warning look. "Unless you should give us reason to withdraw it."

Janell lifted her chin. "I assure you that I'll be as discreet and proper as you could wish." She stood. "Now, if you gentlemen will excuse me, I must get back. It is time for their sign-language lessons."

As Janell strolled down the sidewalk she congratulated herself on how well the meeting had gone. It was well worth a few minutes of bearing under their scrutiny to make certain her good name did not suffer and, by association, her job.

She'd already had a taste of that and it wasn't something she ever wanted to experience again.

Janell lifted her chin. No good was to be had in looking back at past mistakes. There was too much pain and deception there. She had the irrational fear that if she dwelled on it, it would follow her to Turnabout to ruin her life here as well.

And that she truly could not bear.

Impulsively, she turned her steps to the Blue Bottle Sweet Shop. She was certain Mr. Chandler wouldn't mind her taking a few extra minutes and she dearly wanted to speak to Eve.

Fortunately, when she stepped into the place the only person in sight was Eve herself.

Her friend's face lit up as soon as she recognized her. "What a wonderful surprise. I usually don't see you this time of day."

"I can't stay long, but I was wondering if you had a few minutes to chat."

"Of course. Come on back to the kitchen and I'll brew us both up a cup of tea."

With a nod, Janell followed her friend into the cozy kitchen. Without waiting for direction, she fetched a pair of cups from the cupboard while Eve took a kettle of water from the stove. In no time at all there was a fresh pot of one of Eve's special teas steeping on the table between them.

"Now," Eve said, "what brings you here today? Nothing serious, I hope."

Janell grimaced. "It depends on what you call serious." She gave her friend a helpless look. "Mr. Chandler proposed to me on Saturday."

That definitely set Eve back in her chair. Then her friend smiled. "It's about time one of the men in this town saw what a special person you are."

Janell waved off that compliment. "He wasn't so

much interested in having me for a wife as he was wanting someone to help with the children."

"And what did you tell him?"

"No, of course. You, of all people, know how impossible such an arrangement would be."

"I know no such thing. The right man for you would look past what happened to you and love you for who you are."

Janell frowned. "I told you, this wasn't offered as a love match, just a matter of convenience."

"And if it had been tendered as a love match?"

"It wouldn't have made any difference."

"And you're happy with that?"

"Let's just say I'm resigned."

Eve poured the tea into their cups. "Well then, if it's all settled and you're comfortable with your decision, why did you feel the need to come talk to me?"

Janell wrapped her hands around the warm cup, shifting in her seat. That was a good question.

She wasn't ready to dig for the answer just yet.

Surely she hadn't formed any sort of attachment to Mr. Chandler in such a short time?

Chapter Eleven

Later that afternoon, Janell answered the door to find a tall, bespectacled broomstick of a woman standing at the threshold. From the top of her tightly coiffed gray hair to the large carpetbag at her feet, she seemed the epitome of stiff propriety.

Janell realized at once that this must be Aunt Rowena. She also realized she didn't know the woman's last name.

She opened the door wider. "You must be Mr. Chandler's aunt. Please, come in."

The woman frowned down at Janell. "And who might you be?"

Did she think she was some kind of interloper? But Janell kept her smile firmly in place. "My name is Janell Whitman, and I'm the town's schoolteacher. I'm keeping an eye on the children while Mr. Chandler is at the sawmill."

"I see." The woman's demeanor remained stiff, her expression suspicious. "If you're the schoolteacher, why aren't you in your classroom?"

"Someone is filling in for me today. Please, do come in where you can be more comfortable and I'll answer all your questions."

The woman nodded, then turned and waved to a man sitting in a wagon parked in front of the house. "Thanks for the ride, Tom." Her voice had a warmth to it that it had lacked before. "I'll telegraph you when I'm ready for my ride home."

The man waved back then gave the reins a shake, setting his wagon in motion. The woman turned back, her stern countenance back in place. She finally stepped past Janell and into the house.

Janell picked up the carpetbag and followed her inside. For some reason she'd been expecting Mr. Chandler's aunt to be a plump, motherly woman, full of smiles and fluttery motions.

This woman seemed to have none of those qualities.

Janell silently chided herself. Mr. Chandler's aunt, who looked to be in her late fifties, had traveled a long distance in a farm wagon to help. No doubt she was weary from the trip. She would surely show a more pleasant face to the children when she met them.

With a smile, she set the carpetbag down and clasped her hands in front of her. "I would deliver this to your room, but as you are to share with Chloe and the children are currently napping in there, I'll just set it here for now."

Then she straightened. "As for your earlier questions, I can understand your confusion, but there is a reason I'm the one here to help today and not someone else from the community."

"And that would be?"

"I assume you know about Chloe's affliction?"

The woman's expression softened and she gave a heavy nod. "Hank informed me."

"As it happens, my own sister lost her hearing as the

result of the measles, so I have some experience that could be helpful."

The woman's demeanor warmed and she gave Janell a more genuine smile. "Then it seems my nephew is lucky that you're available to be here. My apologies if my hesitation made you uncomfortable."

"No need for apologies. You're just looking out for your family." Janell returned the woman's smile. "It was good of you to come here to help Mr. Chandler and the children as well."

The woman let out a couple of sneezes and then smiled apologetically as she pulled out a handkerchief. "Must be dust from the road. Is there a place where I can freshen up?"

"Of course. Since Alex is on the extra bed in Chloe's room, perhaps you can use his room for now."

"That would be most welcome."

With a wave of the hand, Janell led her down the hall. A moment later, she pushed open the door. "Here we are." She stepped back so the woman could pass. "While Chloe and Alex are napping, I would be glad to share my thoughts on them and their needs with you. But first, may I offer you something to eat?"

"I'd like that."

Janell smiled at her show of interest. "Take whatever time you need. When you're ready, the kitchen is—"

"I know where it is. I've been here before."

"Of course." Janell stepped away from the door. "I'll be in the kitchen if you should need me." As she moved toward the kitchen she heard another, louder sneeze. Was the woman coming down with a cold or something worse? That was the last thing poor Mr. Chandler needed right now.

Janell grabbed a clean bowl and moved to the stove.

She'd serve Mr. Chandler's aunt an extra large bowl of the soup she'd made for lunch—maybe that would help her feel better.

Just as Janell set the bowl of the soup on the table, Mr. Chandler's aunt joined her. She pulled out the woman's chair and waved her into it. "What should I call you?" she asked diffidently.

"My name is Rowena Collins."

Janell took the seat across from her. "You asked about the children and I'll be glad to tell you what I know of them. I only just met them two days ago myself, but I've already grown quite fond of them. Alex is eight and is a bright boy who is very concerned for his sister. He's grieving but wasn't physically injured since he was not at home when the accident occurred."

Mrs. Collins nodded as she dipped her spoon into her soup. "But I'm sure this has affected him emotionally."

Janell was relieved to hear Mrs. Collins understood that Alex would need watching as well. "Chloe is ten years old and very scared and confused by what's happened to her."

The woman glanced down at her soup as if looking for answers there. "I've never dealt with anyone who was totally deaf before."

Janell detected a note of anxiety in the woman's voice. "I was very scared when my sister went through this. I was afraid we wouldn't be able to reach her and that she would be permanently locked into her own lonely world."

Mrs. Collins sneezed again and gave her a probing look. "How old were the two of you at the time?"

The woman's sneezing seemed to be getting worse instead of better. "Lizzie was seventeen. I had just turned twenty."

"So young." She shook her head with a sympathetic tsk. "And how is your sister now?"

"Lizzie is doing well. She now has a husband and two children and from all reports leads a very full life." She was so proud of how far her little sister had come. "But it wasn't an easy road for her."

"Or for you, either, I suspect."

Janell traced a circle on the table with her index finger. "Our whole family went through a great deal of training to help us come to terms with what Lizzie was facing—things like learning sign language and how to speak so that she might read our lips."

"Then Chloe is lucky to have you here."

"Thank you, but Chloe will need all of us to help her through this."

Mrs. Collins nodded. "I will do my part—doing what I can to keep everyone well fed and comfortable while I'm here."

"They will need that, of course, but I was speaking of something else."

The woman gave her a wary look. "Such as?"

"Mr. Chandler has agreed to let me teach him and the children how to sign." She straightened. "I would be glad to also include you in the lessons."

The woman dropped her gaze to her bowl. "Perhaps I should stick to doing the cooking and housekeeping. I'm not sure how good I'd be at learning such a thing. Besides, I'm only planning to be here for a few weeks. Hardly enough time to learn something so complex."

Janell was disappointed by Mrs. Collins's response. She tried another tack. "The more people who learn to communicate with Chloe, the less shut out she will feel."

"I suppose that makes sense." More stirring. "We shall see how it goes."

Janell reached across and touched the woman's hand. "Thank you, ma'am. I'm certain Chloe will appreciate your efforts, regardless of the outcome."

"Since you haven't had a chance to teach them that sign language yet, how have you been communicating with the child?"

Janell stood and fetched the slate where she'd left it on the counter. "I write whatever I wish to communicate to her on this slate."

The woman's eyes brightened. "Now, that seems like a very sensible solution. I can certainly work with that."

"It's also important that when you're speaking, your head is turned so that she can see your lips move and that you enunciate your words clearly."

"She can read lips?"

"Not yet. But that's something I intend to help her learn."

Janell tapped on the bedchamber door. Alex's "come in" let her know they were awake.

She stepped inside to see Alex playing with Smudge and Chloe reading a book.

She'd have to speak to Mr. Chandler about subscribing to Abigail's library in town on Chloe's behalf.

But that was for later. "Your great-aunt Rowena has arrived. Come along so you can meet her." She wrote an abbreviated version of her words on the slate and turned it so Chloe could read it.

"Is she going to live here now?"

Alex's question gave Janell pause. How much had Mr. Chandler told them? "I believe she'll be staying for a while, but I'm not certain how long."

Alex's expression fell. "Does that mean you're not going to stay with us anymore?"

Alex's concern touched her. Strange how close she felt to these two children in such a short period of time. "Perhaps not as much as before, but I will still come by to work with you on learning sign language and such." She realized she was going to miss spending so much time here as well.

Alex didn't look totally reassured. She understood how difficult it was for him to cope with loss of any kind right now and she wished she could make things easier for him—for both of them. "And of course, you'll be with me most of the day once you start school."

Enough on that topic for now. She waved them forward. "Come along. Great-Aunt Rowena is waiting to meet you."

They obediently got out of bed and followed her. If their feet dragged a bit, she decided it would be best to just ignore it.

"Children, this is your great-aunt Rowena."

Rather than returning their greetings, Mrs. Collins stared in horror at Chloe's feet as she let out three violent sneezes in rapid succession. "No wonder I've been sneezing." Her voice was thick with congestion. "Hank didn't tell me there was going to be a cat in the house."

Uh-oh. "Is that a problem?"

The woman took a step back. "I can't be around cats without sneezing."

"Oh, dear." This was *definitely* going to be a problem.

Mrs. Collins let out another sneeze as she grabbed the knob on the outside kitchen door. "Excuse me. I need to get some fresh air."

What did they do now? Janell grabbed the slate and quickly wrote *Smudge makes your aunt sneeze. Please put him in your room.* She showed it to Chloe and the girl lifted her cat and held it protectively against her chest, staring at Janell defiantly.

"Smudge lives here," Chloe said out loud.

At least the girl was speaking more. Janell erased the slate and wrote *Just for now, while we figure things out.*

She hoped Mr. Chandler had a solution for this, because she certainly didn't.

The poor man was certainly going through a rock slide worth of challenges right now.

Would he be able to bear up under one more? And what could she possibly do to help?

Chapter Twelve

Hank decided to shut down the mill a little early today. Thoughts of what might be going on at home had distracted him most of the afternoon.

Had Aunt Rowena arrived yet? If so, how had she and the children got along? And how had she and Miss Whitman got along?

For some reason it was important to him that these two women like each other.

But they both had such strong opinions and neither one was afraid to share them.

When his wagon pulled into the lane, there was no indication of whether or not his aunt had arrived. He unhitched the horse and took care of Hector as quickly as possible.

When Hank finally stepped inside the house, he paused on the threshold. There was a tension in the air different from the one introduced by the children.

Aunt Rowena stood at the table, slicing apples. Her eyes were red and puffy and her shoulders, usually drawn back in military manner, were slumped. What had happened to make his usually stalwart aunt cry?

Had the kids upset her? Or had it been Miss Whitman's bossiness?

Only one way to find out. He stepped forward. "Aunt Rowena, are you okay?"

A part of him realized Chloe and Alex were nowhere to be seen. Also conspicuously absent was Miss Whitman. Had she and his aunt had a row?

His aunt turned to him with an expression that was a curious mix of accusation and contrition. "No, I'm *not* all right. Why didn't you tell me there'd be a cat here?"

Had the cat scratched her? He'd known that feline would be trouble. "I'm so sorry if Smudge did something to harm or upset you. I'll make sure the kids keep better control of him in the future."

She waved a hand irritably. "You don't understand. I can't be in the same house with a cat."

What was going on here? "If the animal bothers you so much, I can make sure they keep him out of your way."

"It's not that I dislike cats, Hank—it's that I can't live with them." She grabbed a handkerchief from her pocket just in time to catch a volley of sneezes. "That's what happens every time I'm close to one."

"But Chloe loves that animal. I can't take it away from her, not right now."

"Of course not. She needs her pet." His aunt waved her hand, her handkerchief fluttering like a flag of surrender. "Besides, it wouldn't make much difference. My friend Willeva has a pair of cats and I can't set foot in her house, even if she locks them away in her back room. If I spend so much as ten minutes in her parlor, I start to sneeze and tear up as much as if you'd tossed a handful of pepper in my face."

Hank rubbed the back of his neck, his mind scrambling for solutions. This was a disaster. "Where are the children now?"

"Miss Whitman took them and the cat for a walk. It helped some, but as you can see, it hasn't completely solved the problem."

"Do you have any suggestions?"

The look she gave him held an apology. "I can try to just live with it for a while, but I'm pretty sure I won't last more than a week. I'm so sorry, Hank. You know how much I wanted to help you out. But I'm afraid you're going to have to find someone else to help you."

Hank swallowed a grimace—he didn't want to make her feel worse than she already did, especially since this wasn't her fault. "I understand. And I appreciate your willingness to persevere. But I don't want to put you through such misery. I'll try to make other arrangements sooner rather than later."

"At least you have that nice schoolteacher to help you."

Hank decided not to respond to that. "In the meantime, since Chloe sleeps with the cat, and Alex's presence seems to bring her a measure of comfort, I think it would be best if you move into Alex's room for the time being."

She nodded. "I appreciate that." She paused and gave him a motherly smile. "It's a good thing you're doing, Hank, taking in Enid's kids. I'm sorry I won't be able to be of more help to you."

"It's not your fault, Aunt Rowena. It was good of you to come in the first place. Don't worry—I'll figure something out."

"What you really need is a wife."

He frowned. "I've come to that same conclusion."

She nodded decisively. "Good. I'd hate to think you're letting that fool Cranford girl continue ruining your life."

Hank mentally winced at that. How could his aunt think his former fiancée mattered to him anymore? That part of his life was in the past—the distant past—and he no longer even thought about it.

His aunt gave him an arch look. "That Miss Whitman seems to be good with the children and fond of them, too. And I didn't see a wedding ring on her finger, so I assume the *Miss* isn't just a courtesy title."

"It's not. But she's one of the schoolteachers here and doesn't seem to be much interested in marriage." At least not marriage to *him*.

His aunt sneezed into her handkerchief again, then gave him a condescending look. "Nonsense. Most every woman—and man, for that matter—has an interest in marriage. It's human nature."

Hank raked a hand through his hair, unhappy with the whole situation. "This is all happening too fast. I've only been back in town a few days. But I'd already decided a wife is the only way to make this work. Miss Whitman isn't the right choice, but I'm looking elsewhere."

His aunt's brows went up. "And why isn't Miss Whitman the right choice? I would think, given her history, that she would be the perfect choice. And you've already said you're not looking for a love match."

"Because she already said no," he blurted out.

His aunt gave him a surprised look, then nodded. "I see. Well, that's that." She moved back to the stove. "You must do what you think best for yourself and the children, of course." She lifted the lid to the large stockpot and stirred the contents. Without looking up, she asked, "Is there perhaps someone else who's caught your eye?"

"No one has *caught my eye*, Aunt Rowena, at least

not in the way you mean." He summoned up a cheeky grin. "But there are a few ladies in town who might look favorably on an offer from me."

She chuckled. "My, my, don't you think highly of yourself."

He grinned back sheepishly. "You know what I mean."

She nodded and turned back to the stove. "I do. And honestly, any girl would be fortunate to have you as a husband."

He began pacing. If Miss Whitman was here, would she offer one of her "suggestions"?

"It would seem that you are not to be given an easy time of this."

He glanced up to see Aunt Rowena smiling sympathetically. "No. But then again, neither have the children."

It was something he tried to remind himself of every time things got tough.

Janell ushered the children into the house through the front door. Hopefully, Mrs. Collins would still be in the kitchen. "Alex, you and Chloe put Smudge in Chloe's room. We'll need to keep him away from your aunt Rowena as much as possible for now." Though from what the woman had said, just being in the same house with the animal was enough to have an adverse effect on her. Hopefully, they'd taken a long enough walk that Smudge would be okay cooped up in Chloe's room until tomorrow.

"Yes, ma'am." Alex turned to his sister and indicated that she should pick up the cat. It seemed the two of them were already developing their own kind of sign language.

As Janell turned to the kitchen she heard voices. One of them was definitely Mr. Chandler's.

Good. His aunt should have given him the bad news by now. Maybe between them they'd come up with a solution.

She paused in the kitchen doorway, not wanting to interrupt the ongoing conversation. But Mr. Chandler saw her almost immediately.

When his gaze met hers there was the briefest flash of emotion in his eyes that she couldn't quite read. It almost looked like embarrassment, but she was certain that couldn't be right.

"Hello," she said, not moving forward. "I just wanted to let you know that we're back from our walk. Please don't let me interrupt your conversation. I'll just go—"

"It's no interruption," Mr. Chandler said quickly, waving her forward. "Please join us."

With a nod she stepped farther into the room, but didn't bother to take a seat.

"Aunt Rowena has generously agreed to stick this out until the end of the week," he said, "assuming it doesn't get just outright unbearable. I have until then to figure out other arrangements for the children."

Was he going to look for another live-in housekeeper and nanny until a wife could be found? Perhaps she could help him with that. Her mind was already turning over potential names.

Before she could offer up any of those names, however, he straightened. "Excuse me. I need to clean up and discuss the new sleeping arrangements with the kids. Or perhaps I should say, inform them that the old arrangements will stand for now."

Janell wasn't sure if she was being dismissed or not. "Would you like me to work with you and the children on the sign-language lessons as we'd planned, or would you prefer to postpone it until tomorrow?"

Mr. Chandler hesitated, glancing toward his aunt uncertainly.

She made shooing motions with her hands. "There's no reason to postpone anything on my account. That's why I'm here, after all, to free you up to do what needs to be done."

Mr. Chandler gave his aunt a kiss on the cheek. "Thanks. You're my favorite aunt, you know."

Mrs. Collins grinned at him. "I'm your *only* aunt," she said drily. But the faint pinkening of her cheeks indicated his words had touched her.

Then he turned to Janell. "As soon as I've cleaned up, I'll get the kids and then we can get started."

Janell nodded, then turned to Mrs. Collins. "Is there anything I can do to help you while I'm waiting?" It seemed strange to turn over control of the kitchen to another woman. Even though it had been only a few days, she'd grown used to being in charge here.

When Mr. Chandler's aunt indicated that she had everything well in hand, Janell slowly headed to the parlor, her mind still mulling over her self-appointed task of playing matchmaker for Mr. Chandler. She hadn't done anything but think about it so far. But she couldn't put it off any longer. The children needed stability in their lives. It was her duty to find someone who could be a true mother to them. And a good wife to their uncle.

And for some reason, she found that challenge didn't excite her as it should have.

A few minutes later Mr. Chandler returned, ushering the children into the room before him.

They worked on learning to sign the alphabet until Mrs. Collins announced that supper was ready.

Janell closed the notebook as the children moved to the kitchen. Mr. Chandler had hung back as well and she met his gaze with a satisfied smile. "I think we made good progress today. Chloe seems to be attacking the lessons with a little more enthusiasm."

He nodded. "I thought so, too. It's a good first step, I suppose."

She stood. "I should be going now."

His brow shot up. "Aren't you planning to have supper with us? I'm sure Aunt Rowena cooked plenty."

She resisted the temptation to say yes. "Thank you, but now that your aunt is here, perhaps it would be better if you ate as a family. You don't need an outsider to—"

He cut her off before she could finish. "You're not an outsider. In fact, at the moment, the children probably consider you as much family as they do me and definitely more than Aunt Rowena."

Did he think of her that way, too? "But—"

"I won't hear of you going away hungry. Feeding you is the least I can do to repay you for your time here."

"Very well," she said. "Thank you for the invitation." Then she stepped past him. "I'll see if your aunt needs any help."

Their arms brushed against each other and she felt a startling shiver of response.

Did he feel it, too?

More important, how could she make sure it didn't happen again?

Hank let Miss Whitman leave the room. Her reaction to his accidental touch just now hadn't gone unnoticed. Not that she'd been alone in that reaction.

But if she felt the attraction, too, why was she being so stubborn about acknowledging it?

At least she'd decided to stay for supper. It was important that this first meal with his aunt go well, and his gut told him that would have a better chance of happening if the schoolteacher was present.

Hank stepped into the kitchen a moment later and one look at his aunt told him she wouldn't last long here. Her eyes were still puffy and watery, her nose still red. She must be miserable. But still she managed to smile at the children and direct them on getting the table ready.

It was good to see that the two women were working harmoniously together.

He wondered if whomever he chose for his wife would fit in here so seamlessly.

Somehow, he didn't think so.

Chapter Thirteen

After supper, Miss Whitman, true to form, insisted on helping his aunt clean the kitchen. "You've had a long day," she said when the woman protested. "This will go faster if we tackle it together."

Hank pitched in to help as well, and in no time the task was done.

As soon as the last dish was put away, Miss Whitman retrieved her shawl from the peg by the door.

"If it's okay with Mrs. Collins, I'll come by tomorrow as we'd planned, to work with the children some more. I'll return to the classroom on Wednesday and perhaps Alex will be ready to join my class by then."

"I'll be pleased to have your company," Mrs. Collins said.

Hank insisted on escorting her, and since his aunt was there to watch the children, she didn't protest.

As they stepped outside, Hank saw the schoolteacher give a tiny shiver, then draw her shawl tighter around her. Dusk had settled in and it was now much cooler than it had been when the sun was high. Without giving it much thought, he shrugged out of his jacket and draped it over her shoulders.

She looked up with wide eyes and a startled expression. "Mr. Chandler, that's very gentlemanly of you but quite unnecessary. I have my shawl and surely you need your jacket."

Why did she have to argue about everything? "You were cold, weren't you?"

Her brow furrowed. "Well, yes, but not unbearably so. And we don't have far—"

He'd heard enough. "Then keep it on. I'll get it back from you when we reach the boardinghouse."

"I..." She paused and looked at him uncertainly. Then she drew the jacket more closely around her. "Well... thank you."

That was better. "You're welcome."

They were silent for a few moments. Then she spoke up. "I'm sorry things are so uncomfortable for your aunt."

"She's willing to try to stick it out but I can't do that to her. I need to send her home by the end of the week, if not sooner."

"You do know it's going to be nearly impossible to find you a wife before she leaves, don't you?"

"I know it's going to be tricky, but surely it's not altogether impossible." Trouble was, he couldn't drum up enthusiasm for another bride when he was in the schoolteacher's company.

"True, but highly improbable. I believe you need to start thinking about a contingency plan."

"Easier said than done."

"Oh, come now. There are a number of things you can do. Hire someone to cook and watch the children, for one."

He jammed his hands in his pockets. "Perhaps for a week or so, but only as a last resort."

She gave him a curious look but, to his surprise, didn't ask him to elaborate. Which, he supposed, was why he did. "Finding extra money is a bit of a problem at the moment."

Janell was surprised by his admission. She hadn't believed him to be a wealthy man, but she hadn't figured him for a man of tight means, either.

Was his sawmill in trouble?

Or did this have something to do with settling his sister and brother-in-law's affairs?

She thought about offering him some money, but men could be quite touchy when it came to financial matters. So instead she changed the subject. "I see the mayor is doing his part to decorate the whole town this year." All of the lampposts in town were sporting jaunty red bows and sprigs of holly.

Hank looked around and grimaced. "Isn't it a bit early?"

She grinned. "You weren't at the Thanksgiving festival this year, so you probably haven't heard. The mayor thinks we should show more Christmas spirit. So he's offered up a calf from his prize bull to the shopkeeper who does the best job of decorating his storefront for Christmas." She cast him a sideways look. "So will you be decorating the mill?"

Mr. Chandler just rolled his eyes.

They'd reached the boardinghouse by then and Mr. Chandler escorted her right up to the front door. It was rather nice to have a gentleman pay such particular attention to her. Perhaps it wouldn't be difficult to find a lady willing to marry this man—despite his rough exterior, he could be quite an agreeable companion.

"Thank you for escorting me home, Mr. Chandler."

"It's the least I can do to repay you for all of your help these last few days."

"Miss Bruder is set to take my class again tomorrow, so I'll visit with Betty June first thing."

"I'd wish you luck but that sounds rather self-serving."

At least he still had his sense of humor.

"But I don't want to take advantage of your generous nature. Aunt Rowena can take care of things while she's here."

"Your aunt is here to help you keep your house running smoothly and to be around at night if you should need her. But she can't teach the children sign language. And with the effect Smudge's presence has on her, she may not be able to stay until Friday."

He gave a reluctant nod. "Very well, but I insist that after tomorrow you don't take any more days off to help us."

She nodded. "If things go well tomorrow, I'll return to my job on Wednesday. I suggest Alex start attending class then as well."

"But not Chloe?"

"To be honest, I think it will actually do them both good to be separated for a day or two."

"I agree, *if* Alex doesn't spend all his time worrying about Chloe."

"I'll do my best to see that he doesn't."

"How do you think Chloe and Aunt Rowena will handle being alone together?"

Janell was flattered that he seemed to want her opinion. "Your aunt seems like a strong woman who genuinely cares for people. It may get a bit uncomfortable at first, but that's not necessarily a bad thing." She fingered the jacket's collar. "But we can talk about it after we see how tomorrow goes."

"I agree." He shoved his hands deeper into his pockets, looking pensive.

She slipped his jacket from her shoulders and handed it to him. "Thank you for loaning me this yet again."

"You're welcome." He shrugged back into it. "I'll see you tomorrow." And with a touch to the brim of his hat, he quickly descended the porch steps.

Janell watched him walk away. His bearing was so confident, his stride so assertive. This was a man who knew what he wanted out of life and wasn't afraid to go after it. Except when it came to the children.

As she climbed the stairs to the second floor, Janell found herself missing the feel of his jacket on her shoulders. It had enveloped her so nicely in its warmth, surrounded her with a scent that was so masculine and wholly him.

Strange that the thought of him marrying another woman left her feeling vaguely bereft. It was only because she'd grown so fond of the children, she told herself. She'd miss her daily visits with them once they were in another woman's care. She'd see them at school, of course, but that wasn't quite the same.

Being in their home, cooking their meals, sitting down to dine with them—it had felt almost as if she had a family of her own.

She'd forgotten just how wonderful and fulfilling that felt.

Janell shook off those melancholy thoughts as she stepped into her set of rooms. She had a good life here. She loved her work and her students, and she'd been welcomed into the homes of many of their families on numerous occasions.

She was truly blessed in the life she'd built here.

Wishing for more, such as a family and home of her own, was just plain selfish.

But oh, how her rebellious heart yearned for more…

Hank pulled up his collar against the cold as he headed home. He'd almost proposed to her again. Not only would marrying her solve all of his problems, but he was also beginning to like having her around.

Not that he'd formed any kind of romantic attachment to her—no indeed, he was long past that kind of foolish nonsense. It was just that he'd got used to her and it would take an effort to get used to someone else.

But he'd known in his gut that if he'd asked, her answer would be the same as before. She just wasn't interested.

So it seemed he'd have to go through the tedious process of finding another suitable woman to wed. To say he was dreading the search was an understatement. But at least he wasn't going through it alone. Having Miss Whitman do the interviewing and offering her opinion on potential candidates, something she seemed uniquely qualified to do, would free him up to focus on everything else clamoring for his attention.

And giving Miss Whitman reason to keep coming around was something to look forward to.

For the children's sake, of course.

Hank looked up from his work at the sawmill as Gus started barking. That was his we've-got-company bark. Was it a customer?

He headed for the entrance, then paused as he caught sight of the visitor. Janell Whitman stood calmly in the yard, eyeing Gus with a cautious but unafraid stare. She was speaking too softly for him to make out the words. And Gus, while still alert, was not braced for any sort of attack.

"That's enough, Gus."

The dog immediately stopped barking and began wagging his tail.

"Hello." Miss Whitman gave him a sunny smile.

"I hope you don't mind me coming here," she said.

"Not at all. I'm just surprised. Did you walk all the way here?"

"It's not all that far and the weather is nice."

He considered two miles a fair distance, especially for a woman in skirts. He helped her up onto the elevated floor of the mill. As soon as she was settled, she looked around. "It's my first visit to a sawmill. Would you mind showing me around before we talk?"

"Not at all. We do more than saw trees into lumber here." He waved a hand toward the right. "Simon is working with our shingle machine. The shingles we make get shipped to cities all over this part of the country and even points east." He started walking again. "And this time of year we also do a brisk business cutting and selling firewood." He also donated quite a bit of that firewood to the church and the school.

The complete tour took less than thirty minutes and then he escorted her into his office—a small room just big enough for a small desk and two chairs.

He dusted off the seat of the guest chair with a rag. "Sorry, in a place like this, sawdust gets on everything." Straightening, he waved her into the chair then moved around the desk to take the other seat. "So what can I do for you?"

"I paid a visit to Betty June this morning."

Hank had almost forgotten about their matchmaking deal. And at the moment he wasn't certain whether he wanted her to say Betty June was the right woman for him or not.

"I was quite impressed with her," Miss Whitman stated. "Betty June would indeed make a good mother for the children." She gave him an apologetic look. "But I'm afraid she won't be interested in the position."

It figured. "Why not?"

"Betty June wants to become a journalist. She has a cousin who lives in Tyler and this cousin has connections with the local newspaper. Betty June plans to move there as soon as she's saved enough money to pay her way."

"I see."

"However, since she's trying to earn money for this venture, she might be open to you hiring her as housekeeper for a time, just until you can find a wife."

"We'll see." His funds couldn't stretch for any long-term commitment, but perhaps he could make it work short-term.

"So, have you been thinking of any other names to add to that list of yours?"

"I suppose I'll have to start a new list." He glanced her way. "Any suggestions?"

She hesitated a moment, then nodded.

"You've thought of someone?"

"Not exactly. But I was thinking that we might apply an organized, systematic approach. Since one of the criteria we discussed was that she be a God-fearing woman, we could look to the women who attend church regularly."

"All right. But that's still a large group to sort through."

"Most everyone sits in the very same place from week

to week. Just mentally picture the people sitting there on Sunday morning, starting in the front and moving back. Then start picking out the single ladies. I suppose we should start with the choir. Eliminating the single women who are either too old or too young."

"Well, there's Hazel Andrews. She seems a bit too flighty for my taste, but she appears to have a good heart."

"Hazel does have an exuberant approach to life. But she can be quite sensible and down-to-earth when called for. You are also correct in that she does have a good heart. In fact, she would make an excellent mother to Alex and Chloe. But I'm afraid she has her heart set on someone else."

Just about everyone in town knew the dressmaker had her sights set on Ward Gleason—everyone but Ward himself, it seemed.

Hank frowned. "I'd think she'd given up on that by now."

Miss Whitman shook her head. "When Hazel sets her mind on something, it takes a lot to dissuade her."

He tried imagining the choir again. "There's Abigail Fulton, but she's too young."

"I agree. You don't want to offer this sort of businesslike arrangement to a young lady who's still looking for romance."

He frowned. "The only other unmarried lady in the choir, besides you, is Addis Floyd, and she's my mother's age, so I think we can rule her out."

She nodded. "Then let's move on to those who sit in the pews. Let's start with the left side of the aisle, going front to back."

He tried to picture the church on Sunday morning. "There's the Hymel family—no marriage candidates there.

Behind them are the Daley and the Sanders families—
again no candidates." Then he sat up straighter. "But Emily
Johansen is in the next pew. I hadn't considered her before, but now that I think on it, she might be a possibility."

His would-be matchmaker nodded slowly. "She seems
to have the right temperament for taking care of children, and since her husband has been gone for almost
fifteen months now, she may be receptive to your offer.
But keep in mind that she has two young children of her
own. Are you certain you're ready to add more children
to your household right now?"

He grimaced at that thought. It wasn't that he disliked
children so much as that he wasn't sure he was ready to
be a father to four kids. "Why don't we keep going and
see who else might fit the bill."

"Very well. The Barrs are in the next pew and the
Parkers and Dawsons are behind them—no single ladies
of an appropriate age in any of those groups."

"But behind them is Hortense Lawrence." He nodded as he mentally dredged up all he knew of her. "She's
about my age, seems to have a good head on her shoulders and she's single." He paused and cut a look Miss
Whitman's way. "No one's courting her, are they?"

"Not that I'm aware of."

Something about the way she said that caught his attention. "Do I detect a note of hesitation in your voice?"

Miss Whitman pursed her lips as if trying to hold
back her words. What wasn't she saying?

"We'll keep her name on the list, and if she makes it
to the top, then you can make up your own mind."

He crossed his arms. "That's not how this works.
Remember, your function is to share your thoughts and

advise me on the candidate's suitability to be a mother to the kids."

"Of course I'll share my thoughts with you. But I don't like to spread gossip. For the sake of our agreement, let's just say she wouldn't be my first pick."

"Then let's scratch her name from the list."

"Just keep in mind, in the end it's you who'll have to marry the woman you choose. I would caution you to take the time to make an evaluation of your own."

"But I don't have the luxury of time."

"I understand. Believe me. But you'll be making a lifetime commitment, and regardless of how pressed you feel, you need to really think before you make any sort of proposal." Her voice nearly vibrated with the force of her passion. "And you don't have to decide today or even this week."

She really didn't understand. "I know I can cut back on some of my hours at the mill. But that's my livelihood. If I don't work, I don't have money coming in to keep food on the table."

"I have a suggestion for something that will work until you find a wife, assuming you do find her by Christmas."

Finally! "I'm listening."

"It's a little unorthodox."

"At this point, I'm willing to listen to *any* ideas."

"Well then, first off, since your aunt is leaving Friday, I think that will be a good day for Chloe to start attending school again."

"You think she'll be ready?"

"Perhaps not fully. But she can come in and read on her own and begin to get used to being around the other children again."

He raised a brow at that. "So you're just going to play nursemaid to her?"

"It's more than that. It's a way to ease her back into the classroom. And since I hope to give sign-language lessons to the other children, she can definitely participate in that activity."

He nodded. "If you think she'll be okay, then yes, that'll be a big help. I can walk them to school in the morning and leave work early to meet them after school."

"There's no need for you to cut your workday short unless you just wish to. I can walk them home after school and stay with them until you return home in the evening."

"But isn't that tying you down quite a bit?"

She shrugged. "As I said, this is just a short-term solution, until you settle on a wife. But it gives you a little breathing room so that you can make the right decision. Besides, I can work with the children on their sign-language skills, and they'll need extra help with their class work until they catch up with the other children." She spread her hands. "So you see, your urgency to find a wife is not as pressing as you believe. You can take the time you need to get it right."

Getting it right seemed mighty important to her. Was it just her concern for the children? "I know there are a good many people out there, mostly the young and foolish, who hold out for a love match. But I'm not one of them." At least not anymore. "And there are many people who marry for other reasons, reasons that have to do with business or convenience, or comfort or security. None of these require that the parties be more than merely compatible."

"True. But it's important that you are more than a little certain of that compatibility."

"Is that why you never married?" he asked impulsively. "Because you couldn't find a man you felt was compatible?"

He was surprised by her reaction. She stiffened and her expression closed off. He'd obviously touched a nerve of some sort.

Janell felt everything inside her constrict and she regretted again that she couldn't explain. He couldn't know her secret, but still his words cut.

"First of all, my personal life is not what's under discussion here. And secondly, it will do the kids no good, and lots of harm, if they grow up in a home where the parents don't get along. And make no mistake, you *will* be as parents to them."

She tried to relax. "Now, let's continue building our list. Behind Hortense is the Douglas family."

They went through the remainder of the church quickly and ended up with three more names for Janell to check up on.

Then she stood. "I'll leave you to your work now. I promised your aunt I would come by and relieve her so she can get out of the house and away from the cat for a little while."

Mr. Chandler stood as well. "I can take you in the wagon."

"No need. I enjoy the walk."

"Well then, I'll walk you there." He held up a hand. "And I won't take no for an answer. I want to check in on Aunt Rowena anyway."

Janell knew he was just using that as an excuse, but she nodded anyway.

They walked without speaking at first, but after a few moments, Janell felt compelled to break the silence. "I just want to say, I think you are more capable of being a father to those children than you believe."

He cut her a startled look. "What brought that up?"

"I just thought you should know, is all."

"Even if you're right, what they really need is a mother."

"And you're working on that. I just want to caution you one more time to make certain you take enough time to make the right choice." She knew all too well how disastrous making the wrong choice could be.

Janell met his gaze with earnest entreaty. "It won't really benefit them if you marry a woman who is wrong for them or for you."

He rubbed the side of his jaw. "I hadn't thought of it in those terms."

"I understand your nervousness about getting them ready in the morning and putting them to bed at night. I have a suggestion that might help."

"Your suggestions are always worth hearing."

She didn't miss the fact that he said worth *hearing* not worth *following.* But she pressed on. "While your aunt is still here to help, start developing some specific routines for both Alex and Chloe. Get them up at the same time every morning. Make it clear there are certain tasks they are expected to perform before they eat breakfast, such as getting the table ready or straightening their beds. Then do the same thing in the evenings. After supper, set a specific time when they should clean up and get ready for bed. Say prayers with them and tuck them in. Set rules around whether they are allowed to read or play quietly or if they must get right to bed."

"And how will that help?"

"It'll provide order and structure to their days. That's important for a child. Before long, they will do these things automatically without you even bringing it up."

She smiled. "And just as importantly, it will give some order and structure to *your* day."

And perhaps ease this headlong race he was running to find a wife before Christmas. She knew all too well how not taking the time to know your future spouse could develop into a disaster that would ruin the rest of your life.

She couldn't bear to think of him falling into that same trap.

She wasn't ready to admit to herself that there were other reasons she didn't like to think about him marrying any of these ladies they'd discussed.

Chapter Fourteen

When Hank returned home for lunch that afternoon, it was obvious that Aunt Rowena was not going to last in this house much longer. Her eyes were watery and even puffier than before, and her sneezes were more frequent now.

Janell pulled him aside. "Since it was such a pretty day, I've given the children their lesson out on the back porch most of the morning, with Smudge, too, of course." She chewed her lower lip for a moment. "But it hasn't seemed to make much difference. Your aunt is determined to stick this out, for your sake, but she is truly miserable."

"I agree. I need to get her away from here."

"Perhaps she can spend the afternoon at my place. I'll be with the children, so there's no pressing reason for her to be here for the next few hours as well."

Relieved, Hank nodded. "Thank you. It seems I'm indebted to you yet again."

At first his aunt refused, but Miss Whitman could be hard to turn down when she put her mind to something. At last Aunt Rowena was convinced. While the schoolteacher escorted his aunt to her place, Hank took the kids for a walk to Abigail's library. As they passed by the various shops, the children slowed to admire the decorations that had gone up in many of them. Even Daisy's restaurant, where the library was housed, had a festive arrangement of gingerbread men strung across the front window.

The joy on Chloe's face when she realized she could check out any book that caught her interest convinced him that this needed to become a weekly trip for them.

And he had Janell to thank for making the suggestion.

He was finding it harder and harder to understand why the woman had never married and didn't have a family of her own by now.

"My nephew tells me he proposed to you. And that you refused him."

Janell almost missed a step at Mrs. Collins's rather tactless statement. Trying to maintain a dignified air as they continued down the sidewalk toward the boarding-house, she nodded. "That's true."

"Forgive an old woman for prying, but might I ask why?"

"My reasons are personal."

"Well, at least you didn't try to lie and tell me it was because you don't love him."

Again Janell was caught off guard by the woman's boldness. "I beg your pardon?"

"Oh, come now. The two of you can't be in the same room without it becoming immediately obvious that there's at least a spark of attraction there—for both of you."

Was that true, that he felt it also?

Mrs. Collins studied her a moment longer, but Janell

held her peace. Finally, Hank's aunt reached up and touched a cameo locket at her neck. "You see this?"

Janell nodded. "It's quite lovely."

"There's a story behind it. It's personal and rather lengthy, so I won't go into it all, but I wear it as a reminder of what havoc false pride can bring into a life."

"False pride?"

"The kind of pride that wears the disguise of humility."

"I'm afraid I don't understand."

"Let's just say there was a time in my life when I refused to take chances, to step out in faith. I told myself it was because I wasn't worthy, because I didn't deserve success and joy the way others did."

She shook her head. "But the real reason, I'm ashamed to say, was that I wanted others to think well of me, to admire my humility. It was pride, pure and simple. And as a result, I missed many wonderful blessings I could have had, had I only lived the life the Good Lord wanted me to."

She fingered the cameo. "My best friend gave this to me the night she made me confront what I'd become."

Why was the woman telling her all this?

Mrs. Collins smiled as if she'd heard Janell's silent question. "I just don't want to see that same sort of pride steal anyone else's happiness."

Did she think that applied to her? Janell knew she was far from perfect, but this, at least, was not one of her shortcomings.

But she gave the woman a smile as she escorted her into the boardinghouse and thanked her for the story.

The next morning, Janell stood in front of her classroom with a nervous Alex beside her. "Children, this is

Alex Hobbs. He and his sister moved here from Colorado to live with their uncle, Mr. Hank Chandler. Let's give Alex a warm Turnabout welcome, shall we?"

Janell kept her hand on Alex's shoulder while she waited for the chorus of "Hello, Alex" to die down, then spoke again. "Alex's sister, Chloe, will be joining us on Friday."

She pointed to an empty desk in the second row. "Alex, why don't you take that seat." Then she smiled at the boy seated in the next desk over. "Jack, please help Alex for the next few days, until he gets used to where we are in our lessons."

As soon as Alex slid into his seat, Michael Greene raised his hand.

She nodded at the boy. "Yes, Michael?"

"Is it true his sister can't hear nothing?"

"Can't hear *anything*," she corrected. "And yes, that's true. An explosion went off close to Chloe and it damaged the part of her ear that allows her to hear things."

"So how are we gonna talk to her?" the boy asked.

"That's a good question." Janell looked around the classroom. "I've never told any of you this, but I have a younger sister, and she, too, went deaf. So my family and I had to find a new way to communicate with her."

"What did you do?"

She looked around the classroom. "Have any of you ever heard of sign language?"

Most of the children shook their heads.

"It's a very special language that allows you to talk with your hands. All of my family, my sister included, learned how to 'talk' to each other this new way. And now I'm teaching it to Alex, his sister and his uncle. Pretty soon we'll be able to hold entire conversations with each other, without saying a word." She lowered her tone conspiratorially. "We can even send secret signals to each other if we like. Like this." She signaled *how are you* Alex's way and he immediately responded with *I am well*.

The students seemed quite impressed. "What did you say to each other?" Lily Tucker asked.

Janell relayed the simple conversation, then gave them her best conspiratorial look. "Is there anyone else here who would like to learn to do that?"

Nearly every hand shot up.

She nodded approvingly. "Wonderful. Any day that we finish our lessons early, we can spend the extra time on sign-language lessons. Those who don't care to learn can either read or work quietly on their homework at their desk."

She'd speak to Mitch Parker about making the same offer to his students. The more people in town who learned the fundamentals of signing, the less isolated Chloe would feel and the more comfortable she would be going out in public. And that was half the battle.

Satisfied she'd taken a strong first step, Janell returned to her normal classroom routine. "Now, let's begin our lessons."

As the school day progressed, Janell couldn't help wondering how things were going with Mrs. Collins and Chloe. She'd promised Mr. Chandler's aunt she'd walk Alex home after school and then let the woman slip away to her room at the boardinghouse for a few hours again today before supper.

And that meant she would be there when Mr. Chandler returned from the sawmill. She wanted to report on how Alex had done at school and see how Chloe had fared without her brother for most of the day.

But a small part of Janell knew that there was more to it than that. She was eager to see Mr. Chandler.

Pushing that thought away, she forced her mind back to the present.

She was pleased to see Alex playing with the other boys at recess. Getting out among other children would be good for him. And it looked as if Jack had taken the boy under his wing.

Then Janell caught sight of Leo on the playground and it reminded her of her conversation with Eve on Saturday. She headed for Mitch Parker's classroom and told him about her idea for a nativity play. Not only did he agree that it was a good idea, but he also suggested letting some of his more creative students help to write the play as a class project.

This year Verity Cooper came to the school three days a week for one hour right after recess to give the children music lessons. This included not just singing, but lessons on how to read music and how to play the small upright piano that had been donated to the school. All students, whether or not they were in the choir, were encouraged to attend.

Except, that was, for those students who'd fallen behind in their lessons. Those students gathered in Mr. Parker's classroom for extra study time, while the music lessons went on in Janell's classroom, where the piano was housed.

Janell was especially happy about this arrangement because it gave her the kind of access to a piano that she hadn't had since she'd moved to Turnabout.

Piano music had been a big part of her childhood. Her mother was an accomplished musician, but more than that, she was very passionate about music in all its forms. She'd tried to instill that same passion in her daughters as well.

Janell didn't consider herself a talented musician but she did enjoy playing, especially when she was anxious or trying to work out a problem in her mind. She would often play the piano after school or on weekends. The music had both a calming and focusing effect on her so that problems didn't seem so overwhelming.

When Verity arrived today, Janell was ready to approach her with the idea of a children-cast nativity play to go along with the Christmas music program. Verity was in enthusiastic agreement.

Before Janell could explain about the choir to Alex, she saw Jack leading the boy over to introduce him to the music teacher. For a moment she wished she could convince him to join the nativity play instead so she could keep an eye on how he was doing.

But she took herself to task for such selfish thoughts. It would be good for Alex to widen his circle of acquaintances, with both children and adults.

And since she wouldn't be a presence in his home much longer, it was really time she started distancing herself somewhat.

That thought put a damper on her spirits. Those two children had grown so precious to her in such a short time—watching another woman step into the role of mother to them was going to be wrenching.

Sometimes she wanted to just scream out that she'd paid enough for her foolish actions, that she should be able to leave the past behind her. But she knew that it would never be behind her.

Chapter Fifteen

~~~

When Hank arrived at home he was greeted by the aroma of food simmering on the stove, the warmth of a fire in the fireplace and the sound of a woman humming as she worked.

A man could get used to coming home to this.

He walked into the kitchen and was met with a cheery greeting and warm smile from Miss Whitman. Aunt Rowena was no doubt relaxing in the schoolteacher's cat-free room at the boardinghouse.

After a quickly exchanged smile with Miss Whitman, he turned to the kids. "So, Alex, how was your first day of school here in Turnabout?"

The boy shrugged. "It was okay. Miss Whitman is a good teacher."

Hank glanced up and met Miss Whitman's smiling gaze. "I'm sure she is."

The boy sat up straighter. "And guess what? She's teaching a bunch of the kids at school how to do sign language, too, so they'll all be able to talk to Chloe."

Hank met her gaze again with a warm smile. "Is she, now? A whole bunch, huh?"

Miss Whitman's cheeks turned pink. Nice to know he could have that effect on her.

"It's purely voluntary," she said, "but the majority want to participate." She grinned. "The ones who normally wouldn't be inclined to join in will be afraid of missing out on something fun."

Then she turned back to Alex. "Don't forget to tell your uncle about the choir."

"Choir?"

Alex nodded. "The choir lady comes to the school three days a week to teach music. And she said I could join the children's choir if I want to."

"And you want to?"

Alex nodded again, more vigorously this time. "Lots of the kids are in it, even the boys."

"Well then, I think it's a good idea." The kids might actually learn to feel at home in Turnabout after all. Or Alex, at least.

Hank turned to his niece. "And, Chloe, how was your day with Aunt Rowena?"

The girl just gave him a blank stare.

Miss Whitman nodded toward the slate. Hank obediently picked it up and wrote out his question.

Chloe read it and shrugged, then bent her head back down over the paper she'd been scribbling on. Was she deliberately shutting him out? Or was it just a normal thing for a girl her age?

He tried again. "What are you doing there?"

Hank grimaced as soon as the words were out of his mouth. It was still hard to remember his niece couldn't hear him.

He moved closer and looked over her shoulder. To his surprise, this was no childish scribble. It was a drawing of a dragonfly on a blade of grass, and while it was by no means perfect, it was obvious Chloe had a talent worth nurturing.

He tapped her shoulder to get her attention. When she looked up he laboriously signed out *good picture*.

Chloe watched his hand movements closely, a little furrow of concentration creasing her forehead. When he was done she glanced up to meet his gaze and gave a shy smile, then ducked her head and went back to her sketch.

He glanced up to see Miss Whitman smiling at him with approval. Why did such a simple act suddenly make him feel ten feet tall?

Janell was beginning to look forward to these few minutes when Mr. Chandler walked her home. It gave them time to talk privately about the progress the children were making, about his search for a wife and about nothing at all.

"Have you seen any of Chloe's drawings?" he asked.

"Yes. They're quite good for a child her age."

"I think so, too. Why didn't I see evidence of this talent before? I mean, I've noticed her scribbling but never paid attention to what she was actually creating."

She touched his sleeve. "Don't take yourself to task. You've had quite a few other things on your mind lately."

He placed his hand on hers and gave it a light squeeze before releasing it. "That's no excuse. I have vague memories of her hunched over a tablet of paper, scribbling away, but I never paid a bit of attention to what she was drawing. I just figured it was another way for her to avoid me."

Janell dropped her hand from his arm, but her fingers still tingled from his touch. She tried to push away that thought. Much better to focus on how vulnerable he seemed at the moment. "But you *have* noticed now, so what matters is what you do with that knowledge."

"I'll encourage her, of course, and let her know how special her talent is." He eyed her quizzically. "Is there something else you think I should do?"

"Mitch Parker, the teacher for the older students, is quite accomplished at sketching. I can ask him for resources that might be of interest to her if you like."

He nodded, and then he changed the subject. "I see most of the shopkeepers in town have got on board with the decorating contest."

Janell smiled. "For once I have to agree with Mayor Saunders. I think the decorations are very festive and cheery." They were currently passing by the dress shop. "Like this one, for instance. That tree decorated with lace and sequins is quite pretty."

The saddle and leather goods shop was next door and Hank nodded toward the lack of ornamentation. "At least Nate Cooper hasn't succumbed yet."

Janell grinned. "Just wait. Verity told me today of some ideas she has for it."

He groaned, then changed the subject again. "Any progress on the wife hunt?"

She ignored the little twinge of dissatisfaction. She refused to think of it as jealousy. "Only to scratch another name off the list, I'm afraid."

He frowned. "Who?"

"Joan Wimple." She watched him obliquely for signs of disappointment. Joan was a very pretty young lady with an infectious smile.

"What was it this time?"

"Joan is the oldest and only female of seven siblings. She's been helping her mother raise her younger brothers most of her life. At the moment Joan's more interested in a bit of freedom than in tying herself down with children."

Mr. Chandler didn't say anything but she thought she heard a smothered sigh.

"Don't worry." She almost put her hand on his arm again, but got hold of herself just in time, brushing at her skirt to hide the involuntary movement. "There are still other names on the list to check out."

They'd arrived at the boardinghouse by this time. But for some reason Janell wasn't ready to go inside just yet.

She paused on the top step of the porch and turned around to face him. "Your aunt is truly a selfless woman. I'm not certain I could have lasted this long, much less be willing to stay for another day and a half."

Mr. Chandler nodded and leaned his shoulder against a support post. "She is a good, God-fearing woman. I've often thought it was a shame she never had kids of her own. I feel bad for putting her through this, even though she insisted."

"No one can blame you for that. You've been put in a difficult position and are doing the best you can."

He crossed his arms over his chest and studied her quizzically for a moment. "I know why Aunt Rowena is going out of her way to help me. She's family. What I can't quite figure is why *you're* going out of your way to help us."

She held her head up, willing herself not to let him see that his question had flustered her. "Why, for Chloe and Alex, of course. Helping children is what I do. It's what I've made my life's work."

"And that's your *only* reason?"

"Of course." Or at least it had been at the outset. In

the past few days it had got a bit more complicated. But he didn't need to know that.

He studied her silently for another long moment, and it was all she could do not to squirm under that steady gaze.

Finally he straightened. "Well, Aunt Rowena will be wondering what happened to me. I'd best be heading back home."

She clasped her hands in front of her and nodded. "Good night, Mr. Chandler. Thank you for escorting me home."

Janell watched him leave, an unsettled feeling jangling inside her.

This was ridiculous. Discounting the fact that he'd been a vague figure who happened to live in the same town as she did, Janell had known Mr. Chandler for less than a week. How could she be developing such strong feelings for him?

She'd known her ex-husband, Gregory, for more time than that, and look what had happened there.

No, she had to keep her distance, had to make certain they maintained a strictly platonic friendship.

But a little voice inside her whispered that it was already too late.

Hank stuffed his hands in his pockets as he headed home. He was convinced the very proper Janell Whitman wasn't as cool toward him as she'd have him believe. He'd felt her reaction when he squeezed her hand earlier and he'd caught her watching him a time or two lately with unmistakable warmth.

So why was she being so stubborn about accepting his offer? Did he not measure up to her standards of what a husband should be? Even if she came from a wealthy background, she obviously led a fairly simple life now.

Or maybe it was something much simpler? She'd been harping on the fact that he shouldn't be quite so abrupt and businesslike when he proposed to whatever candidate made it to the top of his list. Perhaps that was what she was looking for—a bit of romance.

He rotated his head from side to side, trying to ease some of the tension in his neck. He supposed he could court her a bit. It wasn't as if she didn't know what his ultimate goal was, so it wouldn't be deception. She, of all people in this town, knew exactly what his intentions were.

But just because he hadn't been acting like some besotted mooncalf didn't mean he couldn't introduce a bit of romance into their relationship. At one time he'd played the part of the love-struck beau, courting a woman who'd gone and made a fool of him.

However, now he'd be doing it with open eyes and guarded emotions.

Yes indeed. If she wanted a proper courtship, he could definitely play the role.

The next morning he put his plan into motion. When he walked Alex to school, he made sure to compliment Miss Whitman on the color of her dress. He held her gaze for a couple of extra beats, just long enough to see her pupils expand. He also made a point of finding an excuse to touch her arm briefly and ask her opinion on a few trivial matters.

That afternoon he left the sawmill early, ostensibly to deliver firewood to the school. It put him in the position to be there while Janell was finishing up the day with the sign-language lessons, and then he could walk her and Alex home.

He caught her casting several confused glances his way. Was that a good sign? Was she warming to him at all?

If so, how long should he keep this up before he proposed again?

Janell wasn't certain what to make of Mr. Chandler's behavior. One minute she thought he was actually flirting with her and the next he seemed distant. Was it her imagination? Or was he just being gentlemanly?

Regardless of what it all meant, she had to hold fast to her resolve. Her peace of mind depended on it. But he wasn't making it easy on her.

That evening, as he walked her back to the boardinghouse, Mr. Chandler opened their conversation with a question. "Are you sure Chloe is ready to go to school tomorrow?"

She heard the genuine concern in his voice and gave him a reassuring smile. "It depends what you mean by *ready.* She won't want to go. She'll be scared and uncomfortable and probably embarrassed. But if we waited until she actually *wanted* to go, she might never leave the house."

He chuckled. "I'm glad I have you to help figure these things out. I'm not sure I could handle it on my own."

"Trust me, you'd do fine. A lot of this is instinct and trial and error. I just have more experience, is all."

"That's no small advantage."

Uncomfortable with his praise, she returned to the original topic. "I promise to make the transition as easy on Chloe as possible."

"I know. That's the only thing that makes this bearable."

This was the last night his aunt would be around to

watch the kids while he walked her home. Janell wondered if that meant this would be their last evening stroll
together. If so, she realized she was going to miss them.

Not that she had any right to his time or his company.
Even though her feelings toward him had changed significantly since she'd turned down his proposal, if he
was to ask her again today her answer would have to be
the same. The past she'd left behind her when she moved
to Turnabout ensured that marriage—to any man—was
not an option for her.

But for the first time since she'd moved here, she
found herself sorely tempted.

The afternoon passed by much too fast, and before
she knew it, they were once more at the foot of the boardinghouse steps.

"Thank you for escorting me home once again, Mr.
Chandler."

He gave her a small, crooked grin. "Don't you think
it's time we used our given names?"

His question caught her off guard. "I don't—"

"It's what friends do. You *do* consider us to be friends,
I hope."

"Yes, of course—"

"Good. Then it's settled. Good night, Janell." And with
that, he tipped his hat and turned back the way they'd
come. The faint sound of masculine whistling floated
back on the air toward her.

"Good night, Hank," she said softly. Then she turned
and slowly entered the boardinghouse.

He considered them friends, did he? That was both
sweet and disappointing. Why did she want more when
she knew she couldn't do anything about it?

"Well, hello, dear."

Janell paused with one foot on the stairs leading up to

the second floor. "Oh, hello, Mrs. Ortolon. I'm sorry—I didn't see you there."

The woman gave a broad smile. "Not surprising. I could see your mind was elsewhere." She waved toward the table in the entryway. "I just wanted to make sure you knew you received a letter. It's from your sister, I believe."

Janell obediently retrieved her letter. "Thank you. I've been waiting for this."

"You've certainly been spending a lot of time at Mr. Chandler's home since he returned with those two children on Saturday."

Was Eunice trying to read something gossip-worthy in her actions? "I'm doing what I can to help him ease the children into their new home."

"And that's mighty charitable of you. And then giving up your room so poor Rowena could find some relief from that cat they brought with them. Why, that went above and beyond in my book." She gave Janell an arch look. "I certainly hope Hank appreciates all you're doing."

She ignored the question, instead giving the woman a distracted nod. "I think I'll head up to my room—I'm eager to read my letter. Good evening."

There was no way she was going to hang around and let Eunice Ortolon drag information from her. But if Eunice had taken note of her time spent with Hank, perhaps another meeting with the city council was in order to nip any rumors in the bud.

Her lips twisted in a mirthless smile as she thought about the fact that rumors such as this were really minor when compared to the truth she'd worked so hard to keep hidden.

Then she sobered. Truth was, her reputation was

something she was determined to guard closely. Much as she wished it were different, she'd never have a family of her own, so her job as schoolteacher was all she had. And she'd do just about anything to protect it.

Chapter Sixteen

Right after breakfast the next morning, Hank walked through town, escorting both children to the school-house. For once, when he'd insisted on holding Chloe's hand, she hadn't argued with him. He could feel the nervous tension radiating from her and knew she was terrified but was trying to hide it. Not even the sight of the festive windows in the various shops could draw a smile from her.

Was this too soon to push her out among other children? Should he keep her home today, even if he had to stay home with her himself?

He took a deep breath. Janell thought Chloe was ready, and he trusted her instincts. She *was* the school-teacher, after all.

He glanced at Alex. Yesterday, when he'd walked the boy to school, Alex had run off to play with the others as soon as they reached the school yard, just like any other boy.

But not today. Today Alex seemed determined to accompany Chloe into the schoolhouse, as if sensing she needed him.

As soon as they entered the classroom, Janell looked

up and greeted them with a smile. He was growing to look forward to that smile.

"Good morning." At the same time she spoke, she signed the words to Chloe.

The only other person in the schoolroom was a young girl about Chloe's age—one of the Tucker children, if he wasn't mistaken. She was stoking the stove that served as a heater to the classroom, but she looked up and smiled a welcome to the new arrivals.

Janell met them halfway and took Chloe's hand, then moved to the front row of desks. She patted the third one from the left. "Chloe, you'll sit here. That way you'll have a clear view of the blackboard."

Had the girl caught all of that?

Whatever the case, his niece seemed to have understood and she slid into the seat indicated.

Hank stood there a moment, knowing he should leave, yet feeling as if he would be abandoning his niece.

Then the Tucker girl stepped forward and approached Chloe. "I sit next to you," she explained. "I'm Lily."

To Hank's surprise, the little girl laboriously spelled out her name in sign.

Janell turned to him, a look of "it's all going to work out" on her face. "Don't worry. She'll be fine. Now, it's about time to call the rest of the students in, so you should probably go on to the mill."

"Of course." She was right—his hovering here wouldn't do anyone any good. Besides, he needed to check in on Aunt Rowena. She'd be leaving as soon as her friend arrived with the wagon this morning, so he wanted to thank her one more time and make sure she didn't need help with anything. Given the circumstances, she'd stayed longer than could have been expected. And if it hadn't been for the knowledge that Miss Whitman was so determined to lend a hand, he might have panicked.

Which reminded him. He reached into his jacket pocket and pulled out a small bundle. "I almost forgot," he said, holding it out to Janell. "Aunt Rowena asked me to give this to you."

Janell accepted the package, but looked at him with a puzzled expression. "What is it?"

"Open it."

She did as he said, then sucked in a breath. It was his aunt's cameo necklace.

"I can't—"

He touched her arm briefly. "She wanted you to have it."

He knew how much that cameo meant to his aunt. He'd never seen her without it. It seemed Janell had made quite an impression on Aunt Rowena.

While the children played outside at recess, Janell stood watching them from a window. Chloe's first day was going about as well as could be expected. The girl was on the playground, but she hadn't really joined in any of the games. She wasn't alone, though. Lily sat with her. Whether she wanted one or not, it appeared Chloe had a new best friend.

She absently fingered the cameo that now rested against her throat. Why had Mrs. Collins given it to her? Had it been a message of some sort? Regardless, it was a lovely piece of jewelry that had been given to her by a dear lady. She would treasure it for always.

Then she saw Mr. Chandler heading toward the school yard. What was he doing here? Not that she minded. Quite the opposite, in fact.

It warmed her heart to see him here in the middle of

the day. No matter how gruff he pretended to be, Hank really did have a soft spot for his niece and nephew.

She stepped out on the schoolhouse porch and he strode forward until he reached the lower step.

After they exchanged greetings, she smiled. "To what do we owe the honor of this visit?"

"I had lunch at Daisy's restaurant and thought I'd swing by on my way back to the mill to see how everything is going."

The school was most definitely not on the way to the mill, but Janell let that pass. "You'll be glad to hear that Lily Tucker has taken Chloe under her wing."

"And how has Chloe responded?"

"She was standoffish at first, but I think she's beginning to thaw a bit."

"Good. Chloe could use a friend."

Janell nodded. "Lily is a bright girl with a very big heart. She'll be good for Chloe."

"Did you prod her to befriend my niece?"

"Not at all. It happened naturally."

Hank set one booted foot on the next step up. "Alex mentioned that Mrs. Cooper comes by to give music lessons after recess."

"She does. Verity should be here soon if you wish to speak to her."

"No. I was just wondering… I mean, Chloe won't be able to participate in that."

"No, but she won't be the only one. Some of the students spend that time studying. And for the next several weeks some of the students will be working on a nativity play."

He raised a brow at that. "Do you truly think Chloe can take part in a play?"

"Yes. But *only* if she wants to. It's not something that can be forced on her."

"I sleep easier at night knowing Chloe has you looking out for her."

The quiet sincerity in his voice brought an unexpected lump to her throat. Before she could collect herself enough to respond, he tipped his hat and turned to go.

Why did he have to make keeping things business-like between them so difficult?

Later that evening, when it came time for Janell to return to the boardinghouse, Hank realized she no longer protested the courtesy. He took that as a sign she was becoming more comfortable with him.

As soon as they were out of earshot of the house, she turned to him with a serious expression. "Now that your aunt has gone, I think it's time Alex moved into his own room and left Chloe to hers."

"They're not going to like it," he said. "And aren't you the one who suggested I turn a blind eye to their room sharing?"

"I am. But that was just during their settling-in period." She nodded. "And you're right—they probably won't like it. But children don't always know what's best for them. That's a parent's job."

But he wasn't their parent; he was their uncle. There was a difference. "And if Alex tries to sneak back into Chloe's room?"

"Then you send him back to his own bed, firmly but with a minimum of fuss." She gave him a sympathetic smile. "I do have a suggestion for something that might make the transition easier for them."

He hid a smile—of course she did. "I'm listening."

"Try making their rooms more personal and welcoming. Right now they have all the charm and warmth of a hotel room. These aren't temporary accommodations, after all. These are rooms they will occupy for many years to come."

She didn't actually expect him to try decorating their rooms, did she? "I can help," she continued. "I'll take them to the mercantile and let them each pick out fabric for new curtains. Perhaps find some toys or keepsakes to set out—did they bring anything of that nature with them?"

"Most of their possessions were lost when their home collapsed." He rubbed his chin. "But the house we're living in is the one their mother and I grew up in. There may be a few of our things still stored up in the attic."

"Then perhaps you could tell them some stories of that time, something that will give the rooms, and the house itself, history and meaning to them."

"I'm not much for telling stories."

"Oh, come now, Mr. Chandler. Everyone can tell stories."

He wasn't so sure he believed that, but he was willing to give it a try. With a nod, he changed the subject. "I can't believe you convinced Chloe to take part in your Christmas play."

"Actually, it's Lily who gets the credit for that. She's one of the angels and she convinced Chloe that she would feel better if she had another angel standing with her. That, and the fact that she wouldn't have any lines, was all it took."

Then it was Janell's turn to change the subject. "You haven't asked about my matchmaking activities lately."

Was she so eager to see him matched with another woman? He'd thought he was making progress with her.

"I figure you'll let me know when you have something to tell me."

"You certainly don't seem to be in as big a hurry as you were a few days ago. Are you no longer looking to have a wife by Christmas?"

"That's still the goal." Though he would prefer it be with one particular woman. "Or at least to have set a wedding date by then. *Do* you have some news for me?"

"We need to scratch Maddy Jean off the list. She is not interested in marriage right now." She pulled the list from her pocket. "I'd like to have a quick discussion about whether you have a preference as to what order I approach the rest of them."

It seemed the schoolteacher had absolutely no trouble remaining unemotional when discussing his future wife.

Hank figured he had to step up his courting efforts.

Chapter Seventeen

Janell arrived at the Chandler home bright and early Saturday morning. As soon as breakfast was over she turned to the children. "The three of us are going on a little shopping trip."

"What are we shopping for?" Alex asked.

"I'll tell you when we get there."

"What about Uncle Hank?"

"Don't worry about me." Hank carried his dishes to the counter. "There are a few things I need to take care of around here."

Was he glad of the opportunity to have the house to himself for a while? She imagined that hadn't happened since he'd returned to town. It must be a big change for a man who'd lived alone for at least as long as she'd lived in Turnabout.

Alex spent most of the walk to the mercantile trying to pry from her what they were shopping for. Even Chloe seemed intrigued. When they arrived, it was to discover Mr. Blakely had decorated his shop window with a toy train, complete with tracks and landscaping. It took nearly five minutes to pry Alex away and lead him to the back of the store.

When she stopped at the fabric section, Alex's face fell. She noticed Chloe, however, was fingering the fabric longingly.

What girl her age didn't like pretty things? And while the clothing Chloe had was no doubt adequate, it looked as though it had been handed down.

Perhaps she would also get a length of dress fabric while they were here.

"What are we doing *here*?" There was a definite pout in Alex's voice.

"We're going to spruce up your rooms and give you a chance to fix them up however you like." She waved toward the bolts of fabric. "And we're going to start with curtains. You can pick out whatever fabric you like." She turned to Chloe and carefully signed out *bedroom curtains*.

Alex gave her a speculative look. "Start with—does that mean there's more?"

She smiled. "It does. But that's going to be a surprise."

Satisfied, Alex turned his attention to the fabric and quickly picked out a dark blue with thin yellow stripes. Chloe took a little more time and eventually picked out a pale green fabric dusted with tiny pink flowers. Janell took note of the other fabrics the girl lingered over. She would be back later to select a pretty piece for a dress.

Later, when they returned home, they found Hank in the parlor, a pleased-with-himself smile on his face. He took a moment to admire the kids' choices in fabric, but she could tell there was something else on his mind.

He finally cleared his throat. "Come on into the kitchen for a moment—there's something I want to show you."

As soon as they stepped into the kitchen, he waved toward the table. "I went up in the attic while y'all were

gone. I dug through a couple of old trunks my ma—
your grandmother—had stored up there and found a
few things I thought you might want for your rooms."

Displayed on the table, Janell saw a set of tin soldiers, a wooden horse that was obviously homemade,
an old rag doll that had seen better days and a small
doll-sized cradle.

Both children drew close to the table but neither
touched the items.

Hank rubbed the back of his neck, as if uncertain
what to do next. "These things belonged to me and my
sister—your mother—when we were kids growing up
here."

"You mean this is where Ma grew up?" Alex stared
at his uncle with wide eyes.

"It is. In fact, she slept in that same bed Chloe's sleeping in now."

"What about my room?"

"That one was mine. I moved into the one that used
to belong to my parents when I took over the house."

Hank picked up the wooden horse. "My pa, your
grandfather, made this for me when I was about five
years old. Carved it with his own two hands. I named
him Captain and he went everywhere with me for a
long time."

Alex's eyes got big. "Can I hold him?"

Hank handed it to him. "If you promise to take real
good care of him, you can keep him."

"Yes, sir!"

He turned to Chloe and picked up the slate. *This is
Penny* he wrote, then pointed to the doll. *It was your
ma's when she was a little girl.*

Chloe picked up the doll, then looked up at him with
questioning, hopeful eyes.

Hank erased the slate, then wrote again. *She's yours if you want her.*

Chloe nodded vigorously and hugged the doll tightly.

Hank cleared his throat. Was that a touch of tenderness Janell saw in his expression?

He touched the cradle and wrote *This is Penny's bed. Your grandfather made it for your mother.*

Then he turned back to Alex. "These tin soldiers were a long-ago Christmas present to me. You're welcome to them as well."

Janell crossed the kitchen and reached for the apron she now kept on a peg by the door. Those three people who had become so dear to her were definitely beginning to draw closer as a family. It was both heartwarming and bittersweet to see. Because more than ever, it made her long to be a part of it, something that could never be.

"Why don't you take your things to your rooms," she told the children, working to keep her voice cheerful. "I'm going to get lunch started and then get to work on these curtains."

Janell grabbed some carrots and potatoes and pulled out the chopping board and a knife. By the time she had everything gathered, the children were gone, but Hank remained.

She glanced up at him, then back down at the chopping board. "The children will treasure those toys for a long time to come."

He shrugged. "I wasn't even aware that my mother had saved those things until I went digging around in the attic."

He seemed uncomfortable with the subject. Perhaps a change of subject was in order. "I've been thinking about the problem of how to enter Chloe's room since she won't hear a knock."

"And you've come up with an answer?"

She nodded, ignoring the touch of dry humor in his voice. "A privacy screen."

"Privacy screen?"

"Yes. You know, a tall, three-paneled—"

He waved impatiently. "I *know* what a privacy screen is. What I don't know is how that solves the problem."

"When Chloe needs privacy—such as when she's changing clothes—she can make certain she's behind the screen. That way, when you or Alex enter her room, you won't inadvertently embarrass her or yourselves."

"I see. Yes, that could work. At least it's something to try."

"If you want to order one, I know the furniture catalog at Blakely's mercantile has them. And there's one in my room at the boardinghouse. You can borrow it until—"

"That's not necessary. It would be simple to make. In fact, I'm sure I have everything I'll need down at the sawmill. I could take care of it today."

She looked up in surprise. "That quickly?"

"It won't be anything fancy, but like I said, it's a simple construction if you already have the materials."

"Perhaps Alex would like to go with you."

He frowned at that. "I don't know. It could be dangerous for him to be around all that equipment."

"Not if you keep a close eye on him. And I'm sure he'd like to spend time with you. I'll fix a cold lunch for the two of you to take with you—this soup will taste better for supper anyway. And while you two are gone, I'll teach Chloe how to make curtains."

He still seemed hesitant, but she was confident. This

was going to be a very good day, especially for Hank and Alex.

Later, once the male members of the household were gone and the kitchen had been cleaned up, Janell picked up the slate and started writing. *Do you know how to sew?*

Chloe frowned uncertainly. "Mother taught me to embroider."

Not a direct answer but it would do. She erased the slate and picked up the chalk again. *Then you should be able to sew something as simple as curtains.*

Janell ignored Chloe's skeptical expression. Her next written message was on a different topic. *While we're sewing the curtains, we'll also work on your communication skills.*

This time the girl shot her a suspicious look.

Janell nodded firmly. *No more slate. While we work, I will sign, and you will speak.*

Chloe bit her lower lip, then nodded.

Janell signed *Good.*

As they got to work, she wondered how Hank and Alex were faring.

Hank helped Alex down from the wagon and the little boy looked around with wide eyes. "This whole place belongs to you?"

"It does."

"Just like the dry goods store belonged to my pa."

Hank felt a tightening in his chest when he realized where the boy's thoughts had drifted to. "Yep, just like that."

Alex kicked at a rock, keeping his head down. "Pa always said the store would be mine someday."

Hank studied his nephew helplessly, not sure what

to say that would ease his hurt. "Your father was a very good man," he said softly. "And he was always very proud of you."

Alex looked up at him without turning. "How do you know that? You weren't there."

"No, I wasn't." He regretted now that he hadn't taken time to visit his sister when he'd had the opportunity. "But your ma was my sister and she wrote me letters. She always told me about the family and how proud both she and your pa were."

"She did?"

"Of course. She told me about the time you won your school's frog jumping contest, and about the time you and your pa caught that huge fish together, and how you were able to count to one hundred before anyone else in your first-grade class."

That seemed to make Alex feel better. The slump left his shoulders and he seemed ready to focus. "Do you know how to run all of this equipment?"

"I do. But of course, I don't run the place all by myself. I have one man who works full-time with me and another who comes in when I have an extra heavy workload."

"But you're the boss."

"That I am."

"Can I see the big saw cut something?"

"As a matter of fact, I'll be cutting some boards to make that screen for Chloe's room. If you promise to be real careful, and do exactly as I say, I may just let you help."

"Yes, sir!"

Hank took his time making the privacy screen, patiently teaching Alex how to use a hammer, sandpaper and paintbrush. The boy was eager to learn and turned out to have a natural talent. The screen they'd constructed was rather plain but well made. He'd deliberately kept it free of decoration because he had something else in mind.

He thought perhaps he'd purchase some paints and see if Chloe would like to decorate it herself.

At the last minute he decided to work on a second project. Together he and Alex constructed a wooden box, complete with hinges and a latch, to hold Alex's tin soldiers.

Alex was as proud of the finished product as if it had been covered in jewels.

All in all, Hank was pleased with how the day had turned out.

It was nearly four o'clock by the time Hank loaded the newly constructed privacy screen on the wagon and helped Alex climb in. He cast a worried look up at the sky. It had become overcast—they might be in for some rain tonight. He'd need to make sure he got Janell home early this evening.

When they arrived home, Hank let Alex help him unhitch the wagon and tend to the horse. The boy chattered nonstop about the sawmill and the work they'd done there.

They carried the screen in through the kitchen door and Hank gave a satisfied smile as he inhaled the savory scent of a stew simmering on the stove.

They had just stepped into the hall when Hank heard a clatter and a yelp, closely followed by a cry from Chloe. He quickly set the screen down and sprinted for Alex's room, where the sound had come from.

He rushed into the room and halted abruptly on the threshold. Janell sat on the bed trying to calm an upset Chloe.

"What happened here? Are you two okay?"

Janell glanced up with a self-recriminating grimace. "We're fine."

Chloe also turned and he could read the fright in her expression. "Miss Whitman fell off the chair and hurt her foot."

He crossed to where Janell sat and looked down at her. "How bad is it?"

Why hadn't the fool woman waited until he got home so he could have helped her hang the curtains?

Because she was Janell I-can-do-anything Whitman, that was why.

If he didn't care for her so much, he'd seriously consider sitting her down and giving her a stern lecture on being aware of her own limitations.

And he might do it still.

Just as soon as he made certain she was all right.

Chapter Eighteen

Janell tried to wrestle control of the situation from Hank. "I just stepped down wrong and twisted my ankle. It'll be fine in a bit."

But he ignored her and stooped down, motioning for her to let him see her foot. "Let me have a look."

"Don't be ridiculous. I told you, it's nothing."

He raised a brow, looking anything but ridiculous. "If you prefer, I can carry you to Dr. Pratt's office so he can take a look at it."

She glared at him, but he maintained eye contact, refusing to budge, and she finally gave in. It wouldn't be good to get into an argument in front of the children.

With a little huff of irritation, she lifted her foot just high enough for Hank to take it in his hands.

He eased her shoe from her foot, with surprisingly smooth, gentle movements. The warmth of his hands penetrated through her stocking and sent little shivers skittering through her.

Then he glanced up, his eyes expressing a concern that touched her on an entirely different level. "This may hurt a bit."

She nodded mutely and he began to prod and massage her foot and ankle. She tried not to show any signs of distress, but a couple of winces escaped her as he touched the tender area of her ankle.

He finally set her foot back on the floor. "I don't think it's broken."

She tugged her skirt back down to cover her foot. "Of course it's not broken. I told you, it's just twisted a bit. Nothing to worry about."

"What in the world were you doing up on that chair? You could have broken your neck when you fell."

She excused his tone because of the worry she'd seen in his eyes earlier. "Chloe and I were hanging the curtains we made. And I didn't fall. I just landed wrong when I stepped down. It's happened to me a few times before and no doubt it'll happen to me again." She smoothed down her skirt. "Now stop making such a fuss—you'll worry the children."

She spotted Alex, still standing in the doorway. "Come on in and tell me how you like your new curtains."

Alex studied the window covering with a critical eye. "They look good."

Janell nodded. "Yes, you did a great job of picking out the fabric—it suits this room perfectly."

Then she waved him closer. "But tell me about your day at your uncle's sawmill. Did you enjoy yourself?"

"Yes, ma'am. Uncle Hank let me help make the screen. I got to use a hammer and sandpaper and everything."

"Oh my. He must really trust you if he let you use his tools."

"Alex was a big help." There was a touch of protective pride in Hank's voice.

The boy's chest puffed out even farther.

Janell braced her hands on the mattress on either side

of her, ready to push to her feet. "Speaking of the screen, let's have a look at it."

Hank frowned. "Do you think you should be up and walking so soon?"

"I'll be limping more than walking for a while, but it'll be fine."

He helped her to stand, then placed her hand on his shoulder. "Lean on me. You shouldn't put any weight on that ankle right now."

She hesitated, not because she disliked the idea of leaning on him, but because she liked it too much. She hoped the warmth in her cheeks didn't translate to heightened color.

As soon as she placed her weight against him, his hand wrapped around her waist. Startled, she glanced up but saw nothing more than patience and concern in his gaze. "Just to steady you so you don't fall again," he said reasonably.

Perhaps she was the only one affected by their nearness.

He led her to Chloe's room at a snail's pace. Not that she minded. Truth to tell, she was enjoying leaning on him this way. He was so close that she could feel the tautness of his muscles through the fabric of his shirt. Could see the tension in his jaw. Could inhale the masculine scent that was so uniquely his—sawdust, resin, fresh air and something faintly spicy that she couldn't quite identify.

She was actually sorry when they reached Chloe's room and she had to let go of him to sit on the spare bed.

"I see no screen," she said, looking around with a mock frown. "Are you gentlemen certain you built it?"

Hank clapped Alex on the back. "Come on—let's go get it."

Once they'd left, with Chloe in their wake, Janell

chided herself for her reaction to Hank's closeness just now. Was she so starved for attention that she would allow herself to act like a schoolgirl? This wouldn't do at all. Thank goodness he hadn't noticed anything amiss.

That would have been absolutely mortifying.

But she couldn't let this continue. Could she?

Hank felt a deep sense of satisfaction as he lifted the screen. His strategy was working. Her reaction to him had been edifying, to say the least.

Of course, if he was being honest, he'd have to admit that his reaction to her had been just as visceral.

When they walked into Chloe's bedchamber, Janell was half-standing, testing her foot with a bit of weight.

"What do you think you're doing?" he asked with a frown.

"My ankle is much better. I should have no trouble walking home this evening."

"Nonsense. I'll take you home in the wagon. But not until after supper."

A horrified look crossed her face. "Oh my! Supper—"

"Keep your seat. I'll check on it. Tonight, we're waiting on you." He turned to Chloe and Alex. "Right?"

Alex nodded vigorously, but Chloe, who obviously hadn't understood him, just stared blankly.

With a smothered sigh, Hank hefted the screen. "But first we set this up." And with a great deal of fanfare, he did.

Later that evening, Hank opened the kitchen door and looked out at the sky, which was much too dark for the hour. The sound of pinging told the story. Ice.

He turned back to Janell, who sat at the table. "That

settles it. There's no way I'm letting you go out in that. You can spend the night in Chloe's room."

"But—"

"No buts. You're staying, and that's all there is to it."

"But it wouldn't be—" she glanced toward the children "—seemly for me to spend the night here."

"I know it's not ideal, but this is an unusual situation. And you have my assurances that I will do nothing to take advantage of the situation."

"Of course." She waved a hand dismissively. "I never imagined otherwise. It's only—"

"And with the two kids here, I'm sure your reputation can survive this."

"But—"

"Look at this weather. I can already see ice forming on the leaves on my pecan tree." He closed the door. "I've made up my mind—you're staying put. If it'll make you feel better for me to bed down with Hector, I will."

"No, of course not."

"Then it's settled."

Janell lay atop the spare bed in Chloe's room, fully clothed except for her feet. But sleep eluded her. She could tell from the sound of Chloe's rhythmic breathing that the girl was sound asleep. Every so often there was a muffled snap and crash as the ice broke another limb from a tree. Otherwise the outside world seemed eerily quiet.

Even without the jarring noise, though, she would have found sleep impossible. It wasn't her ankle bothering her—that pain had gone away, just as she'd told Hank it would. No, it was the reminder of the concern in his eyes when he'd learned of her injury, the memory of the way his strong but gentle hands had cradled her foot, and the memory, too, of the way his expression had, just for a moment, changed from concern to something deeper, warmer.

He'd been in the parlor tending to the fire when she and the children had retired to their beds. She found herself listening for the sound of his footsteps in the hall. But that sound never came.

What was keeping him up so late? Or was he planning to spend the night in the parlor?

She must have drifted off to sleep at some point, because she suddenly woke, jarred from sleep by a loud noise.

She heard that snapping, cracking sound again, this time much closer than what she'd heard earlier. Before she could register exactly *how* close it had been, there was a loud crash just outside, closely followed by the sound of a child crying out.

Alex!

She scrambled to her feet and paused only long enough to make sure Chloe was still asleep before she bolted from the room. She stepped into the hall but Hank was already there, rushing into his nephew's room just ahead of her.

Hank barely made it to the bed before Alex launched himself at his uncle and wrapped his arms tightly around the man's neck, burying his tear-streaked face in his shoulder.

"It's okay," Hank said. "You're safe. It was just a branch breaking off from that tree outside your window."

The boy only clung tighter and his little frame trembled with emotion.

Janell sat down on the bed next to the pair and Hank met her gaze over the boy's head. There was a look of helplessness in his eyes that tugged at her every bit as much as Alex's distress.

She placed a hand lightly on Alex's back. "You're thinking of the explosion, aren't you? About what happened to your parents?"

Alex nodded without moving his face from Hank's shoulder.

Hank's expression softened as the light of understanding dawned. "It's okay for you to be sad that they're gone now, Alex. You loved them very much and you miss them."

"But I didn't get hurt like Chloe did."

Janell put a hand on his arm. "Alex, you can't compare your loss to your sister's. You suffered something awful as well—you lost your parents and your home. It's okay to be sad about that and to be angry as well."

The boy pulled back from his uncle slightly. "It is?"

"Absolutely. You just can't let that be all you feel. You have to look at the good things around you, too."

Janell could see he was still shaken by the eerie sounds of the ice storm, so she gave him a smile. "I tell you what. I'm not very sleepy right now. I was going to sit up in the parlor and do a bit of mending by firelight. Why don't I make up a comfy pallet for you on the floor in front of the fireplace, where you can be all toasty warm and keep me company? Would you like that?"

Alex rubbed his eyes with his knuckles and nodded.

"Good. Then just give me a moment to make up your pallet and we'll be all set."

Hank stood. "I'll get a spare blanket. Why don't the two of you gather up the pillow and bedding from here and take it to the parlor."

Janell did her best to make Alex's move from his bedroom as cheery as possible, comparing the pallet to a sleeping bag one would use on a camping trip.

Once Alex was settled in, Hank headed for the back of the house.

True to her word, Janell gathered up her sewing basket and some stockings of Chloe's she'd noticed needed darning. She started humming softly as she went to work, and in no time at all, Alex was sound asleep.

Hank approached the sofa and stood looking down at her, wishing he had the right to sit next to her and take her in his arms. "You can set that aside now and try to get some sleep," he said gruffly. "I'll stay in here with Alex."

She flashed him that warm, sweet smile he liked so much. "I'm not sleepy and this needs doing."

Hank raked a hand through his hair. If she wasn't going to distance herself, so be it. "In that case, I think I'll fix us both a cup of hot cocoa."

She smiled up at him. "That sounds good. And if you want to bring a small piece of the pecan pie left from supper, I wouldn't turn it away."

He returned her smile with a grin. "I'll see what I can do."

While Hank worked in the kitchen, his mind replayed that moment when Alex had launched himself trustingly into his arms. It had made him feel almost like a dad.

That wouldn't have happened if he hadn't spent the day with Alex. And that had happened because Janell had prodded him to invite the boy along.

It seemed every good thing to happen to him lately originated from her.

By the time he carried the cocoa and pie into the parlor, Janell was putting away her sewing. Was the light of welcome in her eyes for him or for the treats he carried?

Janell sipped on her cup of cocoa, enjoying the companionable silence between them while they watched the fire and the sleeping boy in front of it.

Hank was the first to break the silence. "I forget sometimes, because his hurts aren't as obvious as Chloe's, that he suffered, too."

"He's a brave little boy, but he *is* just a little boy."

Hank nodded. "I really enjoyed spending time with him today."

He said that as if it surprised him. "It's obvious he enjoyed it, too."

He made a noncommittal sound but she could tell the thought pleased him. She touched his arm lightly, then dropped her hand. "You're going to be a very good father to these children."

"I hope so." He didn't sound convinced. "But that won't make up for what they really need—a mother's touch."

"We're working on that." If she'd felt a decided lack of enthusiasm for that job lately, she'd just have to get over that. He was right—these kids needed a mother.

Time to change the subject.

"Christmas is just three weeks away. Have you thought about how you'll celebrate it with them?"

He raised a brow in surprise. "Do you really think they'll want to celebrate? I mean, their folks haven't been gone that long, and this time of year is bound to bring back memories of happier times."

"That's precisely *why* you need to celebrate. Perhaps include a few of their traditions, but build new ones as well. Don't let them wallow in the memories of what was. Let them find joy in what is. Christmas is a time to remember the great gift our God has given to us. And the message of hope and joy."

"You make it sound so easy."

"Of course it won't be easy. Most things worth doing take effort. But ignoring it will only make things worse."

"Do you have any suggestions?"

"For starters, you should get them as actively involved in both the planning and the doing as possible. Let them handcraft decorations for the house and ornaments for the tree. Tell them stories of other Christmases spent in this house when you and your sister were children. When it comes time to cut down a tree, let them help pick it out."

He rubbed his chin. "That all sounds easy enough." Then he gave her an almost-challenging look. "Since we want to build new memories, perhaps you could share stories of some of your Christmas traditions."

She nodded. "I'd be happy to."

"And are your Christmas memories happy ones?"

"Absolutely. My sister and I looked forward to Christmas as soon as Thanksgiving was behind us. Mother loved to decorate the house with evergreens and ribbon. Father brought candy canes and ribbon candy home for us. It was all very festive and exciting."

She smiled as the memories came flooding back. "Lizzie was always the creative one. She had a flair for needlework, watercolors and music. I was more of a dreamer."

"Come now. I won't believe you didn't participate in the festivities."

She grinned. "I helped string the popcorn and decorate the parlor." She gave a faraway kind of smile. "There was one thing I was better at than Lizzie, though, and that was decorating our baked goods. Sugar cookies, gingerbread men and especially gingerbread houses. In fact, some of my favorite memories are of me and Lizzie making gingerbread houses."

He couldn't remember if she usually stayed in town for Christmas or not. "Do you and your sister still do that?"

She shook her head. "No. I stay here for Christmas and Lizzie stays back in Dentonville. Turnabout is my home now."

"And where is Dentonville?"

"Illinois."

Her whole bearing belied the casualness of her tone. There was a story here; he was certain of it. And it was more than just the distance separating her from her family. He'd dearly love to hear more about it, but perhaps now was not the right time.

He took a sip of his cocoa, then changed the subject. "I noticed you were no longer limping. Ankle all better?"

She nodded. "I told you it would be all right."

"Still, it wouldn't hurt to take it easy for a day or two."

"I promise to give it all the care it requires."

And he knew that meant she would go on doing just as she pleased.

She stared down at her cup, as if trying to read answers there. "Speaking of families and Christmas, I've been thinking that I might invite my sister and her family to come down for a visit for the holidays this year."

She watched him from the corner of her eye as if looking for his approval, though for the life of him he didn't know why. "I'm sure it'll be nice to have time to visit with your family." Then one reason occurred to him. "And don't worry about continuing the signing lessons while they're here. We can get by on our own."

"No, you don't understand. I want Lizzie to meet you and the children. I think it would be good for Chloe to spend time with someone who has gone through something similar to what she has."

Was that why she was inviting her sister to visit? Why wouldn't she have done it for her own sake? "I agree that Chloe would benefit from knowing your sister, but isn't that a lot to ask of your sister? Perhaps it would be better if we traveled to her. And it wouldn't have to be at Christmas—"

"No."

The vehemence of her response surprised him. Was there some reason she didn't want him traveling to her hometown? Or maybe she just didn't want him and the kids intruding on her parents' hospitality?

She took a breath, then said more calmly, "I mean, I don't think it would be a good idea to uproot the children right now, not when they're just settling into their new surroundings and new routine. Much better that Lizzie come here."

That made sense, but he got the distinct impression there was more to it than that.

"I've been corresponding with my sister regularly since you returned to Turnabout with your niece and nephew, and she's taken a keen interest in Chloe's situation. I think Lizzie would be quite open to taking a trip down here—in fact, she's all but hinted as much."

"Then by all means, invite her to come." He smiled her way. "I imagine you'll be happy to have time to visit with her yourself."

She nodded.

"How long has it been since you last saw her?"

"Four years."

That surprised him. Was there some reason she'd allowed so much time to pass? Was there some sort of rift between her and her family?

But it wasn't his place to ask so personal a question. "You said her family—who all does that include?"

"She has a husband and two children. Elliott is four and Olivia is not quite one."

Did that mean she'd never seen her niece and barely seen her nephew? For a woman who obviously loved children, so much of this seemed out of character. The more he learned about her relationship with her family, the more curious he became.

For the first time it occurred to him to wonder how a woman of obvious genteel upbringing had ended up in Turnabout. Had she run away from something?

There was another snap and crash of a branch falling in the distance, causing Janell to jump. She quickly glanced Alex's way, but the boy barely stirred. Shooting him a slightly embarrassed grin, she stood and padded over to adjust Alex's covers before returning to her seat.

For the first time he noticed she was barefoot. It reminded him of how slender and delicate her foot had felt when he'd held it earlier.

He cleared his throat, deciding it was best not to linger on such thoughts. "It's late. Why don't you go back to Chloe's room and try to get some sleep? I'll stay in here in case Alex wakes again."

She shook her head. "If you don't mind, I'd like to sit up awhile longer. I don't think I could sleep right now and I don't relish the idea of lying there staring at the ceiling."

"I don't mind." Not one bit.

She sat back down, her eyes still on the slumbering child. "I think Alex is really starting to settle in here. He's made friends at school and joined the choir." She turned to him, her eyes alight with approval. "And it's obvious he's formed a connection with you. You should be really proud of the difference you're making in these children's lives."

"Perhaps I would be, if I didn't know that I owe all of that to you. I could never have accomplished so much without you." Did she have any idea how deeply he meant that?

But she brushed aside his praise. "Nonsense. It might have taken you a little longer, but you would have gotten there." Then she placed her hand on his. "You truly care for these children and that's what matters. Some part of them responds to that."

"They're family," he said simply. At least that was all it had been at first—a nebulous connection to his sister. But now these kids were his and he felt fiercely protective of them.

But the feel of her hand on his—warm, soft, gentle—was eliciting an entirely different kind of emotion. Yes, he felt possessive and protective and ready to slay dragons for her. But in an entirely different way. The fact that she left her hand there, didn't withdraw as she had in the past, only strengthened those feelings.

He had a sudden, almost overwhelming urge to kiss her. What would she do? Push him away? Accept his overture? Kiss him back?

With an effort he resisted the temptation and leaned back. But he was careful to keep his hand touching hers. "So tell me a little more about your childhood Christmases."

"Only if you share some of your stories as well."

"It's a deal."

Chapter Nineteen

Janell woke with a start. For a moment she wasn't certain where she was. Then she looked around at the shadowy room and memories of the night came flooding back. She was half sitting, half reclining on the sofa in Hank's parlor. Sometime during the night she must have dozed off.

Someone—Hank, of course—had draped a blanket around her. She glanced toward the window and saw a faint hint of gray in the blackness. It would be daybreak soon.

Alex still slept on his makeshift bed, but Hank was nowhere to be seen. Had he gone to bed after she fell asleep?

Then she caught the aroma of freshly brewed coffee and quickly tossed off the blanket. She still wasn't wearing her shoes, but they were in Chloe's room and she didn't want to wake her up. Ah well, she had her stockings on and that would do for now.

Janell padded into the kitchen and found Hank sipping on a cup of coffee.

"Good morning, sleepyhead," he said with a smile. "There's more coffee, if you'd like some."

With a nod, she fetched a cup and filled it with the steaming liquid.

"Is Alex still sleeping?" he asked.

She nodded. "Chloe, too, as far as I can tell."

He leaned back against the counter. There was something different about him this morning—a new confidence, an air of happiness she hadn't noticed before.

Could it be from his newfound relationship with Alex?

"I took a look around outside a little while ago," he said. "Even in the dark I could tell there are a number of large limbs down. Frank Meecham was outside and told me the church has a hole in the roof due to some fallen limbs. There likely won't be a service today."

She nodded. "It's probably best to keep Alex and Chloe inside today anyway." She studied him a moment. "I assume you're going to want to head out and help clean up some of this mess the ice created."

He grinned. "You assume right."

"Then I'll stay with the kids."

He set his cup in the sink, then turned back around. "I was thinking last night, after we took care of Alex, that we certainly seem to make a good team."

She nodded. "I suppose we do at that."

He crossed the room, took the coffee cup from her and set it on the table, then took both her hands in his. "I was also wondering if you'd reconsider my proposal."

The warm cozy mood of a moment ago vanished in an instant. The desire to say yes was so strong that she actually ached. But how could she? It wasn't just that she feared disappointing him the way she had other important people in her life. She also feared telling him that she was a divorcée and that she'd been living a lie all these years. Seeing the affection in his eyes change to contempt was more than she would be able to bear.

Almost of their own accord, her fingers touched the cameo at her throat and she again heard Mrs. Collins's words about false pride.

Then she dropped her hand and lifted her chin. "My feelings on the matter have not changed," she said coolly. "My role is to find you a wife, not to become one."

Hank's jaw tightened and everything about him seemed to harden. He gave a short nod. Then he grabbed his coat from the peg by the door. "I'm going to help clear the fallen limbs from the church. There are probably others in town who need help as well. I assume I can still count on you to stay with the children while I'm gone."

It was more statement than question. "Of course."

He was still buttoning his coat as he marched out the door, as if he couldn't get away from her fast enough. Was he angry because her refusal of his proposal had robbed him of the opportunity to end his bride hunt early?

After all, it wasn't as if he really cared about her in a romantic sense. She was just a known quantity; convenient, nothing more. Holding firmly on to that thought had made it easier to refuse him.

Of course, even if he'd uttered the most romantic proposal in the world, she couldn't have accepted. She'd kept her secrets buried for too long and had no intention of revealing them now.

Especially knowing he would no longer want her if he knew.

Janell carried her cup to the sink and stared out the window. The sun had risen without her noticing. The children would be up soon. Time to get their breakfast ready.

But she didn't move.

Not until Alex came pitter-pattering in from the parlor a few minutes later, rubbing his eyes.

"Is the storm over?" he asked.

She gave him a smile that she hoped didn't reflect any of the turmoil she felt. "It is." She held a hand up to her ear. "Hear that dripping sound? The sun is up and the ice is already starting to melt."

"Is breakfast going to be ready soon?"

She moved toward the pantry. "I'm getting to work on it right now. Why don't you go get dressed and then get Chloe up so y'all can set the table?"

Grateful for something to occupy her mind, Janell went all out, cooking them a grand breakfast.

But even that wasn't enough to stop her traitorous mind from screaming at her that she'd made the wrong decision.

Hank brought down the ax on the fallen limb with unnecessary but extremely satisfying force. Should he have waited a few more days before he proposed again? Had his impatience cost him his chance to win her heart forever?

They'd talked for a long time last night, the room lit only by the flames from the fireplace as they'd exchanged stories from their childhood. Hers had been a happy one. As he'd suspected, her family was well-to-do. Her father owned several fancy hotels and enjoyed pampering his wife and daughters. Whatever had alienated her from her family had happened later in life.

The talk had tapered off and Janell had finally drifted to sleep. She'd slumped toward him as she slept and he'd wrapped a supportive arm around her shoulders.

But as he'd held her, listening to her soft breathing,

feeling her nestle against him so trustingly and inhaling the floral fragrance that was uniquely hers, something inside him shifted, warmed. He found himself wanting to cherish and protect her, to be able to hold her like this every night.

As soon as he realized where his mind was going, it had scared him badly. He wasn't supposed to fall for the woman he married; he was just supposed to be able to work with her. He'd carefully released her and positioned her on the sofa. He'd covered her with a blanket and then fled to the kitchen. He'd built up a fire in the stove to chase the cold from the room, but it hadn't chased the chill from his mind.

He'd tried to distract himself by making a pot of coffee but it hadn't worked. It seemed his plan to romance her had backfired on him.

He told himself he wasn't really in love. The feelings that had hit him with such force were due to nothing more than the atmosphere or her closeness.

A little time and distance would clear his head and give him the perspective he needed.

Then, as he sipped on the hot cup of coffee, he'd had a change in perspective.

Why was he treating this like such a catastrophe? The fact that he found her company pleasant wasn't such a bad thing. After all, if they were to marry, they would be spending the rest of their lives together. Under the circumstances, getting along with her would make their partnership much easier.

And he'd picked up on a number of signs last night that she wasn't indifferent to him, either. It looked as though everything was finally coming together.

He'd planned to wait at least a few more days before he proposed again, but when she'd walked into the kitchen, still shoeless and tousled from sleep, the words had left his mouth almost of their own accord.

How could he have so misread her?

He understood her refusing his first proposal. After all, she'd barely known him. But this time it was different. True, it had been just over a week since his return from Colorado, but he felt as if they'd developed a strong friendship that had nothing to do with time, but with mutual goals, mutual respect.

Well, he'd definitely got the message now. She wasn't interested—her refusal had been immediate and firm.

It was time for him to move on and find someone who was open to accepting his offer.

And the sooner, the better.

Janell glanced out the window. Hank still hadn't returned. Should she hold lunch for him? Or go ahead and feed the children?

Had her refusal of his proposal upset him so much that he was deliberately staying away? Or was it that there was so much cleanup work to be done that he hadn't had time to take a break yet?

Maybe she should bundle up the kids and take a short walk outside to judge the extent of the damage for herself.

Before she could make up her mind, the door opened and Hank stepped inside. He stomped his feet a few times on the rug by the door to knock off most of the mud, then came the rest of the way into the kitchen.

"You look tired."

His shrug was slightly hampered by the armload of firewood he carried. "It's been a long morning."

Without another word, he set some of the wood near

the stove, then headed for the parlor, apparently to add more wood to the fireplace.

It seemed he had not yet forgiven her. How long would he keep her at a distance this way?

A few minutes later Hank returned to the kitchen and poured himself a cup of coffee.

For a moment he leaned back in his chair and closed his eyes, weariness carved into every line of his face. He must have pushed himself quite hard. And she'd guess he hadn't got much sleep last night.

A moment later his lids flew open and he was staring straight into her eyes. There was no emotion there. No affection, no contempt, no admiration—nothing.

It sent an uncomfortable shiver skittering across the back of her neck.

Janell turned back to the stove, more to get away from that gaze than because the food needed her attention. But she could still feel his eyes on her.

Finally, she couldn't stand the silence any longer. "How bad was the damage to the church?" she asked.

"One of the windows is broken and there's an area of the roof that'll require patching, but we have everything covered against the weather for now."

He took a sip from his cup. "I looked at the schoolhouse and there's some large limbs scattered about the school yard, but no damage to the building itself that I could see."

"That's a relief." Perhaps he didn't hate her completely. "Is there any other major damage around town?" The question felt stilted, but she wanted to keep him talking to her.

"Reggie Barr's carriage house has a bit of damage but her photography wagon is okay. And the roof over Mrs. Halverson's back porch is down, but the house itself is okay. Otherwise, at least here in town, the majority of the work is going to be repairing fences and clearing the fallen limbs."

Silence reigned for another few moments. Janell almost wished the children would join them, just so it would relieve some of the tension in the room.

Finally, he got up, set his cup in the basin and crossed his arms over his chest. "Have you made any progress with the names on my wife-candidate list?"

So they were back to that. He certainly didn't seem to be harboring any lingering feelings for her. "A little. But trying to be both discreet and thorough takes time."

"Then perhaps we shouldn't worry so much about discretion and just focus on thoroughness. Keeping secrets is a lost cause in this town anyway."

Not true—so far she'd managed to keep hers. "If that's your wish, then of course I'll do what I can to speed things up." He was right. The sooner he had a wife, the better, for both of them.

"I need to establish a normal household for Alex and Chloe as soon as possible. They're already getting too used to having you around—it'll be difficult for them when another woman takes your place."

The words *takes your place* stabbed at her with a keenness that surprised her. She'd known that was what would happen; she had, in fact, encouraged it. So why did it hurt so much?

Then another thought drew her up short. Was that why he'd proposed to her this morning—because he didn't want the children upset again? It was a noble reason, but he could've been more honest with her.

"As I said when we started down this road," he continued in that same hard voice, "I want this matter of a wife settled by Christmas, if not sooner. If you don't think you can accomplish that, I can always go back to my original plan and try to do it myself."

"I promised you I'd handle it and I will. I'll move forward with more vigor in the next few days."

"Very well." He pushed away from the counter. "It looks like lunch is ready. I'll fetch the kids and get them to clean up and set the table."

As he left the room, she slumped over the kitchen counter. How had things between them changed so abruptly—from the sweet companionship of yesterday to the cold distance of today?

She closed her eyes.

Please, dear Jesus, help me to get through this. I know I don't deserve another chance at marriage, but I don't want to lose this good man's friendship and respect.

There'd been very little fallout from Janell's unexpected overnight stay at Hank's place. Mrs. Ortolon made a few sly comments when Janell returned to the boardinghouse late Sunday afternoon, but no one else did, at least not to her face.

It seemed she wasn't the only one who'd been trapped away from home by the ice storm, and since the two kids had been in the house as well, most folks seemed to feel sympathy rather than be scandalized at her predicament.

To be on the safe side, though, she sent a note to the mayor, explaining what had happened and offering to meet with the council to answer any questions they might have for her. She wanted to make it clear she had nothing to hide, at least in this matter, and was willing to account for her actions.

By the time school was called to order Monday morning, there was very little trace of the ice storm remaining, other than some fallen limbs and trees that had yet to be cleared. It was cold, but well above freezing and all the ice had completely melted away.

Hank didn't so much as stick his head inside her classroom when he dropped off Chloe and Alex. Was he deliberately avoiding her, or was he rushing off to the sawmill because the winter storm had generated some extra business?

It took a while to settle the children down—everyone was abuzz with stories about the ice storm.

After recess, when Verity showed up to conduct music class, Janell asked Mitch to take care of the students who were practicing for the play while she ran an errand.

She took advantage of that time to visit with Edith Lawrence, the next name on Hank's wife list. Edith, who had just turned twenty, heard Janell out, then shook her head.

"I understand why Mr. Chandler wants a wife, ma'am, and I ain't saying as he won't make some woman a fine husband. But to be honest, when I get hitched I'd prefer it to be to someone closer to my own age."

That took Janell aback. This was the first objection she'd heard to the man himself. "But, Edith, Mr. Chandler is far from old. In fact, he's not yet thirty. And he has a lot to offer a wife—a home of his own, an established business, good standing in the community."

"Exactly. He's built his life just the way he wants it and is probably set in his ways. I want to marry someone who I can help build a life together with."

She wanted a boy when she could have a man, a *good* man. Janell just didn't understand. But Hank could definitely find someone better suited.

"Besides, after what happened the first time, well, one can't help but wonder..."

Janell sat up straighter. "First time?"

"Yes, ma'am. The first time he tried to get married, I mean." She traced a circle on the table with her finger. "It might be wrong of me to think this way, but I just got to wonder about why his fiancée ran off and left him that way, practically at the altar."

Janell's thoughts whirled as she tried to process what Edith had just told her.

Edith apparently noticed something in her expression because she launched into an explanation. "Oh, I forgot—it must have happened before you moved here. I was only about eleven or twelve at the time myself, but I could tell something big was going on. Mr. Chandler was engaged to Agnes Insley. They grew up together and everyone thought they were the perfect couple—it was quite romantic. Then, the day before the wedding, she ran off with another man."

Janell's stomach twisted and her heart stuttered painfully. Poor Hank. That must have been so terrible for him. How could a woman who supposedly loved him have done such a thing? Janell wanted to go find him and hug his hurts away.

Only she had no right to do so.

"It was all people talked about for weeks afterward," Edith continued. "There were lots of rumors about what happened but I don't reckon that anybody knows for sure. And Agnes and Barry have never returned to town in all that time. Like I said, it just makes me wonder if maybe there was a reason she changed her mind about marrying him."

"Based on what I currently know of Mr. Chandler, I think it's safe to say he did nothing to drive her away."

Edith shrugged. "Well, I do wish you luck in helping him find a wife. I know those two little kids need a mama something fierce."

Janell made it back to her classroom just as Verity wrapped up her lessons. She tried her best to focus on what she had to teach the rest of the afternoon, but her mind kept tugging Edith's disclosure to the forefront.

Should she say anything to Hank when she saw him this evening—let him know that she knew? Or would he prefer to not have it dredged up again?

Of course, this information wasn't really a secret. It seemed everyone who'd lived here at the time knew what had happened. And unlike her, he'd stuck around to face the gossip and the uncomfortable scrutiny. He'd probably consider her a coward for the way she had acted.

And he wouldn't be wrong.

Chapter Twenty

Hank said a quick hello to Janell when he got home from the sawmill, then headed for the parlor, where he could hear the kids playing. He'd dug out his old checkerboard and checkers yesterday and given it to them. It was a game they could play together and one where being deaf was not a disadvantage. They'd played dozens of times since he'd pulled it out. He had to admit it was gratifying to have got this, at least, right.

They looked up when he entered the room and he discovered something else to be gratified by.

Alex greeted him with a big grin. As for Chloe, she wasn't as enthusiastic as Alex, but she no longer seemed as belligerent or closed off. He considered that definite progress.

"Who's winning?" he asked. At the same time he signed the question to Chloe. It wasn't as graceful or quick as Janell would have done it, but he felt a sense of accomplishment in knowing he'd done it properly without referring to the book.

He stayed with the kids, watching their games, occasionally testing both his and their signing skills and just getting them used to seeing him in a relaxed setting.

He would like to think it was all for the kids' sake, but he knew that at least part of it was because, for his own peace of mind, he was avoiding being alone with Janell. Much as her refusal had frustrated him, he knew deep down that this was not her fault. She'd been nothing but generous in helping him and the kids. It wasn't her fault she didn't love him.

But he'd tried to make her feel it was.

He owed her an apology.

And putting it off wouldn't make it any easier. Hank stood and left the children to their game. But before he could cross the room, Janell appeared in the doorway.

"Supper's ready," she announced.

The kids popped up to join him and the moment was lost.

Later, as they ate their meal, Hank could sense something was troubling Janell. Was it because he'd proposed to her again? Or because of the way he'd acted when she turned him down? Regardless, he had to put an end to this before the kids noticed something was amiss.

Hank had talked to Glenda about setting up a regular schedule between now and Christmas for her to watch the children while he walked Janell home. In return, he'd provide her family with a half cord of firewood.

So at six thirty Hank and Janell stepped out his front door, and he was secure in the knowledge that the kids were being looked out for.

Hank gathered his thoughts and his courage, then cleared his throat. "I believe I owe you an apology."

Her head swung around and he saw the surprise in her eyes. But she didn't say anything, just waited silently for him to continue.

"I didn't react well when you refused my suit. In fact,

I was an oaf, and if that caused you any distress, then I am most sincerely sorry."

She nodded slowly. "Thank you." Then she took a deep breath. "But perhaps I'm not totally blameless, either. It wasn't my intent to mislead you, but if I did, then you have my apologies."

She'd succeeded in surprising him yet again. "Apology accepted." He raised a brow in question. "Perhaps we can just call it even, then."

She nodded.

"One other thing. I want you to know that you don't have to worry about me pressing my suit with you again. You've made your feelings quite clear, and I'll honor that. In the future it's friendship between us, and nothing more." He'd watched her face as he spoke and saw the relief he'd expected. But was there also a touch of regret?

If so, it was quickly gone.

"Thank you," she said, then changed the subject without further comment. "I paid a visit to Edith Lawrence today."

One of the names on his possible-wife list. "And?"

"And I'm afraid we need to scratch her off the list."

Hank grimaced. He hadn't expected this to be such a difficult quest. He wasn't the town's most eligible bachelor, but he didn't consider himself totally unacceptable, either. "What reason did she give?"

"She's looking for someone younger."

He winced. "I didn't realize I was considered old."

"I think that's just Edith. She didn't strike me as particularly mature."

At least she seemed ready to defend him—he supposed that was something.

A moment later he realized she still seemed tense and was struggling with something.

"Did Edith say anything else? Don't worry—I've got a thick skin."

"Yes, but not like that. It's about something in your past."

"Oh." That again.

"I didn't invite her to tell me this, and I should have cut her off as soon as I realized it was gossip, but I was just taken so off guard—" She took a deep breath. "Anyway, I'm sorry."

The last thing he wanted from her was pity. "No need to apologize." He managed a smile. "I assume we're talking about my former fiancée and our aborted wedding?"

She nodded.

"As I said, no need for apologies." He'd rather not go through the whole story again. "To be honest, I assumed you already knew, just like everyone else in town." He heard the touch of bitterness in his tone and wished it back. It wouldn't do for her to think it still smarted.

He mustered up another smile, hoping it looked genuine. "So I'm too old, am I? I suppose I should look into getting a cane and a rocking chair."

"I told you, Edith is a silly goose. You and the children are better off without her."

"Perhaps. But that still leaves me without a wife. Who's left on our list?"

"Norma Crandall and Selma Winters. Do you have a preference as to which one I speak to first?"

Hank thought about that for a moment. Norma was about two years younger than him and helped her brother run the hotel. She was rather bookish and dour, but she seemed to be a good person, and as long as she got along well with the children, he supposed he could overlook the rest.

Selma Winters ran a laundry business. She owned

her own home and lived alone. His impression was that she was a hard worker and very independent.

So if he had his choice of the two, whom would he prefer? There were pros and cons to each woman. He tried not to think about the fact that the biggest con was that neither of them was Janell.

"No preference. Just whichever one you can get to first."

She gave him a curious look, then nodded. "Of course. You've made it very clear that speed is of the essence."

He frowned at her tone, trying to figure out why she would sound so irritated by that deadline when she'd known what it was all along.

"Miss Whitman?"

Janell looked up to see a young woman standing in the doorway of her classroom. It was Wednesday and class was done for the day. It was just her, Chloe and Alex left in the building. She'd stayed to work on some papers and had asked the two children to work on their lessons until she was ready to go.

Janell put her pencil down. "May I help you?"

"I was hoping I could have a private word with you."

Janell stood. "Of course." She turned to the children as she moved around her desk. "Please continue with your lessons. I'll be right outside." She signed an abbreviated version of this at the same time and she was pleased to see that Chloe appeared to understand.

Janell escorted the visitor out to the porch. When they were out in the sunshine, she turned to the visitor.

"Is there something I can help you with, Miss…?"

"My name is Cassie Lynn Vickers."

The last name at least was familiar. "Are you related

to Norris and Dwayne Vickers?" She'd taught both boys in the past but they were now in Mitch Parker's class.

"They're two of my brothers."

Why had she never met Cassie Lynn before? "If you don't mind my asking, how old are you?"

"Turned twenty last month."

Then she was young enough to have still been in school when Janell started teaching here—albeit as an older student. But now was not the time to ask her about that. "Neither of your brothers are in my class any longer. Perhaps it's Mr. Parker you need to speak to."

Cassie Lynn shook her head. "It's not my brothers I'm here to talk about."

"Then what *are* you here to discuss?"

"I live on a farm about five miles north of town with my pa and four brothers. I had to quit school when I was twelve to help around the house when Ma passed. And Pa doesn't believe in going to church like Ma did, so we don't make it to services much."

So that was why she'd never met Cassie Lynn. Sounded as if the young lady had led a rather isolated life since her mother had died.

"My oldest brother, Verne, is getting married Saturday, and his wife will be moving into our place with him. Dinah, his wife-to-be, is a nice girl, but I figure there ought to be only one lady of the house."

"So you're planning to move out."

"I am."

"I still don't see—"

"I heard some talk that you're trying to help Mr. Chandler find a woman to get hitched to."

Janell stilled. "That is true."

"Then I'd like to add my name to your list."

A willing candidate at last. Janell wasn't certain if

she was relieved or disappointed. "And have you ever met Mr. Chandler?"

"I've seen him across the way once or twice. He seems like a respectable kind of man. Besides, if what I heard is true, he's looking for someone to help with those two kids and to run his household, and that's something I know how to do. And to be honest, a practical rather than romantic arrangement like that is fine by me."

Just what Hank was looking for. Janell glanced toward the doorway leading into the classroom. "Do you know about Chloe's condition?"

Cassie Lynn nodded. "I've heard. I also heard that you're teaching folks how to talk to her with sign language." Her tone and expression held the hint of a question.

"I am."

"Then I reckon you can teach me, too. I may have had to quit school early but I promise you I'm a fast learner. It would please me no end to be able to bring a little joy to both those kids' lives."

Janell had to admit she liked Cassie Lynn. Reading between the lines, it sounded as if the young woman had dealt with a lot in her short life, yet she still seemed to have a positive attitude.

And Janell hadn't heard anything to make her think Cassie Lynn wasn't a good choice for Hank. In fact, she seemed to meet most of his criteria. She'd helped raise her brothers, so she knew about children. She'd run her father's household, so doing the same for Hank shouldn't be an issue. And it appeared she had the right spirit to help Chloe deal with what life would hand her in the years to come.

"So you see marrying Mr. Chandler as a way to get out of your father's home?"

"I won't lie to you, Miss Whitman—that's part of it. But I wouldn't be here talking to you if I didn't intend to do my very best to be a good wife and mother. I think I have a lot to offer this family. But I'm confident the Good Lord has this whole business under His control. If Mr. Chandler decides I'm not what he wants, then I'll find some other way to get by."

She gave Cassie Lynn a smile. "Let me speak to Mr. Chandler this afternoon and, if he's agreeable, then perhaps the two of you could meet and discuss the matter."

"Thank you. I appreciate you considering my request. Maybe me and him can have that talk on Saturday, after my brother's wedding." She smiled apologetically. "I don't get the opportunity to leave our place much."

Janell felt sympathy for the girl. But she admired her, too. There was a quiet courage and strength about her that would make her an excellent mother for the children.

Had she truly found Hank's future wife?

And why wasn't she happier about it?

Hank took a seat at the kitchen table and leaned back in his chair. He'd looked in on the kids when he got home from work, but then he'd wandered back in here. He found he liked watching Janell cook—her efficient movements, her pleasant humming, the intriguing little sounds she made when she tasted her foods. It was like watching a musical performance.

"Are you familiar with the Vickers family?"

Her question pulled him back from those inappropriate musings. "Not well, but I've had a few business dealings with Alvin Vickers. Why?"

Rather than answering his question, she asked another. "More specifically, do you know Cassie Lynn Vickers?"

"Alvin's daughter?" He tried to picture her and all that he could summon was the hazy image of a girl who was totally unremarkable—brown hair, average height, commonplace features. "Even less well than Alvin."

"I met her today."

"Oh?" Where was this going?

Janell cut him a sideways look. "She heard I was helping you look for a wife."

He straightened at that. "You mean she wants the job?"

Janell's brow sailed up a notch. "You consider being your wife a *job*?"

He waved a hand dismissively. "You know what I mean. Anyway, last time I saw Cassie Lynn she was just a kid."

"Well then, it must have been a long while. She tells me she just turned twenty."

"And she sought you out?"

"She did. Apparently her brother is bringing a new bride home and Cassie Lynn feels she's going to be in the way."

"So I'm her way out." He wasn't sure how he felt about that.

"I have a feeling whether she marries you or not, Cassie Lynn is strong enough to find a way to escape her current situation."

"Sounds as if you like her."

"I do. She has a lot of spirit."

"So she has your approval?"

Janell nodded but her expression had closed off. "I think she'd make you a fine wife and the children a very good mother."

"So what's the next step?" It seemed he was about to get what he'd asked for. But not what he wanted.

"The two of you need to talk so you can see if you think you'll be able to make a marriage between you work."

"As long as she meets those requirements I gave you, and you think she'll be a good mother to the children, then the rest doesn't matter to me." Especially if the woman in question couldn't be Janell.

"But it may not be all the same to her. You forget, she needs to be comfortable with you as a husband as well."

He hadn't thought of that. "But surely, if she came to you…"

"Of course. And I got the impression that, as long as you weren't an ogre, she would be willing to marry you in exchange for a home of her own."

Not an entirely flattering proposition. And there had to be a catch. "But?"

"But you said yourself that the two of you don't know each other. And before making such a solemn commitment, you really need to take the time to get to know each other."

She spoke with such conviction it made him wonder if perhaps she'd been close to someone who'd been trapped in such a situation.

But Janell wasn't finished speaking. "She asked if you'd be willing to chat with her after her brother's wedding on Saturday."

"Of course." He held her gaze. "And I'd like you to join us for that chat."

She paused for a split second, turning to stare at him in surprise. "Don't you think this is something best handled by the two of you alone? I'd be glad to watch the children while—"

"No. You agreed to give me your input on this and I'm going to hold you to it." Before she could argue further, he pressed on. "We can meet here so there's no need to worry about the children—they can play in their rooms. If things work out, I'll want them to meet her anyway."

"Very well. But I plan to be a silent observer only. The two of you need to do the talking."

Hank nodded, then leaned back as she turned back to her cooking.

So this was it. She'd found him a woman who not only met all his requirements, but who was also willing to marry him. He could actually be married by Christmas.

It was what he'd wanted.

So why wasn't he happy?

For Janell, the next few days were busier than ever. She received some good news on Thursday from her sister. Lizzie and her family should arrive in Turnabout the following Thursday. Janell was elated at the prospect of seeing her sister again after so long. But a small part of her worried that, with both Lizzie and Wilfred here, her past would somehow get out.

The children's Christmas Eve program was coming together but they definitely still needed more practice. The nativity play was a very simple enactment of the Bible story of Christ's birth, with few lines. But the children were also spending part of their time working on the costumes and props, things like wings for the angels, staffs for Joseph and the shepherds, gift containers for the wise men and some large canvas-and-wood backdrops that had to be painted.

Mitch Parker, with his artistic skills, was a big help with that project. And when she told him about Chloe's budding talent, he made sure the girl was involved as well.

She was also very pleased with the way the sign-language lessons were going. Most of the schoolchildren were already picking up some rudimentary skills, and those who were highly motivated—Lily and Jack, for instance—were doing exceptionally well.

But always in the back of her mind was a ticking clock, telling her that her time as part of Hank's household was coming to an end.

She didn't want to think about the lonely days looming before her.

Saturday finally arrived. To cut down on the speculation, it was Janell who met Cassie Lynn at the church and escorted her to Hank's house rather than Hank himself.

As the women stepped into the parlor, Hank studied the young woman closely. He detected no signs of nervousness or coyness in her, both positive signs.

He stepped forward. "Miss Vickers, thank you for agreeing to meet with me. Please have a seat."

Once they were all settled, he waved a hand Janell's way.

"I hope you don't mind that I asked Miss Whitman to join us."

"Not at all. I have no secrets to hide."

Hank leaned back. "So tell me, if we were to marry, what do you think you would do here?"

"Well, naturally I'd take care of our home and cook our meals. But most importantly, I'd take care of the kids."

"And what does taking care of the kids mean to you?"

Cassie Lynn didn't hesitate. "I'd see that they had a good Christian upbringing, and that doesn't just mean taking them to church on Sunday. We'd read the Bible together and say prayers and learn what it means to be honest and charitable. And I'd make sure they got their schoolin' and help them with their lessons if need be. I'd take care of their clothes and care for them when they get sick. But most of all I'd make sure they knew they were loved."

Janell was impressed and she could tell Hank was, too.

He cleared his throat. "And Chloe? How do you plan to help her?"

"I don't have experience dealing with deaf people, but I can learn. And I'll ask Miss Whitman to help me do it right." She leaned back in her seat. "Do you mind if I ask a few questions of my own?"

"Of course not."

"Do those two young'uns know you're looking for a wife?"

"No. I didn't want to add any other big changes in their lives until I knew it was going to happen."

"But they're going to be as affected by this as you and I will."

"Surely you're not suggesting I let them have a say in this matter."

"Not exactly."

"Then what *are* you suggesting?"

"A trial run of sorts." Hank saw the startled expression on Janell's face, a reflection of his own reaction.

"I beg your pardon?"

"Hear me out. I'd like to suggest that I come to work for you as a housekeeper for the rest of the month. That'll give the children time to get used to me being around and will give the two of us time to get used to it as well."

Hank rubbed his jaw. What she was saying made sense.

"That should give us time to see if we'll be able to get along as a happy family."

Now she sounded like Janell. "And if we don't get along well?"

"Then we walk away, with no regrets and no recriminations."

Hank stood, extending his hand. "I agree to your plan. How soon can you start?"

"Will Monday be okay with you?"

Janell spoke up. "But I thought you were eager to move out of your father's home?"

"I am. When I start work here on Monday I won't be going back to the farm."

Hank frowned. "Are you planning to sleep here? I mean, I suppose I could bed down in the horse barn with Hector—"

She shook her head vigorously. "Oh, no, I wouldn't think of turning you out of your own home. I figure I'll talk to Reverend Harper about sleeping over at his place for a couple of weeks. He's told me before that if I ever need anything at all, I should come to him. And their daughter is back East at pharmacy school, so I figure they'd be okay with putting me up for a little while, especially if they didn't have to feed me or nothing."

Cassie Lynn really *had* been thinking this through. Hank was impressed with her maturity and resolve.

Cassie Lynn looked from him to Janell. "Would it be possible for me to meet the children?"

Janell stood. "Of course. I'll fetch them."

Hank tried to read her expression but couldn't. Was she relieved things seemed to be working out for him? Her life could finally go back to the way it had been before he and the kids had taken it over.

Of course, she'd still have Alex and Chloe in her classroom.

But would she miss spending time with him at all?

Chapter Twenty-One

Hank found Miss Vickers to be both competent and pleasant. She kept his home spotlessly clean, cooked tasty, filling meals and was very good with the children.

If the children themselves were a bit standoffish, that had more to do with the fact that they missed Janell, not that they had anything against Miss Vickers.

He understood exactly how they felt.

Janell only came around now for about an hour in the afternoon to help them with the sign-language practice. She left before supper, telling him that it would be best if the children started to see Cassie Lynn as the lady of the house. The first evening, when he offered to walk her home, she wouldn't have it.

"The sun is still up and you're supposed to be getting to know Cassie Lynn better. Besides, if you keep walking me home, folks will think we're courting."

He had no response to that, so he let her go home alone. By Wednesday, however, he was better prepared. He followed her out the door, shrugging into his coat as he went.

She gave him a severe, disapproving look. "Where do you think you're going?"

"I just need a word with you. In private."

When she didn't move, he added, "It's about Miss Vickers and the children."

Her expression immediately changed to one of concern. "Is something wrong?"

He started to walk and she fell into step beside him. "I'm not sure I'd say wrong so much as troubling. The children aren't warming to her the way I thought they would."

"Oh, I see."

"You don't sound particularly concerned. Don't you think it's important that they like the woman I choose to be their mother?"

"First, be careful of how you refer to her. The children probably aren't ready to look on another woman as their mother yet—they may never be."

He'd thought they were reaching that point with her.

"And yes," she continued, "of course it's important that they grow to like, and someday love, the woman you marry. But I think you're rushing things."

"It's been three days."

She gave him an exasperated shake of her head. "Chloe and Alex have been through a tremendous amount of change in a very short period of time. And remember, you haven't told them that you're considering making Cassie Lynn part of the family. So it's difficult for them to trust that this arrangement is going to grow into anything permanent."

He mulled over what she'd said. "So how will I know if this will work out between them?"

She placed a hand on his arm, then withdrew it quickly. Looking straight ahead, she cleared her throat. "I've seen Cassie Lynn with them. I have every confidence that they'll get along quite well together. Just don't try to force it. Give them some time for it to happen naturally."

He was silent for a moment, then quietly said, "I've missed our little evening walks."

"Me, too." Her lips clamped shut as if she wished to take back the words. "But if that's all you needed to speak to me about, I'll leave you here to return to your home."

He ignored her words. "Your sister arrives tomorrow afternoon, doesn't she?"

She nodded, her expression brightening. "On the three o'clock train." Then she cut him a diffident glance. "If you don't mind, I probably won't come to your place tomorrow afternoon as I usually do."

"Of course. Your sister is coming a long way to see you and you'll want to spend as much time with them as you can." He noticed the way she was gripping her hands together tight enough to turn her knuckles white. "Are you nervous about seeing her again?"

She nodded. "Nervous and excited all at the same time."

That urge to protect her came stampeding back in. "Would you like some company?"

A number of emotions flitted across her face. "But… your work?"

"One of the benefits of owning your own business is that you can leave early occasionally if you want to."

"Then yes, I would very much like to have a friend with me when my sister and her family arrive."

The fact that she wanted him with her raised his spirits considerably. Then he had another thought. "Will I need to sign to communicate with her?"

Janell shook her head with a smile. "Lizzie is quite adept at reading lips. Just make certain you face her and enunciate clearly when you speak and she should have no trouble understanding you."

"Do you think Chloe will ever be able to do that?"

"Lizzie warned me that reading lips is not an easy skill to master, but I'm hopeful."

"Which brings me to my next question. I understand that part of the reason you invited your sister was to give Chloe a chance to spend time with her. How do you plan to make that happen?"

She grimaced. "I haven't planned anything specific. Perhaps we could have an outing of some sort on Saturday."

"What kind of outing?"

"I'm not sure. It's too cold for picnics or sporting activities. I'll come up with something." Then she grinned as if she'd had an idea. "Perhaps I can talk to Mr. Crandall about letting us have the use of the hotel dining room for the afternoon. That way we could comfortably eat together and afterward visit and play parlor games."

"Edgar would probably go along with that, but he'd likely charge a fee."

She waved that away as if it was of no concern. "Don't worry—it'll be my Christmas present to you all."

Just how much money did Miss Janell Whitman have, anyway?

Janell halted and set her lips in a hard line. "Now, I'm sure Cassie Lynn is holding supper for you. You really should get on home before you ruin everyone's meal."

Hank nodded, said his goodbye, then turned and walked back toward his place.

Distancing herself from Hank and the children was proving even more painful than she'd thought it would be. And his thoughtfulness didn't make this easier.

The fact that he'd even thought to ask about the best way to communicate with Lizzie touched her more than any gift he could give her personally. Then his offer to meet her sister's train with her, just to be supportive, was touching in a whole different way.

That he could still show such concern for her on a personal level, after the way she'd turned him down— twice—without explanation, both humbled and pleased her.

He was going to be a great husband to some woman— and oh, how she wished it could be her!

The only bright light in this was that she felt Cassie Lynn was truly going to be a good mother to Chloe and Alex. Her claim to be a fast learner was proving true. From the amount of progress she was making with sign language, she had to be practicing when she was home alone.

Oh, how she wished things could be different, that she'd met Hank before she'd married Gregory and her world fell apart. But her warning to him to make sure he really knew Cassie Lynn before he married her came from hard-won experience. She wished someone had given her that advice all those years ago.

Then again, would she have bothered to listen? She'd been so sure she'd found the perfect man and that they would live happily ever after.

Nothing could have been further from the truth.

Thursday afternoon Janell hurried to the train station as soon as school let out. The idea that she would be seeing Lizzie again after so many years was adding speed to her steps.

The train was not yet in sight when she arrived at the depot. Neither was Hank. Janell had to consciously plant her feet firmly on the platform floor to prevent herself from nervously pacing.

Would Lizzie and Hank like each other?

Had Lizzie truly forgiven her for her last visit?

Would Lizzie keep her secret?

Hank showed up a moment later. While he wasn't wearing his Sunday best, it was obvious he'd taken the time to stop by his house to clean up. The fact that he'd care enough to do that pleased her. But more important, she was glad of his company. It wasn't that she was afraid to see her sister alone. It was just that having a friend at her side made her feel somehow more grounded.

That he'd sensed this need in her before she'd even admitted it to herself said something about what a truly caring man he really was. Cassie Lynn was one lucky lady.

Before she could do more than greet Hank, the first rumbling of an approaching train sounded. She waited impatiently for the train to pull into the station, winced at the loud shrillness of the whistle, then tried to watch all four passenger cars to see which one her sister would step out of.

There she was, two cars down, dressed in a stylish blue traveling suit—Lizzie always took pleasure in nice clothes—and holding the hand of a little boy.

Janell hurried forward and threw her arms around her sister, and she almost broke into tears when her sister's arms came around her just as tightly. A moment later she moved back enough so her sister could see her lips. "It's so very good to see you."

"Oh, Nelly, I've missed you so much."

Janell gave her sister another quick hug, then looked past to the man behind her. "Hello, Wilfred."

"Janell. You're looking well. It appears Texas agrees with you."

"That it does." It was nice of Wilfred to compliment her. She knew, compared to Lizzie, she was no beauty, and her own frock was more serviceable than stylish.

Pushing those thoughts aside, Janell belatedly remembered the man behind her. As if responding to her thoughts, Hank stepped forward.

She placed her hand lightly on his arm. "Lizzie, Wilfred, this is my friend Mr. Hank Chandler." She smiled at Hank. "Mr. Chandler, this is my sister, Lizzie Hastings, and her husband, Wilfred."

The three of them exchanged greetings, and then Lizzie drew the little boy forward, claiming his hand once more. "Allow me to introduce our son, Elliott."

Janell stooped slightly to greet him. "Hello, Elliott. I'm your aunt Janell." The last time she'd seen the boy he'd been only a few days old.

Her nephew's face scrunched up in a frown. "But Mama says we were coming to see my aunt Nelly."

She smiled. "Nelly is what your mama calls me."

"You're my mama's sister."

"That's right. Her *big* sister."

"And the little sweetheart sleeping on Wilfred's shoulder is Olivia."

The eight-month-old had pudgy hands, rosy cheeks and a riot of golden curls on her head. "She looks just like you."

Lizzie nodded proudly, then turned to Hank. "Janell's told me all about you in her letters. My condolences on the loss of your sister."

"Thank you, ma'am."

"Please, call me Lizzie."

Hank nodded then turned to Wilfred. "I assume you have more luggage than what I see here."

Her brother-in-law nodded. "Several trunks in the baggage car."

"Come on, then. I'll help you make arrangements to have them delivered to the hotel."

Wilfred handed Olivia to Janell and followed after Hank. The baby fussed for a moment at the transfer, then snuggled down on Janell's shoulder without ever opening her eyes.

She glanced up to see her sister watching her.

"You should have a houseful of babies of your own by now."

A sharp pain pierced her at those words. Pain for what could never be. "I have a classroom full instead."

"But that's not the same."

No, it wasn't.

"Are you truly happy here, Nelly?"

"I am." Or at least she'd thought she was, until Hank and his two young charges came into her life, reminding her of what she didn't—would never—have. "But I miss you and Mother and Father very much."

"Then why don't you ever come home to visit?"

"You know why." Why would Lizzie dredge up those old hurts?

She tried changing the subject. "I'm sorry you have to stay at the hotel, but since I live at a boardinghouse—"

Lizzie gave a limp-wristed wave. "Fiddlesticks. We don't mind at all." She squeezed Janell's hand. "I'm just so happy to be here. You don't know how long I've waited for you to issue the invitation."

Was there a hint of a reproof in that statement? "I'm sorry. I didn't mean to shut you out."

"Well, we're here now." Then it was her turn to change the subject. "I like your Hank."

Janell rolled her eyes. "He's not *my* Hank."

Lizzie made a noncommittal sound and Janell cringed inwardly. She hoped her sister didn't take it in her head to do some matchmaking. At the first opportunity, she'd explain the situation with Cassie Lynn.

The men rejoined them and they headed for the hotel at a leisurely stroll. Janell pointed out the livery in case they wanted to rent a carriage during their stay. She also pointed out the boardinghouse when they passed nearby so they'd know where she lived. Lizzie exclaimed over the jaunty red bows on the lampposts and many of the decorations in the windows of the shops and businesses they passed along the way, declaring Turnabout to be a charming town.

Once they were checked into the hotel, Hank took his leave. "It was a pleasure meeting you folks, but I'll leave you to your visiting. I trust I'll be seeing more of you during your stay."

Lizzie gave him one of her dazzling smiles, the kind of smile Janell had feared to never see again during those dark days after her illness.

"Thanks for taking time to welcome us to your lovely town. I also look forward to getting to know you better."

Olivia had finally decided to take notice of the world around her and, based on the loud wail she let out, she was not pleased.

Janell smiled at her sister. "It seems that she takes after you in more than one aspect."

Lizzie made a face before she took her daughter. "It's time to give my lamb-kins her feeding."

Janell nodded. "Then I'll leave you to get settled into your rooms and rest up from your trip."

Lizzie frowned. "But you're going to join us for dinner, aren't you? I insist. We haven't had near enough catching-up time."

"Of course, if you think you'll be up for company that soon."

"It *was* my idea."

Wilfred shook his head. "Lizzie has spoken of nothing else since she received your invitation. Believe me, she's planning to take up a great deal of your time while we're here."

"Which suits me just fine. I'll return in time for dinner."

As it turned out, when Janell stepped into the hotel dining room, only Lizzie was there.

"Wilfred said he was tired and preferred to eat in the room, so he volunteered to watch the children while we ate." She smiled fondly. "I think he was just trying to give us some time to talk in private."

"Wilfred is a good man."

"Yes, he is." Lizzie settled in her seat with an expression of deep satisfaction. "And your Hank seems like the same sort of man."

"I told you, he's not mine, but yes, he's a good man."

Lizzie gave her an exasperated look. "Not yours? From the way you wrote about him, and the way he looked at you, I just assumed—"

"Lizzie, you, of all people, know that can never be."

Her little sister drew herself up as if she'd been challenged. "I know no such thing."

Janell loved that her sister wanted her to be happy, but she had to face facts. "Please, let's not talk about such things today. I want this to be a happy reunion."

Lizzie smiled. "Very well." Then she gave Janell an arch smile. "But be warned—we *will* revisit this topic."

Of that, Janell had no doubts.

Just then, the waitress came by to take their orders. Janell could tell the woman wasn't facing the right direction or speaking clearly enough for Lizzie to read her lips. But before she could say anything, Lizzie spoke up.

"Excuse me. I know you're not aware of this, but I'm deaf. For me to read your lips, I need you to face me and speak clearly." Her sister's tone was pleasant and nonaccusatory.

The woman's face reddened and she immediately turned to face Lizzie more fully. "I'm so sorry. Is this better?"

Lizzie smiled warmly. "There's no need to apologize. You didn't know. And yes, that is much better. Thank you so much for understanding."

Janell leaned back, admiring the way Lizzie had handled the situation with such confidence and kindness. Oh, yes, she was going to be very good for Chloe.

When the waitress had returned to the kitchen, Janell leaned forward slightly. "The food here is good, but for breakfast tomorrow you really should try Daisy's restaurant. She's a fabulous cook and I think you and Wilfred will really enjoy it."

"You'll be joining us, won't you?"

Janell shook her head. "I have to work tomorrow. But it's the last day of class until after Christmas, so we'll have lots of time to be together before you head home."

Janell settled back. "Which reminds me. I hope you don't mind, but I've rented this dining room for all day Saturday. I was hoping all of us, Hank's household included, could get together here for the afternoon, including lunch. Sort of an indoor picnic."

"I don't mind at all. In fact, it sounds lovely. Is there a special occasion I'm unaware of?"

"No, I just thought it would be a good way for you to spend time with Chloe in an informal situation."

Lizzie nodded. "So, tell me what I can do to help Hank's niece."

"As I wrote in my letters, Chloe is certain her life is over. And no matter how much I try to tell her otherwise, I don't think she quite believes me."

"I well remember those feelings."

"My hope is that she'll believe it if it comes from you. I'd like her to spend time with you, to observe the rich life you've built for yourself, to see the confident, accomplished, *social* woman you've become, so that she can see the possibilities for her own life."

"I'll be glad to do what I can. But you *do* realize no one can force her to believe something—it has to come from within herself."

"I know. But a little nudge from a person who's been through something similar certainly can't hurt."

"You seem to care a lot about this little girl that you only met a few weeks ago."

"She reminds me of you. How could I not love her?"

"Are you sure that's all it is?"

"Lizzie, you promised."

"I promised not to discuss your ridiculous assertion that marriage is out of the question. I didn't promise not to discuss your feelings for Hank."

Janell let out a frustrated breath. "All right, let's get this out of the way. I like Hank. I like him a lot. But nothing more than friendship will ever come of it." She saw the protest forming on her sister's lips and held up a hand. "He has someone else in mind to share that part of his life with."

Her sister's expression fell. "Oh, Nelly, I'm so sorry. I would never have brought it up if I'd known. It's just, the way the two of you look at each other…"

How had Lizzie sensed something like that in the brief time she and Hank had been together in her company? Janell thought she'd been doing a good job of hiding her feelings. Perhaps Lizzie was just seeing what she wanted to see.

She waved away her sister's apology. "Enough about Hank Chandler. Tell me about how Mother and Father are doing."

To Janell's relief, Lizzie accepted the change of subject and the conversation moved onto safer ground for the rest of the evening.

But as she and her sister got reacquainted over their meal, Janell's mind kept wandering back to Lizzie's statement. *Had* Hank been watching her with love in his eyes? Could he possibly care for her in that way after the way she'd treated him and with the knowledge she'd found him an ideal wife candidate? Could it be that he truly cared for her?

Then she pushed those thoughts away. It. Didn't. Matter. She couldn't marry him, no matter how either of them felt.

Chapter Twenty-Two

Hank escorted Cassie Lynn to Reverend Harper's home, then headed back to his own place. These past few days had shown him that Cassie Lynn was going to make a very good wife. He came home every afternoon to a delicious meal, a warm, clean house and kids who seemed content. She was making their costumes for the Christmas pageant, and she was earnestly working on her sign-language skills.

So why wasn't he happier? Walking her home in the evening was more of a duty than a pleasure. Other than a few updates about the children or questions about household matters, the two of them really had nothing in common to discuss. He was never tempted to touch her arm or linger on her doorstep.

Though Janell had told him Cassie Lynn was twenty years old, he still saw her as an adolescent, a mature adolescent, but an adolescent nonetheless.

Could he really go through with marrying her?

His thoughts turned to Janell and the joy he'd seen in her face when she first caught sight of her sister this afternoon. The siblings obviously shared a strong bond—it made him more curious than ever as to why she'd stayed away from her family for so long. All his protective urges came to the fore as he contemplated possible reasons.

He wished she would trust him enough to share her past with him.

Janell glanced at the clock. It was thirty minutes until the school day ended. She'd spent most of the day wondering how Lizzie and her family were getting along and now she was considering sending the students home early.

But before she could decide, the door opened and a familiar face peeked inside.

"Hello," Lizzie said with an impish smile on her face. "I hope I'm not interrupting, but I bring treats." She held out a large box tied with a string. If Janell wasn't mistaken, that box came from Eve's sweet shop.

It appeared, based on the number of students bouncing in their seats, that several of the children recognized the box as well.

"Class, I'd like you to meet Mrs. Elizabeth Hastings. Better known as my sister, Lizzie."

Lizzie joined Janell at the front of the classroom. "Hello, everyone. I made a visit to a wonderful little sweet shop today and I thought perhaps I'd share some of what I found there. Would someone like to pass these out for me?"

Several hands shot up and Lizzie selected Peggy Richards, one of the girls in the second row. While Peggy began her important task, Alex raised his hand. When Janell indicated he could speak, he turned to Lizzie. "Is it true that you're deaf, just like my sister?"

Lily, as usual, was making sure she did her best to help Chloe understand what was going on. She used a combination of signing, gesticulations and writing on the slate. Chloe had sat up taller and was looking from Lily to Lizzie with intense interest.

Lizzie nodded. "It is." She signed as she spoke.

"Then how come you can tell what I'm saying without me using sign language?"

"Because I can read your lips." Again she signed her response.

That elicited a lot of excited reaction from the class with several of the students speaking out at once. Lizzie finally held up her hand for silence and the room quieted. "Because I can't study all of you at the same time, lipreading doesn't work well when a lot of people are talking to me at once."

Janell addressed the class. "Now, if you all will take your treats, and thank Mrs. Hastings, I think it is close enough to dismissal time to let you go home. Those of you who are waiting for someone to walk you home may wait on the playground."

As the students began gathering their things to leave, she made one more announcement. "And don't forget, even though there is no class next week, we *will* have practice for the Christmas Eve program on Monday, Tuesday and Wednesday at eleven o'clock."

"A Christmas Eve program," Lizzie said. "That sounds like fun. Do you remember the plays we used to do for Mother and Father?"

Janell smiled at the memory, but before she could respond, Chloe stepped up. "Is learning to read lips hard?"

Lizzie moved to the blackboard to write her response as she spoke it aloud. "It's more difficult than signing, and it's not perfect, but with a lot of time and patience, it can be learned."

"Can you teach me?"

"I would be glad to help you get started and to work with your uncle so he can help you after I leave."

Chloe cut a quick glance Janell's way. "Could you work with Miss Whitman, too, so she can help me?"

Lizzie gave her a smile. "Of course."

Cassie Lynn showed up just then to fetch Alex and Chloe, and Janell made the introductions.

"Pleased to meet you, ma'am," Cassie Lynn said. "The whole town is happy that your sister moved here to be with us, but I imagine you all back in her hometown do miss her."

"That we do. But I'm glad she's found a new home among such fine, caring people as I've met here in Turnabout."

Cassie Lynn took each child by the hand. "Time for us to be getting home. But don't worry—we'll be seeing them again real soon."

Once they'd gone, Lizzie turned to her. "Is that the woman Hank is currently courting?"

Courting was definitely not the word she'd use. "It's not my place to speak of Hank's personal business," she said primly. "I probably shouldn't have said as much as I did already."

Then she changed the subject. "What did you think of Chloe and Alex?"

"They seemed like sweet children. Alex is protective of his sister, as you mentioned in your letters. But Chloe doesn't seem quite as rebellious as I'd expected based on your letters."

"She's softened some since she arrived. Now she's more resigned than outright belligerent."

"I see she's made a friend—I'm certain that's helped."

"Lily's a sweet girl and she's really taken a liking to Chloe."

Lizzie linked arms with Janell as they moved to the door. "So tell me more about this 'indoor picnic' you have planned for tomorrow. Exactly what activities, other than eating, did you have in mind for us?"

As they stood in the school yard together, watching over the remaining children and discussing plans for Saturday, Janell found herself dwelling on thoughts of Cassie Lynn and her upcoming marriage to Hank.

How could she bear to stand aside and watch that happen?

Janell sat off to one side of the dining room, happily playing with little Olivia while Lizzie stood in the middle of the room, directing her husband and a frazzled-looking hotel manager on how to rearrange the tables so that everyone could sit together.

Hank, accompanied by the children and Cassie Lynn, arrived before things were arranged to her sister's satisfaction, and he quickly made the introductions then rolled up his sleeves to help the men do Lizzie's bidding.

By the time the matter of the tables was settled, it was time to eat.

The meal became a large, loud affair, the kind Janell remembered with such longing from her childhood. The children sat with the adults, the food and conversation flowed freely and stories were exchanged. Janell made sure Chloe sat across from Lizzie so that she could observe how this other deaf individual lived with such exuberance.

Wilfred and even Elliott could sign as easily as they spoke, and they instinctively spoke in a manner that facilitated the reading of their lips.

Once the meal was over Lizzie stood to get everyone's attention. "Nelly and I have a surprise for you. When we were children, one of our favorite things to do during the days leading up to Christmas was build gingerbread houses. And we used to compete to see who could build the prettiest and fanciest."

"Who won?" Alex asked.

"My mama," Elliott said with supreme confidence. "She makes one for me every year and they're the best."

Janell smiled. "She does make very colorful houses."

Lizzie ignored their side conversations. "Today we're going to build our houses together for the first time in a very long while. And we want you children to help us. What do you think?"

The children immediately voiced their support for the project.

Janell took up the announcement. "Lizzie and I already baked the gingerbread this morning, and we also stopped at the mercantile yesterday and picked up gumdrops, licorice whips, candy canes and other candies we can use for decorations."

Alex was practically bouncing in his seat in excitement.

Lizzie tapped a finger against her chin. "I think I should like Chloe and Elliott to be my helpers."

"Then I shall have Alex and Cassie Lynn," Janell said quickly.

"And what about us menfolk?" Hank asked.

Janell spread her hands. "We only have enough gingerbread for two houses, but you two can be our judges if you like."

"Now, that sounds like a thorny proposition if I ever heard one." Wilfred glanced Hank's way. "Why don't the two of us see if there's more of that apple pecan pie in the kitchen."

Hank gave Janell a wink as he got up to follow Wilfred.

Now, what in the world was she supposed to make of that?

Chapter Twenty-Three

As they worked on the gingerbread houses, Janell noticed how naturally Elliott communicated with his mother. When he spoke, he made certain she was looking at him and he enunciated properly. And he was also adept at sign language. She could tell that Chloe was taking notice as well, which was the whole point.

As for her own team, she, Alex and Cassie Lynn worked surprisingly well together. There was a lot of friendly banter and some challenges levied. Once they had the four walls put together, they had to take a break to let the frosting dry properly before trying to attach the roof, so Lizzie suggested a game of charades. It was an activity that Chloe and Lizzie could participate in on nearly equal footing with everyone else.

It was nearly two hours later before the gingerbread houses were deemed complete. Olivia had long since gone down for her nap on a soft pallet set up in one corner of the room. Elliott was yawning but he'd refused to lie down for his nap until they were finished with the gingerbread houses.

Hank and Wilfred were called on to judge the results,

but they took the coward's way out and declared it to be too close to call.

Lizzie declared herself so happy with the gathering that she talked Wilfred into renting the dining room for their exclusive use during the rest of their stay.

"That way we can all get together whenever we like without inconveniencing anyone." She clapped her hands as an idea occurred to her. "In fact, why don't we plan to all spend Christmas Day together right here? We can all go out and select a tree to set up in here and then decorate it together." Then she sobered. "Unless you have your own traditions you'd prefer to celebrate. I don't want to step on any toes."

Hank looked at Chloe and Alex. "Actually, our family is hoping to discover some new traditions this year," he said.

"And we can have our gingerbread houses for dessert," Alex added.

"That's a wonderful idea," Janell said. It would definitely be better than the past few Christmases she'd spent alone in her room at the boardinghouse.

A real family Christmas. Attended by some of her favorite people.

Janell couldn't wait.

After the children's practice for the Christmas pageant on Monday, Cassie Lynn was there to walk Alex and Chloe home. Janell had offered to do it for her, but Cassie Lynn had insisted on doing it herself. Janell could tell that, now that the children had grown used to Cassie Lynn, they were getting more and more comfortable being around her.

It appeared Cassie Lynn was going to be a good fit

for the Chandler household after all. Janell was happy
for all of them.

Really, she was.

This sick feeling in the pit of her stomach was more
about her own selfish feelings than anything else.

Janell stayed behind at the schoolhouse after everyone
else had gone. Lizzie wanted to meet her at the boardinghouse today so she could see where Janell lived, but
that wasn't for another hour, and she wasn't in the mood
to return to the boardinghouse on her own.

She drifted over to the piano and fingered a few ran-
dom keys. The disjointed sound—she couldn't call it
music—echoed the unsettled feeling inside her. A feeling she was ready to give a name to.

She sat down on the piano bench and began playing,
her fingers seeming to make the selection of their own
accord. It was a sonata her mother had composed many
years ago, a piece that had always been a favorite of hers.

Her fingers danced across the keys, but it didn't bring
her the peace it normally did. It did, however, bring
clarity.

She was in love with Hank. In fact, she'd been in love
with him for some time now; she just hadn't wanted to
admit it to herself. Because acknowledging her feelings
didn't change anything. She couldn't marry him, not
even if he asked her again. And really, what man would
propose to a woman three times in as many weeks, especially when she'd turned him down with such firm
determination the first two times?

No, her chance was lost, and, though it didn't feel like
it right now, that was probably for the best. She wasn't
sure she was strong enough to refuse him a third time.

She'd reached the crescendo of the piece and she
pounded it out. There were some missteps, but she didn't

care—this was for herself alone, and she was pouring all her emotion and angst into the music. When the piece transitioned into a quieter, slower section, she felt almost sorry.

A sudden crash made her jump, then spin around to find the cause. Hank stood there, a load of firewood in his arms...with one large piece at his feet.

Hank mentally kicked himself for his clumsy handling of the firewood. When he'd heard the music from outside he'd thought it must be Verity Cooper. Why hadn't he known Janell could play, and play with such uncharacteristic abandon? Watching her, he'd been entranced by the tumultuous emotions she'd expressed, not only with the music, but also with her whole being.

And then he'd dropped that chunk of firewood and spoiled the moment. "Sorry," he said, apologizing for interrupting, but not for witnessing what had obviously been a private moment for her. "I didn't mean to startle you. I didn't expect anyone to still be here until I heard you playing."

Looking suddenly shy and vulnerable, she slid from the bench. "That wasn't intended for an audience."

He'd already figured that out. "Why hide your talent—you're very good."

She tilted her chin up, her eyes narrowing suspiciously. "My feelings aren't so tender that you need to pretend. I know that my performance was less than perfect. The fumbled notes should have been obvious to anyone listening."

Did she really feel technical perfection was what mattered? Or was she just embarrassed at his having seen a part of her she tried to keep hidden? "But you played it with such passion. That's better than perfectly hitting all the right notes." He could tell she was still upset by the interruption. Or was it the spying? He supposed he shouldn't have intruded on her that way, but he'd been caught off guard as well. And then he'd been trapped by the beauty of her performance.

Deciding to give her the privacy she obviously wanted, Hank crossed the room toward the stove. "Let me just set this down and I'll leave you to your playing."

"No need. I was just about to put away a few things here and then meet Lizzie at the boardinghouse."

That seemed a nice, safe change of subject. "It's good that you're getting to spend so much time with your sister."

"We had a lot of catching up to do."

For a few moments nothing more was said as he carefully stacked the wood.

Then Janell decided to break the silence. "Thank you for bringing the firewood inside."

"I don't mind."

He watched from the corner of his eye as she retrieved a small stool that she then carried to the closet. As she retrieved a parcel from her desk, he tried not to think that he was lingering just because she was there.

Because that would just make him a besotted fool.

As soon as she stepped up on the stool, he straightened and crossed the room in a few quick strides. "Here now—you shouldn't be climbing after what happened last time. Why don't you let me do that for you?"

She gave him a don't-be-ridiculous frown. "I've done this dozens of times." She placed the box on the top shelf, then turned to smile at him. "There, all done." But she turned too fast and she wavered, seeming to lose her balance, and she grabbed reflexively for his shoulder.

"Whoa there." His hands reached for her waist to steady her.

He was loath to release her, even after it was clear she'd regained her balance. She had such a slender waist, one ideally suited for holding on to.

He noticed her hands remained on his shoulder as well.

With her perched on the stool they were nearly eye to eye. And what beautiful, expressive eyes she had. The green flecks were more pronounced at the moment, shining like stars in a cloudless night sky.

The clean, fresh scent of her surrounded him, and the sight of one tendril curling on her forehead made his fingers itch to release the rest of her hair and watch it spill over her shoulders.

Suddenly her eyes widened, and she inhaled, and it was all he could do not to pull her to him. Her face mirrored the same tumultuous emotions she'd displayed earlier when he'd caught her playing the piano. Did she have any idea what she was doing to him?

Then everything inside him stilled. Was that a look of longing, of invitation, in her eyes?

Or merely wishful thinking on his part?

The urge to finally hold her in his arms grabbed him and wouldn't let go. He placed a hand on her cheek and she leaned into it, snuggling against his palm with a heavy-lidded gaze that finally did him in.

Holding her gaze, making sure there was no hesitation or withdrawal there, he slowly leaned in to kiss her.

He was going to kiss her.

And, even though Janell knew she shouldn't, she was going to let him.

When their lips met, she wasn't disappointed. She'd

been kissed before, but never like this. It was as if those other kisses had been pale imitations of what a kiss should be.

This aching tenderness, this gentle claiming, this sweet, sweet feeling of being cherished and needed was something she'd never experienced before.

And she knew, deep down inside, that this was what real love should feel like.

Her hands moved from his shoulders to slip around his neck. He responded by pulling her closer and deepening the kiss, as if he couldn't get enough.

When they finally pulled apart, Hank couldn't suppress the wide grin splitting his face. She loved him. There was no way she could kiss him like that if she didn't.

He stroked her cheek, loving the soft feel of it. He also loved the responsive hitch in her breath at his touch. He'd never felt this tender, this protective, with anyone before.

"Janell Whitman, will you marry me? And before you answer, you should know that I'm not asking for the children's sake this time, but because I can't imagine myself marrying anyone else."

The soft, dreamy expression she wore suddenly changed to a regretful, wounded wall of denial. It was as if she'd been awakened from a pleasant slumber to find her world had turned to ashes.

To his disbelief, she shook her head and took a step back. "I'm sorry. I truly do care for you, but I can't marry you."

Hank clenched his jaw. He'd thought for sure this time she would say yes. Had he misinterpreted her feelings again? Had that kiss truly meant nothing to her?

The fact that she'd used almost the same words both

Agnes and Willa had did nothing to boost his confidence or his spirits.

"Are you telling me I've been reading you wrong, that you don't have feelings for me?" He couldn't quite mask the spark of disappointment surging through him. Whether it was aimed at Janell for her mixed signals, or aimed inward for putting himself in this position yet again, he wasn't certain.

She reached a hand out as if to touch his face, then let it fall back to her side. "I didn't say that."

"Then what is it?" Why did the women he cared for, and who claimed to care for him, fall short of making a commitment to him?

She turned away from him and his anger ebbed as concern took its place. It wasn't like the outspoken schoolteacher to hide from a confrontation. Whatever was troubling her, he needed to get to the heart of it—for her sake, if not for his.

He placed his hands on her shoulders. "Help me understand."

She nodded with an air of resignation rather than true agreement. "There's something I need to tell you." Her voice wavered and she took a breath. "Something I tried to leave behind me when I moved here." She turned around to face him again. "It's something I've only ever told one other person here in Turnabout."

Whatever it was, he could see it wasn't going to be easy for her to talk about. He felt honored that she would trust him, if not with her heart, with this at least.

Her jaw tensed. "And once I tell you, you'll understand why marriage is impossible for me."

Not marriage to him, but marriage in general. *That* he could fight. "You're not going to tell me you're already married, are you?" he teased. He'd expected her to either smile at his statement or give him an offended look. What he hadn't expected was the guilty flush coloring her cheeks.

"Not exactly." Her gaze didn't meet his.

"Not exactly? What in the world does that mean? Either you are or you aren't."

This time she did look up, her gaze troubled. "I *was* married."

"You're a widow?" Why would she hide such a thing— it was nothing to be ashamed of.

She shook her head.

"Then what—"

"I'm a divorcée."

That set him back on his heels. Divorced.

And she'd kept it secret from everyone here for all this time. Would the town council have even considered her as a schoolteacher if they'd known?

More to the point, how did he feel about it? He tried to fit what he knew of Janell with the image the word *divorcée* conjured up, and it didn't seem possible.

He glanced up and saw her watching him, resignation and hurt cloaking her normally outgoing spirit. And just like that, he knew exactly how he felt about it.

He took her hands. "Janell, I'm so sorry some poor excuse of a man put you through this. But believe me, that doesn't change how I feel about you one whit. Whoever this lout was that you married, whatever he did to force you to take this step, losing you is his loss and my gain."

Her eyes widened in surprise. "But don't you understand what I said? What it means? What if word got out? You can't want your name linked with someone with such scandalous history. And you definitely don't want the children bearing that burden."

"You're not giving me, or the people of Turnabout,

enough credit. Think about it. Two of our leading citizens spent a number of years in prison. Several local marriages over the years have been the result of social pressure. Yet no one treats these individuals like pariahs. So why would you think they would treat you differently?"

"Because I've experienced it firsthand."

The bitterness in her voice shocked him. Her former husband must have done something truly reprehensible to force her to take such drastic action. Already he felt his anger at this unnamed ex-husband burn inside him.

"Well, you won't get that sort of reaction from me, nor from most of the townsfolk, I'd venture. It's obvious you wouldn't have divorced the man if you hadn't had good reason to do so." What had the man done? So help him, if the low-down skunk had hurt her physically, he'd track the man down and—

"You still don't understand." Her voice sounded small, miserable. She withdrew her hands and turned her back to him again.

He placed his hands on her shoulders once more, feeling the tension radiate from her. "Then explain it to me."

She took a deep breath, then blurted out her confession. "I didn't divorce him. *He* divorced *me*."

Again Hank tried to make sense of her words. There were very few reasons he could think of that would compel a judge to grant a divorce. And he couldn't imagine Janell would be guilty of any of them.

He drew her to her desk and seated her in the chair before propping a hip on the desk itself and facing her. "Will you trust me enough to tell me the whole story?"

She nodded and tucked a strand behind her ear with fingers that visibly trembled. "I was nineteen when I married Gregory. I could tell my father had reservations about him, but Gregory was such a dashing, charismatic gentleman that I felt I was the luckiest girl alive. After the wedding we moved thirty miles from my parents so that Gregory could take a job with a prestigious law firm."

Hank felt an intense dislike for the man. But he was also worried. She admired a man because he was dashing and charismatic? If so, his suit with her was doomed from the outset.

"During that first year of our marriage," she continued, "I was able to make only one visit home, because Gregory was trying to establish his career and he didn't like the idea of me traveling without him. I missed my parents and Lizzie, but Gregory and I were building a new life together." She paused a moment. "Gregory was very busy with his career, but I understood that. And I was determined to be the perfect wife."

Something about the way she said that told him she hadn't had an easy time of it.

"Then, shortly after our first anniversary, Lizzie took sick with the measles. It was a very bad case and I received several telegrams telling me she was asking for me. I wanted to go to her, but Gregory kept putting it off, saying we would leave the next day, but something always came up to delay our departure. And he kept reminding me that there wasn't anything I could do that the doctors weren't already doing."

She was wringing her hands now. "Then I got word that complications from the measles had rendered Lizzie deaf. This time, when I read the telegram, I didn't give Gregory a chance to stop me. I packed a bag, left him a note and departed immediately for Dentonville."

Good for her. "And your husband objected?"

"He was angry that I had left without consulting him.

But he also sent wishes for Lizzie's recovery. I immersed myself in helping my sister get back on her feet. It was awful. Partly because in her anger over her situation, she blamed me, saying if I'd only come when she asked me to, the results might have been different."

"You can't truly think she still believes that. It's clear as day that she loves you."

Janell only shrugged. "Regardless, that was how she felt at the time, which made it difficult for me to get through to her. My vibrant little sister retreated into her own world, a shadow of her former self, withdrawing to the point of shutting out everyone who loved her."

Based on what he'd witnessed with Chloe, he could imagine.

"As for Gregory, after a week had passed, he became insistent that I return home, saying that I'd done all that could be expected of me. I explained to him that Lizzie wasn't dealing well with her situation and that she and my parents needed my support. But Gregory was angry that I considered helping with my sister more important than resuming my role as his wife, as if the two things were mutually exclusive. I received several letters from him demanding that I return home. By the third week, he came in person and tried to force me to go back to our home in Havington with him."

Hank could hold his tongue no longer. "The man is a self-centered lout."

She gave a tiny smile at that. "Perhaps so. But he was also my husband. When I refused to leave, backed by my father, Gregory told me I'd be sorry. Then he stormed out and headed back to Havington without me."

He took her hands. "You did the right thing. A better man would have understood and supported you during such a time, not made matters worse for you."

"Gregory didn't see it that way. He filed for divorce on the grounds of my having abandoned him and our marriage. And since he was a well-respected lawyer, with all the right connections, he won. Before I really knew what had happened, I was a divorced woman."

Seeing her vulnerable, shamefaced demeanor made Hank want to track down this fool Gregory and pound him into the ground. Instead, he gave her hands a gentle squeeze. "Listen to me. This was not your fault. The man is lower than a dung beetle. You're well rid of him."

She shook her head. "I'm a failure as a wife and an embarrassment to my family."

He raised a brow at the last part of her statement. "They told you that?"

She waved a hand dismissively. "No, of course not. My family loves me and always stands behind me, come what may. But whenever I am home, the stigma of divorce comes with me and the whispers and speculation bleed over to my family. I can't allow that to happen. That's why I don't go home anymore. At least with me here, far removed from Dentonville, they aren't burdened with such unpleasantness."

"If what I've observed from your sister is any indication, I think they would rather bear with the gossip than be apart from you for so long."

She didn't say anything at that, merely made a noncommittal sound. Then she returned to the original topic. "So you see, I'm not really the kind of woman who should be marrying anyone."

"You haven't said anything to make me believe that. I've already told you, I don't see any of this as your fault. Any man worth his salt, who would care for you as you deserve, would have understood and supported your desire to be with your sister."

She shook her head. "I appreciate you're trying to make me feel better, but it's not true that I bear no blame. I said my vows before God to honor and obey my husband until death us do part, and I failed."

"But he made vows as well. And his violation of those vows was the more egregious."

She smiled regretfully. "Perhaps so, especially since he remarried and now has children. But his failing does not offset mine." She glanced down at her hands. "Besides, a small part of me, I'm ashamed to say, resisted going home with him because I no longer loved him."

That softly spoken confession gave him renewed hope. "Do you love me?"

Her gaze flew up to meet his. "What?"

"I asked, do you love me? Because to me, nothing else matters."

"I do. I do love you. But I can't marry you."

"If you can't marry me because I'm not the kind of man you're looking for—if I'm not rich or sophisticated enough, if I'm not dashing or charming enough—then just say so. If, like Agnes and Willa, you think of me as a good man, just not a good husband, then say that as well."

She placed a hand lightly against his chest. "Oh, no, please don't think that. You're the kind of man any girl would be blessed to have as a husband. It's just that…"

Hank focused on the I-do-love-you part of her statement, confident he could overcome whatever arguments she could summon. "Just what?"

"Just that I *can't*. I let my father down, I let my husband down and I let my sister down. Three people I was closest to and wanted to bring joy to. Instead I brought them nothing but pain and disappointment. If I allowed myself to marry you, it would happen all over again. I can't go through that another time. I can't find myself breaking the heart of someone I love."

"Why don't you let me worry about that? Besides, there's nothing that says it will happen again. If we truly love each other, we can work through anything."

"I thought Gregory and I were in love. I dearly love my father and my sister. And still I hurt them deeply."

He couldn't believe it. How could the usually clear-sighted, no-nonsense woman be so completely blind? It was almost as if she didn't want to see the truth. "Don't you think you're being a bit melodramatic?"

She stiffened. "I beg your pardon."

He'd got her riled. But he liked her this way much better than cowed and dejected.

Perhaps now he could finally talk some sense into her.

Chapter Twenty-Four

Janell couldn't believe he'd turn on her this way. Didn't he understand how serious this really was?

Before she could gather her wits about her enough to respond, he spoke again. "Disappointments happen," he said. "I'm sure, at one time or another, those you love have hurt or disappointed you, perhaps deeply. But something tells me you've forgiven them those hurts, have gotten beyond those disappointments. So why do you think when the reverse happens that your loved ones won't be strong enough to extend you the same trust? I'm sure your father and your sister forgave you long ago. As for your ex-husband—" he nearly spit out the word "—he doesn't qualify as a loved one."

He was obviously oversimplifying matters. "You just don't understand." She heard the querulous note in her own voice and it brought her up short.

"You're right—I don't. Because it sounds to me as if you've grown comfortable with being a martyr."

She shot out of her chair and glared at him. "You are entitled to your opinion, Hank Chandler, but I don't have to sit here and listen to it. So, if you will excuse me, I need to meet Lizzie at the boardinghouse." Then she spun on her heel and walked away.

But she could feel Hank's gaze on her for the entire time it took her to reach the door.

Her irritation with his totally undeserved accusations carried her all the way to the boardinghouse. As if she actually could ever be comfortable with being a so-called martyr—ridiculous! He didn't know her at all if that was what he thought.

She stormed up the boardinghouse porch steps and had her hand on the door before she realized Lizzie was sitting on the porch swing with Olivia on her lap.

Lizzie gave her a knowing smile. "It looks like someone had an interesting morning."

Janell deliberately calmed her breathing and put Hank, along with his outrageous accusation, out of her mind. "Nothing to be concerned with. You should have waited inside in the parlor."

Lizzie stood, resting Olivia against her shoulder. "It's such a nice day, I was happy to wait out here. I can't believe the weather here is so mild at Christmastime."

As Janell led her inside the boardinghouse, Lizzie's words conjured up memories of other Christmases, memories of her and Lizzie wearing fur-trimmed coats and snug woolen hats, playing in the snow or skating on the ice. Life had been a lot simpler then.

They hadn't made it as far as the staircase when Mrs. Ortolon came bustling forward from the direction of the kitchen. "Oh, hello, Janell. I see you have a couple of visitors."

"Eunice Ortolon, I'd like you to meet my sister, Elizabeth Hastings, and her daughter, Olivia." Janell turned to her sister. "Lizzie, Mrs. Ortolon is my landlady." She'd warned Lizzie earlier that Eunice was a bit of a busybody.

Lizzie nodded to the other woman. "Pleased to meet you, ma'am. From what I've seen so far, you have a lovely place here."

Eunice preened a bit. "Well now, aren't you a dear. I do pride myself on keeping a nice place. In fact, I'm thinking about entering the town's decorating contest."

Janell frowned. "But I thought that was just for businesses."

The woman drew herself up. "A boardinghouse *is* a place of business."

"Yes, of course." The last thing Janell wanted was to get into a war of semantics with the landlady.

Olivia started fussing to get down and Lizzie gave the woman one of her more charming smiles. "I hope you'll excuse me. Nelly is taking us up to see her room and this little tyrant is eager to do some exploring of her own."

"Of course. You have a nice visit and feel free to use the kitchen if you should like a cup of tea."

Janell hid a grin. She'd never seen Mrs. Ortolon let a target of her curiosity go quite so easily. But Lizzie had always been able to charm even the stodgiest of souls with that smile of hers. It seemed the years and circumstances hadn't done anything to dim that talent.

As she escorted her sister upstairs, by necessity their conversation ceased. Lizzie couldn't read her lips if Janell walked ahead of her.

So she was left with her thoughts, thoughts that turned back to her conversation with Hank. He'd been so achingly sweet and supportive when she'd told him her secret. She hadn't believed how quickly he'd brushed aside any qualms. His immediate reaction to believe the best of her, to try to defend her, had touched the wounded places inside her and provided a much-needed balm.

Then to have turned on her so abruptly simply because she wouldn't change her stand had felt like a slap in the face.

When they reached the second-floor landing, she was able to turn and talk to Lizzie again. "Just down here," she said, sweeping her arm to the left. She quickly moved to the second door and opened it, allowing her sister to precede her inside.

As soon as Lizzie stepped across the threshold, she set down her daughter. Olivia happily began to crawl around and explore her new surroundings.

Lizzie straightened and looked around and Janell tried to see it from her sister's eyes. It was a large room, with her sleeping area, off to the right, taking up about a third of the space. The rest of the room was divided between a seating area with a love seat and two comfortable chairs flanking a low rectangular table, and a work area that had a desk and chair. It wasn't fancy but it was well suited to her life.

Lizzie gave her a delighted smile. "It's charming."

Janell smiled as she fetched a little rag doll one of her students had made for her last Christmas and gave it to Olivia to play with.

She turned to find Lizzie examining her current sewing project that lay atop her desk.

Her sister held up the nearly finished girl's dress. "Is this for Chloe?"

Janell nodded. "It's her Christmas present. Most of her things were destroyed in the explosion and I thought she'd like to have something pretty to wear."

Not wanting to think about the Chandler household right now, she changed the subject. "So where are Wilfred and Elliott?" she asked.

Lizzie plopped down in one of the overstuffed chairs and Olivia immediately began crawling in her direction, dragging the doll with her. "Wilfred found out there's a good fishing spot just north of town, so he took Elliott out to have a go at it." She grinned as she reached down to stroke her daughter's hair. "I'm not the only one enjoying the milder temperatures you have down here."

Janell smiled. "Just one of the many lovely things Turnabout has to recommend itself."

"I can see you love it here."

Janell nodded. "I am blessed to have landed here when I left home. God was truly looking out for me."

"I'm happy for you, but we've all missed you. *I've* missed you."

"I've missed you, too." Janell hadn't realized just how much until she saw her sister step off that train.

Lizzie's expression sobered, turned diffident. "Your invitation for me to come here... Was it just for Chloe's sake, or dare I believe you've finally forgiven me?"

The question set Janell back. "Forgiven you? Whatever for?"

Lizzie made a sharp movement with one of her hands. "Don't pretend. I know you blamed me for what happened. If I hadn't been so selfish and needy, Gregory would never have divorced you."

Janell hurried over to her sister and knelt in front of her chair, taking her hands. "Oh, Lizzie honey, I *never* blamed you for that."

"Didn't you? I said awful things to you, things that gave you little choice but to stay with me. And because you stayed, Gregory divorced you."

"What happened was more about the kind of man Gregory was, about his need to control and to be the center of attention, than about anything you did. My staying may have been the catalyst for him seeking a divorce, but the choice to return to him when he demanded it was always mine to make."

Lizzie's gaze searched her face, as if seeking the truth there. "Are you sure you never blamed me, aren't still blaming me?"

"Of course I'm sure. And I'm so sorry if I ever made you feel that way. It wasn't my intention."

Lizzie threw her arms around her. "Oh, Nelly, you have no idea what a burden you've just lifted from me. All this time I've been thinking—"

Janell gave her a squeeze then gently pushed back so her sister could read her lips. "If only I'd realized sooner, I would have cleared the air long ago."

Lizzie gave her shoulders a squeeze, then leaned back. "The important thing is that it's behind us now." Then she frowned. "But if you didn't blame me, why ever did you stay away?"

"Surely you noticed all the whispering and finger-pointing that happened after the divorce." Janell stood. "Some of Mother and Father's friends stopped coming around and Mother withdrew from some of the social and charitable groups she'd belonged to for years. All because of me." She tried to keep the bitterness out of her voice. "I figured if I stayed away, eventually people would forget and all of you could regain some of what you'd lost."

It was Lizzie's turn to stand and take her hands. "Nelly, do you honestly think any of us value even one of those shallow friendships above you?" She gave Janell's hands a squeeze. "And it's not just me. Mother and Father miss you, too. Father insists we must respect your wish to stay away, but every year at Christmas he makes certain Cook prepares some of your favorite dishes, just in case you have a change of heart and return for a visit." She made a face. "Even Aunt Dorothea's awful fruitcake recipe that none of the rest of us will eat."

Janell tried to absorb what her sister was saying. It was throwing her world off-kilter, rearranging long-held perspectives on what had happened six years ago and the aftermath since.

"As for those so-called friends," Lizzie continued, "a few of the groups have invited Mother back in, but she's declined. She says that she won't belong to any organization that wouldn't let her daughter in as well."

Had she truly endured this self-imposed exile from her family all this time for no reason?

"Did you love him?"

Lizzie's out-of-the-blue question caught her off guard. "What?"

"Did you love him—Gregory, I mean?"

Janell thought about how to answer that as she studied her niece, sitting on the floor in the middle of the room, happily gumming the rag doll. Then she turned back to her sister. "I thought I did, especially at first. But I know now that that was just a youthful infatuation, not a true, abiding love."

"Like the one you have for Hank, you mean."

There was no point denying it any longer, so Janell nodded. "Yes. Not that that matters."

"Of *course* it matters. Especially because he loves you, too. It's plain as day in the way he looks at you and acts around you. You deserve to be happy, Nelly. Truly happy, the way Wilfred and I are."

"But it's too late."

"Of course it's not too late. Just let him know how you feel. Sometimes all a man needs is a little encouragement."

"Actually, he proposed to me this morning, just before I returned here."

Her sister drew herself up. "Janell Catherine Whitman, are you telling me you turned him down? No wonder you looked so upset when you stormed up the front porch a few minutes ago."

Janell nodded. "For the third time," she admitted in a small, miserable voice.

"*Third* time." Lizzie tugged on her hands, drawing her to the love seat and then sitting beside her.

"And this time I had to tell him about the divorce, so he would understand."

Lizzie's expression hardened. "And that made him pull back? Oh, Nelly, I'm so sorry."

Janell shook her head. "Actually, he was able to get past that with more ease than I expected. He said it didn't matter to him."

"And *still* you turned him down. Why would you do such a thing when you both so obviously love each other? And don't try to tell me he prefers Cassie Lynn because I won't believe that."

"I don't want to make another mistake like I did with Gregory. And I don't want to disappoint him the way I did you and Father."

Lizzie gave her a stern look. "First, do you honestly think he's the same kind of man as Gregory? Or that you could go into a marriage so blindly again?"

Janell shook her head.

"And second, what in the world do you mean, disappointing me and Father?"

"Father didn't want me to marry Gregory. I'll never forget his expression just before he walked me down the aisle. He actually told me it was okay if I wanted to back out, even at the last minute."

"He was only trying to protect you. How could you think it would make him love you less just because you were unable to see past Gregory's facade the way he could?"

Janell was finding it difficult to keep from squirming. This was beginning to sound uncomfortably similar to what Hank had said earlier. "Not love me less, exactly. But be hurt and disappointed by my actions."

"Perhaps. But if so, he's long since forgiven you. And to be honest, he's been much more hurt and disappointed by the fact that you've stayed away so long."

That set her back on her heels, figuratively speaking. Had her efforts to protect her parents only heaped hurt on them instead?

"And as for you disappointing *me*, that's ridiculous. After the way you stayed by me when I needed you most, at great personal cost, and me acting so unappreciative at the time, I'd say it was the other way around."

"But when you asked for me, before you lost your hearing, I didn't come. Perhaps, if I'd been there—"

"Nothing would have changed. I'd still be deaf today."

"You don't know that. If my being there had kept you from getting so agitated and overwrought, perhaps the disease would have taken a gentler toll on you."

"But probably not. Nelly, my being deaf is not your fault. And yes, I have regrets and fears about never hearing music or laughter or even my babies' cries. But there's a huge blessing this has brought me as well. Because if I'd never lost my hearing, I would never have met and fallen in love with Wilfred, and I wouldn't have our two wonderful children. So no, I wouldn't trade the life I have now in order to get my hearing back."

Lizzie shook her head. "You've taken on too much of the responsibility for our happiness on yourself—no one expected or even wanted you to do that. Let it go. Allow yourself to find the same happiness Wilfred and I have."

Janell stared at her sister. What she was saying was what Janell longed to hear, but she knew believing such things would be akin to wishful thinking. She had to hold tight to what she knew to be true.

She finally gave Lizzie a promise to think it over and her sister left, only slightly mollified.

Once alone again, Janell became restless, unable to focus on anything. Deciding she needed some fresh air, she headed out to take a walk. Janell closed her eyes, trying to focus on everything she'd been told today. Were Hank and Lizzie right? Had she deliberately sought out the role of martyr, perhaps to punish herself for the failure of her marriage? Then she remembered Mrs. Collins's words about pride disguised as humility and the cost it could exact. Her fingers toyed with the cameo as she began to understand a bit of what Hank's aunt had tried to tell her.

She looked up and found herself standing outside the Blue Bottle.

With a nod of determination, Janell stepped inside.

Chapter Twenty-Five

Janell sat across the table from Eve, sipping on a cup of tea in her friend's kitchen. She'd just poured out a jumbled explanation about the conversations she'd had with Hank and Lizzie and her own confused thoughts and feelings.

She leaned back, waiting for a response, and thought wryly that it would be a miracle if Eve could make any sense of her ramblings at all.

Eve fingered the rim of her cup. "So he finally kissed you, did he?"

Janell shot her friend an exasperated glare. "Didn't you hear anything else that I said?" Was that an amused twinkle in her friend's eyes?

"You finally admitted to yourself that you are in love with Hank. He proposed to you for the third time. You confessed your past to him and he didn't think the less of you for it. You and your sister cleared up all the misunderstandings between you, and she never resented you as you thought she did. And, oh yes, Hank's aunt warned you against the dangers of false pride. It sounds to me as if things are finally working out for you as they should."

Janell frowned. "You're simplifying matters."

"And you'd prefer it be more complicated?"

"It *is* more complicated. Don't you see? I'm worried about disappointing Hank and the children."

"What I see," her friend said gently, "is that what you're really worried about, deep inside, is getting hurt again."

Janell stiffened. "How can you say that?"

Eve reached over and took her hands. "Opening yourself up to people is scary because it makes you vulnerable. But, Janell, don't you see? It is also one of the most beautiful and fulfilling things you can experience. Don't cheat yourself of that gift just because you were hurt once before."

Janell let her friend's words settle inside of her and slowly her defensiveness melted. All of them—Hank, Lizzie, Eve, even Mrs. Collins—had been trying to tell her the same thing; she just hadn't wanted to listen.

But she was listening now.

She met her friend's steady gaze. "What if it's too late?"

Eve smiled. "I don't know Hank very well, but I think he might be open to a change of heart on your part." She smiled archly. "But if he's already proposed three times, then it might take a little more than a few dropped hints to get him to do it a fourth time."

Janell agreed—there wasn't any *might* about it. After the way he'd looked at her just before she walked out of the schoolroom, she knew he wouldn't make it easy on her.

"Does this mean you're going to stop hiding behind your past?" Eve's question held a note of hopefulness.

"Maybe. I don't know." Janell was still afraid to trust her feelings just now. "There's someone I need to speak to first."

Eve stood. "Well then, there's no time like the present. And remember, the true, cherishing love of an honorable, God-fearing man is something worth fighting for, regardless of the outcome."

Janell couldn't agree more.

Hank kicked at a rock whose only sin was being in his path. When he'd left the schoolhouse earlier he'd turned away from town, needing a long walk to clear his head, but it hadn't helped much. Janell had trusted him with her story and it had been something so unexpected he was still trying to digest it all. She'd been hurt, and hurt deeply, and he had wanted nothing more than to go out and slay her dragons for her. Only it turned out the biggest dragon was one lodged deep within her own heart.

He knew his words had hurt her, and a part of him deeply regretted that, but he'd hoped to shock her into seeing what she was doing to herself, to both of them.

But he'd failed. In fact, had only succeeded in pushing her further away. He wasn't sure where he could go from here.

One decision he *had* made during his long walk, however, was that he couldn't marry Cassie Lynn. It wouldn't be fair to the young girl to trap her into a loveless marriage, no matter how willing she might be at the moment. She should have the chance to find someone who would love her as she deserved. He planned to tell her that as soon as he arrived home—no point in dragging this out now that he'd made the decision.

It probably wasn't going to be an easy conversation to have, especially since she had such strong feelings against returning to her father's home. But he hoped his assurances that she was welcome to continue in their current arrangement until she could find other work would go a long way toward easing any disappointment she might feel.

He entered through the back door and found Cassie Lynn in the kitchen, placing a pie in the oven. Smudge was in a corner near the stove, licking at one of his paws.

He and Cassie Lynn exchanged greetings. Then he looked around. "Where are the kids?"

"There's some new puppies over at the Tucker place and they wanted to go see them. Don't worry. The oldest Tucker girl, Fern, is with them. She promised to keep a close eye on them and walk them home later. You don't mind, do you?"

He shook his head. A part of him was a little concerned about their being out on their own, but he knew that was foolish. Children their age freely roamed among neighboring houses all the time. Mostly he was pleased to know that they were beginning to act as if this was home.

He jammed his hands in his pockets and met her gaze. "Actually, that's good because there's something I need to talk to you about."

"Before you do, there's something I need to tell you as well."

Hank leaned back against the counter and crossed his arms, willing to delay his news by a few minutes. "I'm listening."

"I'm afraid I can't marry you after all."

Hank straightened and dropped his hands. This wasn't at all what he'd expected. "May I ask why?"

"Because it's obvious to anyone who has a pair of eyes in his head that you're in love with the schoolteacher and she's in love with you, and I don't aim to get in the way of that."

She said all of that in the most matter-of-fact manner,

as if it was a well-known fact. Were his feelings really so obvious to everyone?

Hank pulled his focus back to the young woman standing in front of him. "So what are you going to do? If you want to stay on here as housekeeper, I won't be able to pay you much, but—"

She held up a hand. "Thanks, but that won't be necessary. I heard Mrs. Fuller was looking for someone to help out at her restaurant since her second baby came along. I already talked to her about it and I'm going to start working with her right after Christmas."

Cassie Lynn was definitely a girl who wasn't afraid to go after what she wanted.

"Then I wish you well. And I want you to know how much I appreciate all you've done for me and the kids this past week."

"I've enjoyed it—I mean that. Those are some mighty good kids you've got yourself, and they're lucky to have you, too. And Miss Whitman, of course."

He was afraid the kids' only interaction with Miss Whitman in the future would be at school. After their conversation this morning, he couldn't see her spending any time here in his home.

"So what was it you wanted to speak to me about?"

Hank looked up and gave her a crooked smile. "The same thing, actually."

She nodded, as if pleased. "Glad to hear it. You and Miss Whitman belong together."

There was no point saying more than necessary. "That remains to be seen."

Before she could say more, he changed the subject. "If you need me I'll be out back, checking on Hector."

It seemed that after Christmas it was going to be just him and the kids. He hadn't figured out how to make that work yet, but he had more confidence now that he could find a way.

And he had Janell to thank for that.

"Please have a seat." Reverend Harper waved Janell toward one of the leather chairs in front of his desk as he settled into his own chair. "Now, what can I do for you?"

"There's a matter I'm struggling with that I'd like to get your perspective on."

"Of course."

How did she start? "It concerns something that happened before I ever moved to Turnabout, something I've put off dealing with." She sat up straighter. "I've gone through a divorce." To her relief, she saw a flicker of surprise in the reverend's face, but no judgment.

"I see. And since I assume the issue you wish to discuss with me relates to this, would you mind explaining the circumstances that led up to your divorce."

Janell gave him a more succinct, less emotional summary of the story she'd related to Hank earlier and then leaned back in her chair. How would he react?

He seemed to ponder her words for a few moments. Then he finally leaned forward. "First, let me say that you have my most sincere sympathy. You were put in a very difficult position at a time in your life when you were quite vulnerable. Based on what you've told me, this divorce was not something you sought or wanted. And let me remind you that the God we serve is a loving and forgiving God." He leaned back with a gentle smile. "But you have yet to tell me what particular issue you are struggling with at this time."

"I've fallen in love with a man who is strong and honorable and God-fearing."

"And you want to know if you are free to marry again."

"Yes."

He put his hand on the large, well-used Bible sitting on one corner of his desk. "The good book is clear on the conditions under which divorce is permissible, which are mainly adultery or desertion. Some argue that these same conditions also make it permissible to remarry. And one interpretation of your story would indicate that your former husband deserted you—especially given that he has subsequently remarried, making reconciliation between you a near impossibility."

He spread his hands. "But ultimately this is a personal decision that is between you and God. Only He knows what is truly in your heart, and only He can give you the answers you seek."

Then he gave her a questioning look. "And of course, it is something that should be discussed with the man you wish to marry."

She nodded. "He knows the truth."

Reverend Harper's face cleared and he leaned forward, placing his elbows on his desk. "Then, if you will allow me, I'd like to pray with you. And be assured that in the days to come I will be praying for you, both that you will discern God's will in this matter and find a measure of peace with whatever that answer may be."

As Janell bowed her head, she already felt some of that sought-for peace wash over her. Whatever the coming days might bring, knowing that she no longer held her secret quite so tightly, and that the guilt she'd carried around with her like iron shackles for so long was misguided, made her feel freer and lighter than she had in many years.

And later, after she left Reverend Harper's office,

she made one more decision. It was time for her to make things right with the town council. She'd taken the job as teacher here under false pretenses. Whether their need to know her private business was right or wrong, she'd lied by omission to them when she'd applied for and accepted the job of schoolteacher.

Telling them would very likely cost her her job, but if it did, she knew that she would be all right. She would find another job, either here or somewhere else. And if that took a while, she also knew that her parents would take her back in the interim.

And just maybe, if she wasn't already too late, there was an entirely different, much more fulfilling position right here in Turnabout that she could fill.

Chapter Twenty-Six

Janell left the mayor's office the next afternoon with mixed emotions. She'd recounted her story to them in as unemotional a manner as she could and had apologized for concealing the facts about her marital status when she'd applied for the job.

The councilmen had been courteous and understanding, and they had all assured her that they thought she had been a fine schoolteacher since she'd moved here. But in the end, the charter they operated under had specific guidelines and they'd asked her to step down.

Though sad to lose her job, Janell understood. Not only did she not meet the stated qualifications for the position, but she'd also knowingly withheld information from them in order to get it in the first place. She suggested they hire Patience Bruder to replace her, knowing the part-time helper would make an excellent full-time teacher for her class.

The councilmen each assured her they would keep her story secret and would allow her to resign rather than firing her.

It was the best she could have hoped for under the circumstances. And now she was headed to talk to Hank. Of her two meetings today, this was the one she was most nervous about.

Hank sat in the sawmill's tiny office, trying to focus on the ledger, without much luck.

They'd been scheduled to have dinner with Janell and her family again last night. But concern that things would be awkward between him and Janell had almost caused him to cancel. Only the fact that it was doing Chloe a lot of good to be spending time with Janell's sister had stopped him.

He'd managed to spend most of the evening in conversation with Wilfred about his and his son's fishing expedition, so he'd avoided interacting with Janell. But that didn't mean he wasn't acutely aware of her presence.

And he'd noticed she seemed to be in a strange, thoughtful mood. She didn't speak much during their visit, but at least she no longer appeared angry with him.

Had she taken any of what he said to heart?

Gus's barking pulled him back to the present. It sounded as if he had a customer. Hank closed the ledger and stood, relieved to have something else to focus on. He crossed the mill floor quickly, curious to see who had stopped by. It was a slow day and he'd let Simon and Calvin go home early, so he was the only one around. He'd hate to lose a customer because they thought no one was present.

He reached the edge of the platform and then stopped in his tracks. Rather than a customer, Janell stood there, calmly talking to Gus. The dog was still in guard mode— no one was going to get by him until Hank gave the word—but his tail had a suspicious wag to it and his hackles were lowered.

Hank understood the animal's mixed response. But

what in the world was Janell doing here? And had she walked the entire two miles from town again?

"Down, Gus."

His command had the immediate effect of turning both heads in his direction. Gus trotted over to get the expected scratch behind the ears for his performance, but Janell stayed where she was, a nervous smile on her face, as if she wasn't sure of her welcome.

Hank stepped down from the elevated mill floor to the ground and absently rubbed the dog's neck, but his eyes never left Janell. "Can I help you?"

"I wanted to talk to you."

"And it couldn't wait until I got home in another hour?"

She fingered the cameo. "Is this a bad time?"

"No. Let's talk." He waved to the elevated floor, indicating she should have a seat.

She didn't hesitate. Relief coloring her expression, she quickly stepped forward and took a seat, arranging her skirts with exaggerated care.

Why was she so nervous? "So what did you want to talk about?"

She finally looked up and met his gaze. "About what you said yesterday."

He'd figured as much. But he still wasn't sure what direction her discussion would take. If it was more of the same about why she couldn't marry him, he was going to get up and leave. "I'm listening."

She fingered that cameo again. "Yes, well." Her hands dropped to her lap and she seemed to collect herself. "After I left you yesterday, I had a conversation with Lizzie. She asked for my forgiveness."

"Forgiveness for what?"

"It seems she assumed I've stayed away from Dentonville all this time because I blamed her for my divorce.

She believes that if I hadn't stayed to help take care of her, Gregory would never have filed for divorce."

"And *did* you blame her?"

"No, of course not. If Gregory was ready to divorce me over this, it wouldn't have been long before he would have found some other excuse to do it."

Was she just now figuring that out?

"I tell you this because it made me realize that perhaps there was something to what you had said, about my holding on to my own sense of blame too strongly." She moistened her lips. "That combined with something else Lizzie said."

"And what was that?"

"That regardless of whatever hurt and disappointment I'd heaped on her and on my father, didn't I realize my shutting them out of my life hurt them much worse."

"I'm glad your sister helped you figure things out, but why was it so important for you to tell me this right now?" He tried not to let it bother him that she gave more credence to her sister's words than to his.

But she was shaking her head. "It wasn't what Lizzie said that cut through my blindness. It was what *you* said. It was just that Lizzie's words reinforced it."

"You still haven't answered my question."

"You were right—about so many things. About my so-called self-imposed martyrdom. About my irrational fears."

She took a deep breath. "About my feelings for you."

His pulse kicked up a notch at that—not only her words, but also the loving way she looked at him. But he'd misinterpreted that look before. "I'm glad to hear that. But I think we already established that you cared for me. I don't see that anything's changed."

Chapter Twenty-Seven

Janell felt her spirits plunge. She *had* been too late after all. Not that she blamed Hank—he'd given her plenty of chances.

She would return to Dentonville, which would make things easier for everyone. It would explain the town council's need to replace her without anyone having to disclose embarrassing confessions. It would give her a valid excuse not to watch Hank and Cassie Lynn get married. And it removed her from his presence as a reminder of her cowardly refusals.

"Was there anything else?" he asked.

She stood and brushed at her skirt, giving her an excuse not to meet his gaze. "Yes. I wanted to let you know that when Lizzie and her family leave, I'll be returning with them to Dentonville."

"I'm sure your parents will be happy to have you visit."

She looked up at him. "I'm not going for a visit. I'm going back to Illinois to stay."

His gaze sharpened at that. "What about your job as schoolteacher here?"

"I spoke to the council today and they are prepared

to hire Patience Bruder to take my place." She didn't plan to tell him it was their idea to let her go. It wasn't sympathy she wanted from him.

He crossed his arms with a frown. "I don't buy it. You love your job and wouldn't just abandon it this way. What are you running away from?"

She ignored his question. "I won't be abandoning you entirely. I'll send some additional books and articles to help you all sharpen your sign-language skills. And there are people who can help her learn to read lips—I can help you locate and hire someone when she's ready."

Janell took a deep breath and pulled out her brightest smile. "I'm certain that with Cassie Lynn's help, you all will make a cozy family in no time at all."

She moved forward. "Now, if you'll excuse me, I need to get back to town. I'd like to change before I meet Lizzie for dinner." She had to get away from here before she broke down. It wouldn't do for him to see her cry.

But he reached out and grabbed her upper arm in a gentle but firm grasp. "Cassie Lynn and I aren't getting married. And I asked you a question."

Not getting married? "But I don't understand. Cassie Lynn is perfect. She met all of your requirements, the children like her and she seemed more than willing. Don't tell me she backed out."

"It was a mutual agreement. She starts work at Daisy's restaurant right after Christmas." His gaze was curiously intense. "Now tell me, why are you really leaving?"

Mutual agreement. Did that mean he had given up on the idea of a marriage of convenience? That thought gave her some small measure of courage. It was now or never. And she really had nothing to lose.

She straightened and looked directly into his eyes. "I was planning to leave because I couldn't bear to see you married to someone else. Because I realized I'd turned away my chance to marry the man I love, not once but three times, and I didn't think I could bear to see the proof of that on the streets of town and in my classroom every day for the rest of my life."

The look in his eyes fed that small spark of hope inside her. And she knew what she had to do.

"But perhaps I'm doing it again, making assumptions that I shouldn't. So, just to be sure you know where I stand, it's my turn to step out on the limb and allow myself to be vulnerable." She placed the back of her hand on his cheek, stroking it, enjoying the rough texture of the afternoon stubble growing there.

The sight of the vein that throbbed at the corner of his mouth emboldened her.

"Hank Chandler, you are dearer to me than my own breath. Seeing you smile brightens my day and being in your company does funny things to my pulse. You can be single-minded, pushy and downright stubborn, but you are the most honorable man I know and when I'm with you I always feel safe and cherished. In other words, I love you. Would you do me the very great honor of agreeing to marry me?"

There, she'd done it. She'd never felt more vulnerable in her life. For the first time she truly understood what her refusals had done to him. She wouldn't blame him if he repaid her in kind by turning her down, but oh, how she prayed he said yes.

But as the silence drew out, her spirits flagged.

Hank stood there, stunned. No one had ever said such beautiful things to him and about him—could she really mean it all?

She'd actually proposed to him. She'd taken the unorthodox step of doing the proposing—something that had required courage.

But her willingness to take action when called for, her spirit and courage, and her occasional shy vulnerability endeared her to him the most.

Seeing the wavering confidence in her eyes, he realized he hadn't answered her yet. He immediately snatched the hand that had caressed his cheek with such aching tenderness and brought it to his lips.

"Nothing would make me happier than marrying you."

With a near sob of relief, Janell launched herself into his arms and gave him a kiss that he returned with equal fervor.

Sometime later, when they reluctantly parted, Hank gently drew her to sit beside him on the edge of the mill floor. She leaned her head against his shoulder and he wrapped an arm around her shoulders.

A sense of rightness filled him, warmed him as nothing ever had before. How had he ever believed he would be happy with a businesslike arrangement? A marriage was meant to be a special kind of partnership, a true merging of lives, where each partner made the other feel whole and fulfilled.

That was the kind of life he and Janell would share; he could feel it with a certainty that settled deep within his heart.

And as he kissed the top of her head, he realized with a smile that he'd actually managed to achieve his goal— he'd found a wife by Christmas.

Epilogue

❧

"Come on, Alex. We're going to be late."

Chloe's complaint brought a smile to Janell's lips. The girl was more verbal now than she'd been before, and she'd even begun to boss her brother around a bit.

The children's Christmas pageant had just ended and Chloe looked beautiful in her angel costume. The program had gone off without a hitch, other than the Davis boy tripping when he walked on stage. Chloe had even managed, with Lily's help, to get on and off stage on cue.

Alex had seemed quite happy to be part of the choir, and now he and Jack Barr were having sword fights with the shepherd's staffs. Thus Chloe's complaint.

But Hank, her handsome soon-to-be husband, stepped in, signing as he spoke. "Chloe, there's plenty of time." Then he stepped between Alex and Jack. "Boys, we do not have sword fights in church."

"Can we go *now*?" Chloe asked.

By this time, Lizzie had made her way up from the audience, Olivia perched on her hip. "You were all wonderful," she exclaimed, waving her free hand. "I do declare this is the best Christmas pageant ever seen."

Janell appreciated her sister's enthusiasm, especially given she'd sat through a performance she couldn't hear.

Wilfred appeared from the crowd, carrying Elliott. "Wonderful performance, everyone."

The mayor took the stage just then, thanking the children for their performance and reminding everyone that there were only a few minutes left to cast votes for the best decorated shop window.

What had the children excited, however, was the fact that cookies and cocoa were being passed around outside while the votes were being counted.

At last Hank gave Chloe and Alex the go-ahead to run outside with the other children. Lizzie and her family, prompted by Elliott, were right behind them.

Hank put an arm around Janell's shoulders as they followed more slowly. She never tired of his protective touch.

She still couldn't believe they would soon be man and wife. And that she would be mother to those two special children. What better present could a woman hope for?

When they stepped out into the churchyard, there were people everywhere. The children were all still in costume and Janell could see two wise men and a shepherd playing tag. There was a large crowd by the refreshment table, so Janell and Hank hung back a moment longer.

For the first time this felt truly like her town. She was no longer living a lie, no longer holding herself apart. On this Christmas Eve, Janell was ready to experience what life had to offer her—both the good and the bad. Because with Hank by her side, she could face anything.

Hank shifted, standing behind her, his arms around her waist. "A penny for your thoughts," he whispered into her hair.

"I was just thinking that I can't regret anything that's happened in my life, because all of it led to this moment, to you. And there's no place I'd rather be than in your arms."

She heard his quick intake of breath, felt his arms tighten around her. "I love you. And it's a good thing we're getting married in three days' time because any longer would be the end of me."

She took his hand, tugging him around to her side. "Then it's a good thing indeed." And standing on tiptoe, she planted a kiss on his cheek, right there in front of the ladies' auxiliary refreshment table.

* * * * *

Dear Reader,

I hope you've enjoyed Janell and Hank's story. Janell first showed up as part of the Turnabout community in the very first Texas Grooms book, *Handpicked Husband*, and she's appeared in most of the books since. So I was very excited to finally be able to give her a book of her own. Hank, however, was much less visible in previous books, though he's lived in Turnabout all his life.

Although the story opens with Hank's life being turned upside down, this was really Janell's story—she's a woman who appeared to be content on the surface but who secretly had a lot of baggage from her past weighing her down. Before Janell could grasp the happily-ever-after she so desperately wanted, she had to find the strength to recognize and separate the lies from the truth in her past.

If you enjoyed this book, I hope you'll look for the next in the series, which will feature the town's flamboyant dressmaker, Hazel Andrews, and the town's sheriff, Ward Gleason.

For more information on this and other books set in Turnabout, please visit my website at winniegriggs.com or follow me on facebook at facebook.com/WinnieGriggs. Author.

And as always, I love to hear from readers. Feel free to contact me at winnie@winniegriggs.com with your thoughts on this or any other of my books.

Wishing you a life abounding with love and grace.

Winnie Griggs

REQUEST YOUR FREE BOOKS!

2 FREE INSPIRATIONAL NOVELS
PLUS 2 FREE MYSTERY GIFTS

Love Inspired HISTORICAL

LIH15

SPECIAL EXCERPT FROM

Love Inspired **HISTORICAL**

*Maddie O'Rourke is in for a surprise when handsome
Michael Haggerty replaces the woman she hired to
escort her orphaned siblings to Seattle—and insists on
helping her care for the children he adores.*

Read on for a sneak preview of
INSTANT FRONTIER FAMILY by **Regina Scott**,
available in January 2016 from Love Inspired Historical!

The children streamed past her into the school.

Maddie heaved a sigh.

Michael put a hand on her shoulder. "They'll be fine."

"They will," she said with conviction. By the height of her head, Michael thought one part of her burden had lifted. For some reason, so did his.

Thank You, Lord. The Good Word says You've a soft spot for widows and orphans. I know You'll watch over Ciara and Aiden today, and Maddie, too. Show me how I fit into this new picture You're painting.

"I'll keep looking for employment today," he told Maddie as they walked back to the bakery. "And I'll be working at Kelloggs' tonight. With the robbery yesterday, I hate to ask you to leave the door unlocked."

"I'll likely be up anyway," she said.

Most likely she would, because he had come to Seattle instead of the woman who was to help her. He still wondered how she could keep up this pace.

You could stay here, work beside her.

As soon as the thought entered his mind he dismissed it. She'd made it plain she saw his help as interference. Besides, though his friend Patrick might tease him about being a laundress, Michael felt as if he was meant for something more than hard, unthinking work. Maddie baked; the results of her work fed people, satisfied a need. She made a difference in people's lives whether she knew it or not. That was what he wanted for himself. There had to be work in Seattle that applied.

Yet something told him he'd already found the work most important to him—making Maddie, Ciara and Aiden his family.

Don't miss
INSTANT FRONTIER FAMILY
by Regina Scott,
available January 2016 wherever
Love Inspired® Historical books and ebooks are sold.

*Desperate for help in raising her niece, Leah Beiler
goes back to her Amish roots in Paradise Springs,
Pennsylvania—and the boy next door who she's never
forgotten. Could this be their second chance at forever?*

*Read on for a sneak preview of
AMISH HOMECOMING by* **Jo Ann Brown**,
available in January 2016 from Love Inspired!

"In spite of what she said, my niece knows I love her, and
she's already beginning to love her family here. Mandy
will adjust soon to the Amish way of life."

"And what about you?"

Leah frowned at Ezra. "What do you mean? I'm happy
to be back home, and I don't have much to adjust to other
than the quiet at night. Philadelphia was noisy."

"I wasn't talking about that." He hesitated, not sure
how to say what he wanted without hurting her feelings.

"Oh." Her smile returned, but it was unsteady. "You're
talking about us. We aren't *kinder* any longer, Ezra. I'm
sure we can be reasonable about this strange situation we
find ourselves in," she said in a tone that suggested she
wasn't as certain as she sounded. Uncertain of him or of
herself?

"I agree."

"We are neighbors again. We're going to see each other
regularly, but it'd be better if we keep any encounters to a
minimum." She faltered before hurrying on. "Who knows?

We may even call each other friend again someday. But until then, it'd probably be for the best if you live your life and I live mine." She backed away. "Speaking of that, I need to go and console Mandy." Taking one step, she halted. "*Danki* for letting her name the cow. That made her happier than I've seen her since…"

She didn't finish. She didn't have to. His heart cramped as he thought of the sorrow haunting both Leah and Mandy. They had both lost someone very dear to them, the person Leah had once described to him as "the other half of myself."

The very least he could do was agree to her request that was to everyone's benefit. Even though he knew she was right, he also knew there was no way he could ignore Leah Beiler.

Yet, somehow, he needed to figure out how to do exactly that.

Don't miss
AMISH HOMECOMING by Jo Ann Brown,
available January 2016 wherever
Love Inspired® books and ebooks are sold.